GOLDA'S HUTCH

ROBERT STEVEN GOLDSTEIN

ISBN: 978-0-98881165-2 (Hardcover)
ISBN: 978-0-98881163-8 (Paperback)
ISBN: 978-0-98881164-5 (eBook)

Library of Congress Control Number: 00000000000

Deft Heft Books
San Francisco, California

For Sandy, my eternal love,

Although I conquer all the earth,
yet for me there is only one city.
In that city there is for me only one house;
and in that house, one room only;
and in that room, a bed.
And one woman sleeps there,
the shining joy and jewel of all my kingdom.

(Sanskrit)

1

BROWNIES AND APPLES

HE NOTICED IT IMMEDIATELY.

As the woman at the lectern spoke, she prefaced each new tidbit of information with a soft monotonic "Okay" followed by a prolonged pause.

He found that itself sufficiently irritating, but she also never quite finalized the offending word's concluding diphthong, so it sounded more like "Okaah."

Craig Schumacher closed his eyes and inhaled slowly. He was in the back row of the small room—its twelve plastic chairs facing the woman in front. He wondered if anyone else had observed the facilitator's vexing semantic tic, and if they had, if they found it quite as annoying as he did. He opened his eyes and looked around. As he expected, no one else appeared particularly bothered.

Craig tried to ignore the woman's voice, and instead studied her visually as she spoke. She was very pretty—with a svelte, wispy frame of the sort that had become so trendy. Craig acknowledged that such women were certainly nice to look at in a hazy mesmerizing sort of way—but for him, they inevitably conjured up a frail and hesitant aura—not at all sexually arousing. He needed strong, robust, assertive women for that. Preferably tall and big-boned—but a more petite woman with an especially powerful personality could obviate his need for that specific anatomical preference.

He realized his mind was wandering.

He looked away and gathered himself for a moment, then shook his head and flashed a barely discernible self-admonishing grimace. *Judge her as a person . . . she's trying her best . . . she seems like a sweet woman . . . maybe she's new to all this . . . give her a chance . . .*

Part of him was concerned that his peers might observe a supercilious facial expression he let slip, and use that to affirm a negative impression they might already have formed. But more important was his sincere aspiration to dwell permanently in the side of him that was gentle, ethical, and compassionate—especially with respect to his treatment of his staff—or people performing a service for him or his department. He believed that the associates with whom he worked most closely knew him to internalize and manifest those qualities at all times, and he was gratified that they did.

The problem was this place. Craig was certain of it. This situation. Being thrust into these oppressive, artificially concocted days of captive bonding exercises—anathema and useless for a shy introvert. It rendered his higher-self moribund, while it unshackled his derisive dark side.

He reminded himself that while his shadow certainly needed to be restrained, it was far better if it could be refocused positively, rather than just willfully suppressed. But how exactly to accomplish that was not always immediately evident.

Craig realized he was again losing himself in thought. He endeavored to refocus.

• • •

After outlining the afternoon's agenda, the facilitator wheezed a particularly extended "Okaah . . ." and moved on to the first discussion item, a recap of the morning's bonding activity and reactions from the group as to how it had been received.

Craig glanced about and reminded himself that he needed to be especially cautious. The corporation took this annual three-day retreat seriously. The division's twelve national vice presidents had been thrown together in this quaint wine-country resort about two hours north of the firm's national headquarters in San Francisco—and all of them, other than Craig, seemed to greatly enjoy the various team-building exercises to which they'd been persistently subjected. Yesterday, when the group had been hauled out into the woods, he'd made a good show of participating jovially in such things as falling backward from the low limb of a tree and trusting a gaggle of his peers to catch him—or navigating a mildly treacherous obstacle path while blindfolded, depending solely on the verbal instructions and encouragement of a randomly assigned colleague. But this morning, as the twelve worked together to build a rudimentary soapbox cart which one of them would triumphantly steer down a steep narrow track when they were finished, Craig had reached the limit of what he could endure. During the midmorning break, he lingered in the toilet stall until everyone was gone, then snuck back to his room and caught up on some work. He rejoined the group quietly for the cart's final run. The work had proceeded by means of small, informal, and constantly morphing subgroups of the twelve VPs, and Craig was pretty certain that his escape had gone undetected.

And he did indeed survive the ensuing discussion unscathed—commenting with rich and humorous detail on the parts of the session in which he'd participated, and remaining silent but seemingly engaged via eye-contact and facial expression when the group discussed the goings-on from which he'd inconspicuously absconded.

When the conversation ended, the facilitator praised the assembled vice presidents on their spirited recap, and then, with two consecutive diphthong-aborted "Okaah's," informed the group that they'd next be taking the Myers-Briggs personality assessment test. She explained a bit about its history as she handed out copies. She told the group to take the twenty or thirty minutes needed to answer the questions, and then to go on a break and help themselves to snacks in the back of the room, while she tabulated the results.

When Craig finished the survey, he grabbed an apple and left the building to stroll alone for a few minutes on the resort's grounds. On his way out, he passed a number of his peers in the hallway outside the conference room, gleefully chatting and munching on cookies and brownies.

When the group reconvened, the facilitator was posting the personality types of the twelve vice presidents onto a huge chart sitting upon an easel in the front of the room. The chart was divided into four quadrants. Blue adhesive dots, one for each executive present, were being pasted into the quadrants, depicting each VP's personality traits.

In the end, eleven dots were crowded into the upper right corner of the chart. One lonely dot sat completely apart, in the extreme lower left.

The facilitator turned toward the group. "Okaah . . . so, here are the results. So—you can see—almost all of you are up here.

People in this quadrant are extroverted—like really hard-driven and very bottom-line-results-oriented. Like—get it done and take no prisoners." She glanced again at the chart, chuckled, and looked back at the audience. "Okaah . . . so, this one dot way down here—this one is yours, Mr. Schumacher. We don't usually see this personality-set in hard-driven executives. It's much more common in—like—priests and therapists."

The room erupted in laughter. Three of the other vice presidents shouted out nearly identical barbs. The comment Craig made out most distinctly amid the din was: "That's how he runs his damn department—like he's a freakin' priest or therapist."

Craig smiled politely as the chortling around him continued. Being seen as different was an issue he had long since learned to cope with. But the fact that these people understood precisely how he treated his staff—coupled with what he knew to be his peers' nagging envy over the fact that Craig's teams consistently outperformed theirs—lent his smile a smirking juiciness that he trusted was indiscernible.

• • •

The discussion that followed, delving into the details of contrasting personality traits, grew tedious for Craig, and went on far longer than he thought it merited.

So, the sense of relief he felt when the facilitator ended the session was palpable, even more so when she advised the group that this concluded the retreat, and that everyone could now get an early start home to avoid rush hour.

Traffic was light as promised.

He made such good time that as he neared the Golden Gate Bridge to enter San Francisco, he decided to stop at the office and get a few things done before heading home. There were indeed some time-critical items to finish up, but more implicit in his decision was his knowledge that the comfort and control he felt at the workplace would help mightily to expunge the painful—nearly claustrophobic—sensibility that this artificially manipulated retreat had elicited in him.

Craig parked in the underground lot and took the elevator up. As he exited and headed toward his corner office, he was surprised to see Byron Dorn further down the hallway. The two men waved and smiled at each other.

"Well," Craig said, as he changed direction and walked toward Byron. "I didn't expect to see you here. I thought you were scheduled to be in Denver this week."

"The assholes in Denver are still playing cat and mouse," Byron grumbled. "I hadda cancel—these jerks'll do anything to delay what's coming."

Craig gazed at Byron and nodded, his lips just slightly parted—an expression designed to gently elicit more information.

"Yeah, I shoulda told you," Byron said. "Maybe you woulda wanted to call the VP out there. But I'm nudging 'em. Trust me—I'll get 'em where we need 'em to go. Y2K has all the regions totally freaked out." A slight grin curled Byron's lips. "Anyway, I knew they dragged you up to wine country—and you hate those damn things—so I figured I'd wait till you got back."

Craig chuckled. "Very kind of you, my friend. It *was* quite dreadful up there."

It was obvious to Craig that Byron was coming down from his pervasive daily coffee-buzz, but had not yet begun the nightly transition to his more genial and expansive vodka-gimlet temperament. Byron's terse daytime conversational demeanor could easily be interpreted as awkward or gruff by those who didn't know him well. Craig worked diligently to mitigate resulting misunderstandings, but felt confident that Byron's remarkable accomplishments as executive director in charge of data interfaces and conversions were well worth those occasional preemptive or corrective strikes.

"Well," Craig said, "let me know when you reschedule the Denver trip. Maybe I can grease the skids with the higher-ups out there before you go." Byron fidgeted, shifting his weight as if eager to be somewhere else.

"Were you on your way out?" Craig asked.

"Yeah. Taking advantage of being in town. Gonna have drinks with a couple of my direct reports. Meeting 'em at Carlucci's."

"Sounds nice. Enjoy. I'll catch up with you next week."

2

GROCERIES

CARLUCCI'S WAS, BY THE CITY'S HIP AND TRENDY standards, an old-school dinosaur of a restaurant. But it had staked out its location on the northern edge of downtown decades ago, and had stubbornly stayed put.

When Byron Dorn ambled out of the Italian eatery, it was half past six, and San Francisco's evening sky was still light. He was alert and animated.

The two men who exited just behind him were considerably younger, taller, and thinner. All three wore nicely fitted suits. Once outside, the men exchanged back slaps, handshakes, and crude shouted wisecracks before Byron set off for his car, a block away.

The other two waited in front of the restaurant for taxis.

It took Byron a couple of minutes to reach the lot where he'd parked.

With the frivolity done, the bawdy stories and obscene reminisces exhausted, the drinks quaffed, and the shoulder-heaving laughter quieted, Byron now relaxed at the wheel of his red Chevy Camaro for a moment before he switched on the engine. As he set off for the freeway, his initial sensibility was one of satisfaction—another (albeit minor and trivial) conquest well-orchestrated—a modicum of healthy bonding and trust once again reinforced with two of the directors who reported to him.

As he reached the on-ramp and maneuvered quickly into the far-left lane, one other source of pride girded his spirits. His two staffers had asked the restaurant to call taxis, fearing that the cocktails had impaired their judgment. But Byron felt vibrant. He believed that unlike others, alcohol focused him—in fact it was during the day at work, sober and gulping coffee, that Byron habitually felt uncertain and hesitant.

He slipped a CD into the car's player—an anthology of fifties pop. He turned it up loud and began singing along to "Istanbul (Not Constantinople)" by The Four Lads.

Without warning, a memory seized him. It was one of the pernicious transgressors in his secret litany of unwanted recollections. His body stiffened. He tried instinctively to fight it, but, as always, it was too strong and persistent. His features contorted. The reminiscence would not let go.

There were more than a dozen such memories all told. Each relentlessly took its solo turn unannounced—its recurrence dreaded yet fully expected—its power to torment undiminished over time.

"Goddammit," Byron screamed over the music. "I'm sorry! I told you a thousand times, I'm sorry. I didn't fucking mean it. Nobody ever gave me a goddamn chance to explain."

He shouted louder now, inundating the interior of the lonely, speeding car. "I'm not a fucking racist. I never have been. You know that!

"I just didn't have the words."

• • •

It was in college when he was a sophomore. He'd met Maria, who lived on the floor above him in the dorm. They'd been dating for only a few weeks, but he felt strongly about her. Maria was Black. In 1970, that sort of liaison was far less common.

A young woman named Sue also lived on the same floor as Maria. Sue, like Byron, was Irish-Catholic. She'd flirted with Byron for weeks at the beginning of the semester. But Byron didn't find Sue attractive, nor did he have the gumption to tell her that, so he took the course of least resistance and acquiesced to a platonic friendship, which she pursued far more zealously than he.

Late on an afternoon which Byron had spent drinking beer and smoking pot, he walked upstairs looking for Maria. But she was in class, so he headed back to the stairway.

That was when Sue noticed him through her open door and invited him in.

Sue was sitting on the edge of her bed. She motioned to Byron to sit beside her, and turned to him when he did. "What's going on with you and Maria?" she asked.

Byron remained motionless, eyes peering downward. "We're seeing each other, I guess."

"You seem to really be into her."

Byron raised his head and glanced briefly at Sue. She looked sad, vulnerable. Hurt and jealous. Byron had no idea what to say. He searched for a comment that would soften the blow, make her feel a bit better. He didn't dislike Sue at all. She was sweet and sincere, and he was flattered that she found him appealing. He grasped for a thought—something—anything.

"I'm just into her because she's Black," Byron finally blurted out. "I was curious how that would be."

It wasn't true, but he thought it would lessen the hurt—spare Sue's feelings a bit. He felt good about coming up with it.

They talked a few more minutes about other things before he went back downstairs.

A day later, Maria was furious when she broke up with him but wouldn't say why. She slammed the door in his face when he begged her for an explanation. She never spoke another word to him after that.

Sue also cut off all further interactions with Byron.

He hadn't known, till afterward, that Sue and Maria were close friends.

Byron's reputation in the dorm soon fractured and decayed. It became so unbearable that he found a small apartment and moved off campus.

He never felt able to talk about the occurrence with anybody he knew.

• • •

He sped south along the freeway with the CD blaring even louder now. The music's volume failed to entirely obliterate recollections of Maria and Sue, whose faces continued to flash sporadically across his mind. But the tension was beginning to subside.

At this time of night, the highway should have been clear, making his ride home quick. However, there had been a bad accident near the end of rush hour, and Byron soon began encountering the residual backup. The slowdown worsened significantly just a few miles from his turnoff. A momentary impulse prompted Byron to dart out of the left lane where he habitually drove and bulldoze his way over to the extreme right just in time to catch an exit.

A handful of drivers were still honking and gesturing angrily at him as he coasted off the ramp. He'd never felt in danger of colliding with them though—he knew from experience that people backed down when he jutted in, rather than risk a crash.

His rash maneuver deposited him in the town of Los Altos, where it soon became obvious that many other cars had taken the same escape route, because the main thoroughfares there were nearly as congested as the freeway had been. So, Byron began wending his way through smaller side streets to reach his house in the neighboring town of Cupertino.

The snafu annoyed him, but it did finally clear his mind of Maria and Sue.

• • •

Byron was driving down a narrow Los Altos street when his head jerked and his car swerved in its lane.

The sight of her had startled him.

The glimpse had been momentary—she was walking toward him on the opposite side of the road, and she was nearly past him by the time he craned his neck to look in that direction.

But Byron Dorn was quite certain. It was Shoshana Schumacher, his boss's wife.

It was unlikely that he'd be mistaken. The two couples spent a good deal of time together. Shoshana was a striking woman—tall, long blonde hair, big-boned and full-figured—voluptuous, yet still somehow slinky.

And there was that dazzling smile.

Byron had fantasized about her. Secretly of course. More than once. Each time he did, he'd conjured her image up vividly—he knew exactly what she looked like.

It was seeing her *here* that made no sense. And why would she be carrying grocery bags?

Shoshana and her husband, Craig, owned a big house in

one of San Francisco's elite nooks, where Byron Dorn and his wife Adelle had shared many dinners, including a couple of sumptuous feasts on Thanksgiving and Christmas. So why was Shoshana lugging grocery bags down here in Los Altos, nearly an hour south of her home?

He made a U-turn at the corner and started back up the street. Slowly this time. Now he spotted her again, a ways up the block. He hung back, crawling forward just enough to follow her progress.

Perhaps the groceries were for a sick friend. Or maybe her mother. No—she'd mentioned that her mother still lived in Philadelphia. Byron remembered that. More likely a sick friend.

He saw her stop in front of a small one-story house. She turned and walked up a few concrete steps to the home's front door.

A townhouse, Byron assumed.

He inched the car closer to get a clearer view. As she leaned forward, her profile revealed itself distinctly in the overhead light. It was indeed Shoshana.

She did not ring the bell. She set the grocery sacks down and fiddled in her purse—evidently for keys. She let herself in.

Odd, he thought. If it were for a friend, she would have rung the bell.

But then again, if the friend were very sick and asleep in bed, Shoshana letting herself in did make some sense.

The entryway into which she disappeared remained dark until she flipped on the lights just a moment later. Before she did though, Byron glanced up quickly at the windows along the side of the house, extending all the way back. No lights on anywhere.

She shut the door.

The two bags had appeared to him to be quite full. But,

if someone were so sick that they couldn't open a door, they wouldn't be eating much. Still, Shoshana could be helping her friend restock the house with other things—paper towels, toilet paper, soap.

A few more lights were turned on, but window shades prevented Byron from discerning precisely what was going on inside. He lingered for a few more minutes—however, there didn't seem to be much else to ascertain. He decided to head off.

But he'd only moved a few feet when he noticed a car pull out across the street from the house. Byron stopped abruptly and stared at the parking space. He was a bit surprised by the urge he felt to take it and stay there longer, and pondered a moment before succumbing. He made a deft three-point turn and maneuvered his car quickly into the empty spot.

It wasn't until he parked and turned the engine off that Byron sensed a slight surge of adrenaline, and consciously acknowledged the visceral intensity of the curiosity that was gnawing at him—why was Shoshana there, and how long would she stay?

• • •

The sun was beginning to set now. Byron waited a good while longer, but there didn't appear to be much else to see. Shoshana was still inside the house. Perhaps she was joining her friend for a late dinner. He was wondering whether his remaining there continued to make any sense—but then something unexpected occurred. It was almost exactly eight when a man walked up to the condo's front door, looked at his watch, waited a few moments before checking the time again, and then rang the bell. He was middle-aged, portly, in a zippered jacket. He glanced about with a furtive expression and shifted his weight nervously from leg to leg. Just a moment later, the door opened and he entered.

Byron's eyes narrowed and his lips separated just a bit as he stared at the concrete landing where the man had been just a moment earlier.

Now Byron had a hunch. But he'd have to stay a good deal longer to see it through.

He pulled his work-issued Motorola from his pocket, flipped it open, and called his wife. She told him she'd just gotten home herself. Byron apologized for being late—he exaggerated the impact of the freeway accident—he affected great annoyance at being caught in gridlock—and he said he'd be home for dinner when he could. Adelle said she was opening a bottle of prosecco and would have a glass ready for him when he arrived.

Byron knew that Adelle took surface streets to and from the nearby doctor's office where she was the front desk manager, so he was confident she'd have no reason to doubt his inflated characterization of the freeway congestion.

He raised the volume on the CD player a bit, reclined his seat, and waited.

Over the next hour, the sun set fully, and the street grew dark.

But Byron's hunch turned out to be correct.

Just a few minutes before nine, the paunchy man departed. As he scurried off, another man got out of a car a few doors down, glanced at his watch, and proceeded to the house. This man was younger, rugged-looking, and tall. At precisely nine o'clock, the man rang the bell and was let in.

As much as Byron wanted to wait till ten and see if another man appeared, he dared not be any later than he was.

He rushed home to apologize to Adelle—and to think a bit about what he'd just witnessed.

3

FISH SAUCE

ONLY TWO TABLES IN THE SMALL VIETNAMESE restaurant were occupied—the rest would surely fill up over the next forty-five minutes. Carolyn Winthrop continued to peruse the menu for another few moments after the waitress returned for the second time.

Finally, Carolyn ordered the seafood soup.

Craig Schumacher, impeccably clad in a dark brown suit and blue patterned tie, had waited patiently while Carolyn decided—he understood she had many options—whereas Craig's order never varied.

"Tofu and vegetables in lemongrass soy sauce," he said when the waitress glanced his way. "I'll have brown rice rather than white." The young Asian woman scribbled on her pad. "And there's no fish sauce in that, right?" Craig asked.

"No fish sauce. Vegetarian," the waitress said with a heavy accent and a broad smile, as she walked away.

The hot Jasmine tea was steeping in its pot on the table. Craig poured some into the small, white porcelain cup that sat in front of Carolyn, and then a cup for himself.

Carolyn took a sip of tea. "You've been ordering that dish for at least three years now from that same waitress," she observed, in her crisp and authoritative London accent. "I think the poor girl understands that you don't want fish sauce, Craig. There isn't even bloody fish sauce in the dish to begin with."

Craig laughed. "A vegetarian can never be too careful."

Carolyn smirked and rolled her eyes playfully. Her wavy blond hair was parted predictably down the middle, and hung down nearly to her shoulders.

• • •

Under most circumstances, meeting at a restaurant at eleven in the morning would have seemed to Carolyn a bit early for lunch, but it was part of Craig's routine, and she habitually accommodated him. Not because he was her boss. She'd been enjoying early lunches with Craig long before that reporting relationship existed.

It was known throughout the IT department that Craig arose at 4:00 a.m. every morning and did two-and-a-half hours of yoga and meditation before dashing to work. So, by eleven, he was hungry. She'd once asked him why he didn't eat breakfast, and Craig explained that his early morning spiritual practice propelled him into an ethereal sort of mind space—the desire for food didn't hit him until hours later. And he'd told her that though mandatory meetings did on rare occasions interfere, he usually managed to escape for an early lunch—invariably taken at one of the little ethnic restaurants near their downtown San Francisco office, where he could find pleasing vegetarian dishes. He said it was a relaxing break in his day.

When Carolyn first joined the team, several years ago, as the executive director for testing and quality assurance, Craig was a peer—the executive director for software development.

He was the only one in the company who made a sincere effort to welcome her—he invited her to lunch, and good-naturedly outlined the department's idiosyncrasies.

They enjoyed each other's company, so it became a regular assignation, every week or two, to dine together at the Vietnamese restaurant they both liked.

When Craig was promoted to vice president, he inherited Carolyn as part of his staff. She was glad that Craig saw no need to discontinue the regular lunch tradition. It became an informal and friendly way for her to check in and keep Craig abreast of the goings-on in her department. He held more formal periodic one-on-one meetings with most of his other direct reports—Carolyn felt privileged to share this more personal time.

• • •

The steaming hot dishes were delivered to the table. Craig refilled both their teacups and they began eating.

"Oh," Craig said. "I wanted to give you an update on that delayed software problem we've been dealing with."

Carolyn sighed melodramatically. "For god's sake," she pleaded, "you need to intervene and start threatening people—or bring in a damn consultant. You keep saying it would do more harm than good to interfere, and the problem will fix itself—but that's a bunch of rubbish, and you know it. It's been two weeks' delay. My team needs time to test the bloody software before go-live."

Craig remained expressionless, and took a sip of tea. Staying calm when Carolyn became agitated always afforded him a momentary spark that felt visceral and sensuous.

"I just learned this morning," he said, "that the software is ready. Their unit-testing says it's working fine, so it should fit into your team's integrated testing and volume testing schedule pretty seamlessly. Your testers should be able to access the code as soon as you get back from lunch."

Carolyn's features tightened into a scowl, and there was the hint of a snarl as she raised her voice just slightly. "You're the most bloody patient man I've ever met."

As Craig laughed quietly, Carolyn added, "And I don't mean that as a compliment!"

"I'm aware of how you meant it," Craig said with a grin. Though he'd lived in San Francisco for decades, his speech patterns still displayed the slightest hint of his New York City boyhood.

Carolyn now laughed along with him.

Her expression turned wistful. "Do you recall," she said, "all that folderol with the prior VP? The scandal with the big consulting firm?" She giggled. "Good god, he was in bed with those bloodsuckers all along! That day he just disappeared from here in disgrace? What was it, a week later that he was installed as a senior partner in that same consulting firm?"

"Right. Just about a week."

"That's when they promoted you, and put you in his position."

"I remember. I was afraid you might be resentful. We were peers then."

"Yes. You were so adorably shy about it. God, when I first saw you enter that giant corner office—it was hilarious—you were so ridiculously awkward and embarrassed." She reached out and touched him lightly on the arm. "But, Craig dear, you deserved it. And you were always the nicest to me of anyone in the department."

Craig put down his chopsticks and stared at her. "It's not like you to reminisce, Carolyn."

"No. I'm not one to wallow in nostalgia."

"So . . . what's going on?"

Carolyn swallowed a mouthful of soup with deliberation before she responded.

"Listen, Craig, I've really dreaded having to tell you this. I've decided to move back to the East Coast."

"Really? That's quite a surprise."

"I've been talking with the people in our Maryland region. They can take me on now. Not quite as high a position. But that's all right."

"Have you become unhappy here?"

"God no. And you know I love you, Craig, and I love working for you on the national team. And we must be sure to keep in touch." She paused, and pursed her lips. "It's my parents. They're getting old—you know, frail. I need to visit them more often. Flying to London from San Francisco is bloody hell. Flying there from the East Coast is at least tolerable. And I'll need to be going frequently."

Craig thought for a moment and finished the mouthful he was chewing. "Well, I understand. And I wish you all the best. I'll miss you. A lot. How long before you have to leave?"

"I'm leaving in two weeks. I'm really sorry it's such short notice. The opening there came unexpectedly, and they need it filled now. They have someone else they can put in, so if I don't take it, god only knows when another spot back there might open up."

"I see." He breathed deeply and nodded. "I'll need to fill your position quickly. There's over a thousand people in the department. And I only have seven direct reports. So every one of those spots is critical to me keeping up with everything."

"Even more so now, with this bloody Y2K deadline looming," she added.

Craig pondered for a moment. "Well, I'm sure you know—the

knee-jerk thing people do in this situation is to look to recruit from the outside. But I really think that's wrong—you and I have talked about this. An organization should always try to try to fill a position from within if they can—I mean it's the fair thing to do—and it's good for morale—and continuity."

"Well, Geoff's ready," Carolyn offered.

"Geoff, eh?"

Craig knew that Geoff had worked for Carolyn in London, and when Carolyn emigrated from Great Britain ten years ago and took a position on the East Coast of the United States, she had helped Geoff come over, and hired him again. He followed her to her next two jobs as well. Although Craig had never met with Geoff one-on-one, they'd been in many meetings together where Geoff had been an active participant.

"You know," Craig said, "I have a couple of hours free on Thursday afternoon, which is unusual, but some things got canceled. How about if I drop by your shop and meet with Geoff, and maybe some of the other folks who report to you."

"That should be fine," Carolyn replied, and slurped down a spoonful of the rich seafood soup. She snickered as she said, "I'm sure everyone will be bloody thrilled to drop what they're doing and meet with the esteemed, charming, well-dressed VP."

Craig grinned. "I'll take that in the best way possible," he said, as he deftly maneuvered his chopsticks to snare a nugget of saucy tofu and an adjacent sliver of shiitake mushroom, and plop them neatly into his mouth. As he began to chew, he gazed at Carolyn. She was wearing that clingy red top he liked, and for just a moment, he imagined her tying him securely to a four-poster bed and having her way with him.

4

EGG SALAD

JUSTINE SILVER DID HER BEST TO APPRECIATE A FEW moments of Oakland's sunshine and balmy breeze as she walked the short distance from her car to the funeral home, lugging several satchels of supplies and tools. She knew that the atmosphere in the home's basement, where she'd be working for at least the next six or seven hours, would be quite different.

"Hello, Ms. Silver," the director of the funeral home said when he greeted her at the door. "Thank you so much for making time for us."

The home's entry room was vast, high-ceilinged, and obligingly sepulchral with its muted stained-glass windows and subdued light. Sample coffins were on display in rows along each wall. The man's son, who served as the home's associate director, stood beside his father. The men's features were similar, but the son was thinner and taller. He smiled and nodded. "Please ma'am," he said, "let me help you with some of those bags."

Justine handed him a couple of the satchels. "Thank you," she said as they took a few steps inside. "It's my pleasure to work with both of you."

The director had gray hair, and his face was beginning to show some wrinkles. He squeezed his lips apologetically, winced, and shook his head. "We did our best to gently advise the family against holding an open-casket viewing, Ms. Silver," he said. "We truly did. But the family was adamant."

"They're devout Baptists," the son added. "For generations, viewings have been a tradition in their family."

The men's staid black suits and ties contrasted pointedly with Justine's frayed blue jeans and high-top sneakers. Her outfit also included an old oversized white shirt, which had been her husband's until a pen sitting in its breast pocket leaked at work and stained it irreparably. Now, vague remnants of other stains discolored the shirt as well—its tails hung down outside her jeans almost to her knees. Justine was in her early forties—tall and slender—she'd grown up in Southern California and retained just a hint of Valley Girl inflection in her speech.

There was a brief moment of awkward silence.

Then Justine asked, "What was his name, and how exactly did he die?"

"Harold Barnes—he was in his fifties," the director explained solemnly, "a longtime security guard at the big refinery, a few miles north—you know the one. Thank god he was the only person on site when it happened. It was terrible—I'm sure you saw it on the news—the huge explosion, and the fire that broke out immediately after."

"They had to retrieve his body in pieces," the son said. "The arms and legs and head were all torn from the torso. And horrible burns over most of his flesh. They told us he died instantly, thank goodness."

The director took a step toward Justine and spoke softly. "You know, Ms. Silver, my son and I usually handle all the embalming and preparation for viewing ourselves. But as soon as we saw these remains, we knew that if the family insisted on an open-casket viewing, it would be far more than we could handle. So we're grateful you could make time for us. You're known as the best in the industry."

"Thank you, that's very kind," Justine said.

"We did manage to give you a bit of a head start," said the father. "Last night we used sectional injections to embalm each part of the body individually. That should all be set now, and ready for your restoration work."

"Yes, your son mentioned that to me on the phone last night," Justine said. "That certainly will save me an extra trip. Thank you." She glanced about for a moment. "I assume your prep room is in the basement?"

"Yes," said the son. "I'll show you the way."

• • •

As they climbed down the stairs, Justine thought about how happy she was to have found this niche in the industry. Her husband Nigel had landed a fairly well-paying position a few years ago, which had enabled Justine to cease working full-time. That had been a great relief. Although she had trained to be a funeral director, and had served as one for several years, she'd found many of the required duties either tedious or objectionable. She had never felt competent trying to counsel bereaved relatives who had descended into deeply shocked or irrational states—she hated assisting in hauling corpses down interminable winding staircases in private homes at all hours of the night—she found it ethically challenging to coax grieving families into purchasing more expensive catering packages, or ornate caskets, when the people were clearly at their most fragile and vulnerable—and she genuinely feared for her safety when she attempted to run interference between violently feuding factions within dysfunctional families.

In any case, funeral cosmetology had always been the aspect of the death care industry to which Justine was drawn. So, for the past few years, she had established herself as a specialist in exceptionally difficult restorations—her unique talent had quickly built her reputation—and she was now able to contribute significant earnings to her marriage, while only working part-time.

"Thank you," Justine said when she'd been shown to the workroom. "I'll be fine here on my own now."

The son nodded deferentially and departed.

• • •

Justine approached the body parts as she pulled on a pair of latex gloves. "My goodness, Harold," Justine said softly, "this certainly is quite a pickle you've gotten yourself into." As Justine gently repositioned the disembodied head at the top of the metal table, she caressed its burnt cheek. "Don't worry though, Harold," she said, now stroking his chest lightly, "I promise that you're going to look very handsome for your friends and family when I'm done."

She started glancing about. "Before I get started on you, Harold, I need to find where they keep the PPE gear. Every prep room hides them in a different place. Don't worry—I have my own, just in case—but, like, you know, you wear those things once and throw them into the biohazard bag—I'd rather not deplete my own stash if I don't have to."

After a bit of searching, she found a box of plastic overalls under a table, and some individually wrapped goggles and facemasks in a nearby closet. A few moments later she was in full regalia.

The hint of a smile curled her lips as she approached the table. "Forgive me, Harold, I know I must look strange—like a space alien or a deep-sea diver. But this won't affect the care I take with you. It's just to protect me from, like, splashes and things. I'm sorry. I promise, I'll feel just as close to you as I would in jeans and a tee shirt."

Justine gazed at Harold's face and stroked his cheek gently. "Considering what you've been through, Harold, your face could actually be much worse. When they told me about the explosion and fire, I thought, oh my god, I'll need to use heat for sure—at least in a few spots—you know, to reduce tissue mass. But now I think I can make you look really handsome with just my cosmetics." She scanned the remains and pondered a moment. "I'm going to save your head for last, Harold. I think it needs, like, just a few more hours to drain." She tilted his head just slightly and set it up on a block, so that gravity could more effectively suck out any remaining fluid. "By the time I'm done with the rest of you, Harold, your head will be ready."

Justine used her gloved fingers to press on various spots along the arms and legs, and checked underneath for moisture. She did the same with the torso, rocking it onto its sides to check the back.

"You've been in really good hands, Harold. The funeral director and his son did a super job embalming your parts. Everything's solid and, like, reasonably dry. So we can get started now."

Justine walked over to inspect the outfit Harold's family had supplied for him when he lay in state. Hanging on wall hooks in the corner of the room she found an impeccably clean, starched white shirt, a blue pinstripe suit, and a red tie. A shoebox on the floor held a pair of dress shoes and high black socks. Underwear sat folded on a chair nearby.

"Oh my god! That outfit will look just perfect on you, Harold. And it will cover everything except your face and hands. That's great. That means we'll only have those two areas to focus on when we get to your skin."

Justine smiled and gazed into Harold's eyes. "Of course, the funeral directors here would have preferred to do all the work on your torso and limbs themselves—and just leave me to the parts that show. They told me so. People always try that the first time they use me—you know, they think they'll save a few bucks. But I always insist on doing all of you. We need that time together, Harold. It's how we get close. And by the end—when I get to your face—I'll really know who you are." She giggled. "I don't tell them all that, of course. I just say I insist on doing it—and that I charge them the same whether I do it or not. They back off after that."

With a loving sigh, she leaned in and repositioned his body parts slightly on the table. "I don't mean to offend you, Harold, but we're going to have to deal with the odor and the leakage. The burns caused a lot of skin damage. I know it sounds undignified, but believe me, it's not your fault. It comes with the territory. I'm going to make it all fine."

Justine retrieved from her satchel several rolls of plastic wrap, a large container of SynGel, a brush, two hefty rolls of flesh-colored duct tape, and boxes containing embalming powder and kitty litter. For the next three-and-a-half hours, she meticulously brushed Harold's torso and each of his limbs with the cauterizing gel, allowing one side to dry before turning it over to coat the other. She then crusted the flesh thoroughly with a mixture of the embalming powder and kitty litter before sealing everything snugly with plastic wrap, and securing each parcel with a wound-blanket of flesh-hued duct tape. The torso and legs were sealed completely, but Justine was careful to wrap the arms only as far as the wrists. Harold's hands would need to be displayed.

"Well, my friend," she said, "there's no way you're going to leak into the coffin or smell now. I'm sorry, Harold, it's the burns that make all this necessary. It's undignified. They just open up everything."

Justine peeled off her latex gloves, facemask, and goggles, disposed of them, and glimpsed her watch. "Oh my god! It's after one. I'm, like, starving, Harold. If you don't mind, I'm going to take a quick lunch break. I'll pull up a chair and we can chat while I eat."

• • •

From one of her satchels, she plucked a neat wax paper bundle containing an egg salad sandwich on whole-wheat bread, garnished with alfalfa sprouts and tomato rounds. She also grabbed a pint-container of carrot juice and a couple of paper napkins.

In her purse she found a small bottle of hand-sanitizer. She rubbed some briskly between her palms and fingers before sitting down about a foot from the work table.

She laughed. "I'll warn you right now, Harold—I talk with food in my mouth. Constantly." She took a bite of the sandwich but barely missed a beat. "I want to finish lunch and get back to *you*, honey. I hope you don't mind the interruption. In the long run, it will give me energy."

She shook the carrot juice, opened it, and took a sip. "Oh, this is good. Like very fresh and still pretty cold. I picked it up at that little health food store on the way over." Her voice grew solemn for a moment. "I'd offer you a sip, but, well, you know."

She set the bottle back down on the floor next to her chair and smiled. "I bet you had a great family, Harold. Beautiful children. And grandchildren. Nice holidays together.

"With us, it's just my husband Nigel and me. Oh, and our dog. People say Nigel and me are a strange mix. I'm a sweet valley girl—Orange County—and Nigel's from 'across the pond' as he would say. Leeds—a few hours north of London."

Justine finished the first half of her sandwich and took a few big gulps of carrot juice. She grabbed the other half of the sandwich from the wax paper on her lap and dug in.

"So far, you look *brilliant*, Harold. That's what Nigel would say. He has all these British slang words. Oh my god, 'brilliant' is tame, believe me. What's really fascinating about it, though, is that Brits have this whole layer of really colorful words, you know, like really potent, but not dirty. We don't have that in America. You have to get vulgar here to be passionate." She laughed.

"Who would have thought my husband and me would last?" She grinned broadly. "No one! I'll tell you that!" She softened her voice to a whisper and leaned in toward Harold's disembodied head. "Oh, and Harold, you can keep a secret, right? I know you can. Nigel's past, you know in Leeds—well as he likes to say—it was a bit *dodgy*. But that's, you know, a really mild way of putting it. He mixed with a very shady element growing up. Most of his buddies wound up in jail." Justine pouted her lips and raised her eyebrows. "I guess Nigel made it across the pond just in time." She leaned back and chuckled.

Justine swallowed the last bite of egg salad, downed what was left of the carrot juice, and brushed a paper napkin quickly across her lips. "Back to work, Harold!" she said as she got up, tugged on a fresh pair of gloves, and unwrapped a new mask and pair of goggles.

• • •

She took a moment to re-examine Harold's plastic-wrap-and-duct-tape-covered torso and limbs. "Hmm," she observed, "you know, this would probably hold, but you're such a sweet man, I want to make absolutely sure that everything stays totally dry."

Justine searched through the cabinets along the wall of the basement and finally found boxes of Kelco plastic undergarments. "Before we put you in the unionall," she said, "I'm going to put one more sleeve on each arm and leg, just to be certain."

After applying the additional sleeves to the limbs, Justine pulled out the unionall and held it, stretching it out in front of her. "I'm pretty sure you're a size medium, Harold," she said, gazing at him up and down. "We need it to fit you tight. You're going to look really handsome in that pinstripe suit."

Slowly, with great care, Justine slipped Harold's fully sealed and taped arms and legs into their places in the unionall, then tugged it up over the torso. She sprinkled the front and back of Harold's taped body with some additional embalming powder before pulling up the plastic zipper. The strong elastic vinyl held tight—it caressed Harold's parts and made him whole from the neck down.

"Wow, Harold!" Justine exclaimed. "You're starting to look pretty damn good!"

Justine walked to the end of the table and lifted Harold's head off the block. She held it up and peered carefully underneath it.

"You're ready!" she exclaimed. "You're about to be whole again, Harold."

From one of her satchels, she retrieved a set of suturing needles and cord, and a wooden dowel. "Promise me, Harold," she beseeched him, "we're going to keep this next part a secret—just between you and me. It's not something anyone in your family would want to know about."

Justine's gloved fingers probed the neck region at the top

of Harold's torso for the channel typically formed by violent decapitation. When she found it, she burrowed the wooden dowel as deep into the hole as her strength allowed. When the end of the dowel butted up against bone, she rested and heaved a cheerful sigh. "Okay!" she whispered. She removed the head from the block and held it for a moment just above the body to be certain that the length of dowel protruding from the torso was about right. "Perfect!" she said, and wriggled the head down onto the stabilizer.

"Harold," she said, softly stroking his chest, "look at you! You're a whole person!" She paused a moment as she chose a suturing needle and cord. "Well, almost."

Justine took a few minutes to systematically readjust the head's angle until she considered it perfect for viewing.

"This technique is called an intradermal suture, Harold," she said as she began to sew. "It takes a lot of time. And frankly, not many people know how to do it exactly right. Or, you know, aren't willing to make the effort." She paused and repositioned herself to get a better angle. "We're going to be working on this for a while. But it's going to be practically invisible when I'm done. And even if a little something shows, Harold, your collar and tie will cover it all up." She focused intently now, and continued to meticulously stitch the flesh on his neck. As she did, without raising her head from her work, she added softly, almost to herself, "And when I'm done, I'll put a little touch of sealant over the crease. Just to be safe."

• • •

When she was barely three years old, Justine came upon her older brother coloring with crayons at the kitchen table. She sat down next to him with a pile of paper, grabbed a bunch of his crayons, and started drawing. Soon, her brother, and everyone else in Justine's family, were gazing in awe at the staggeringly lifelike faces and landscapes the young child was churning out.

Justine progressed to oil paints in her teens. When she graduated from the same Catholic high school in Orange County that her father and his siblings had attended, she won the school's art medal.

And just a few weeks before that, she had been awarded a scholarship from the Roski School of Art and Design at USC—an institution which her father, a motorcycle officer with the California Highway Patrol, and her mother, who'd been out of work for years due to mental and emotional instability, would never have otherwise been able to afford.

Her teachers and professors had told her that her gifts would take her far.

So when Justine announced, at the end of her freshman year, that she was dropping out of USC and transferring to Cypress Community College to study Mortuary Science, everyone in her family was taken aback. Her older brother and younger sister both warned her that she was making a huge mistake. Two of her cousins visited and sat with her for hours, sharing a bottle of jug wine, as they tried to convince her that she'd regret this decision for the rest of her life.

Justine's mother was apoplectic for months.

Only Justine's father, who had seen more than his share of death while patrolling the freeways of Southern California, took her aside, and said, "Honey, if this is what you really want to do, then you go ahead. Don't let anybody tell you different. Death comes to every family, and helping people through it is a noble thing. My god, somebody's got to do it."

• • •

Her skills at all aspects of restoration were exemplary, but it was funeral cosmetology to which Justine had always been especially drawn. In the past, when she had painted portraits, her innate feel for color and tone was startling, and in certain of her works, literally breathtaking.

Her gift remained intact.

But her canvases now were the sallow sunken faces of the dead.

Before starting on Harold's cosmetics, she took a restful bathroom break, envisioning her finished work as she sat. When she came out, she pulled a crisp apple from her bag. She took just a few bites and chewed each one slowly and quietly, consciously refueling while she turned inward.

Then she stood up and donned fresh gloves, goggles, and mask.

She worked silently now.

Her consciousness had fully shifted. There was no more chatty talk. Justine had entered her artistic trance, and would not break free of it until her composition was complete.

As would a painter, she needed to prepare her canvas before applying pigments. She pulled from one of her satchels a box of plastic eye caps, a wire injector, cotton, and glue.

She began her inspection at Harold's crown, and noted that the mortuary director and his son had made various small repairs in the process of embalming the head—all were very professionally done. The most visible stitches were those around the left ear which looked to have been nearly completely reattached—fortunately it would be facing away from the viewers and not noticeable.

She moved next to Harold's eyes. They would be closed. But his eye sockets had become sunken and disfigured. They needed to be expanded.

With a wad of cotton, she made certain the eyeballs and surrounding areas were completely dry. Two eye caps—plastic half-spheres—were slid into each eye like prodigious, barbed contact lenses. When she gently pulled Harold's upper and lower eyelids over them, their spiked plastic tops held the skin fast, and a narrow ribbon of glue on the lower lid's edge made certain they'd stay.

Harold's mouth was next. Once Justine was sure it was dry, she used her needle injector to shoot wiring into the upper and lower gums, and twisted the two cables tightly together to close his jaw.

For the first time today, she took a moment to study the photograph of Harold that had been sitting beside his suit of clothes. Carefully noting the shape and slant of his smile, she methodically packed cotton into his hollowed cheeks and under his upper and lower lips. She then glazed them with humectant to discourage further desiccation and painstakingly glued the lips into a perfect alignment—impeccably dignified, but suggesting the barest hint of a knowing smile.

A few small troughs and imperfections in his face needed to be built back out with injected tissue builder or bits of superficial wax, but Justine made quick work of those.

Her canvas was now ready to be painted.

Justine stocked only the best coloring-cremes, sprays, pencils, lipsticks, and pigment-lotions, which, unlike cosmetics for the living, were designed specifically for the dry, cold skin of the dead. She used brushes, sponges, combs, cloths, and sometimes her gloved fingers for her applications.

She toiled over Harold's face and hands silently for hours, correcting small details dozens of times, working tirelessly to achieve the most lifelike tints and shadows.

When she was done, she dressed him, combed his hair, and positioned his arms. She then removed her mask and goggles and gloves, and stood back and admired him.

She was motionless for a time as she gazed—then her lips trembled slightly, she grew short of breath, and she began to cry.

5

BLOOD SAUSAGE

NIGEL SILVER WOULD SURELY HAVE PREFERRED starting each day in his robe at the kitchen table, enjoying a full English breakfast, while Winchester sniffed about and did his business in the backyard.

But Nigel's wife, Justine, insisted that both he and Winchester would benefit from a regular dose of exercise. The ensuing bargain she'd struck with Nigel was that while he was out each morning, taking Winchester on a brisk forty-five-minute walk around the hilly outskirts of San Rafael, she would cook up the proper English breakfast he'd grown up with and loved so much.

Nigel had named the dog after his beloved collection of antique Winchester lever-action repeating rifles from the late 1800s, which he kept in a glass case in the den. Winchester was a purebred and pedigreed Akita, a guard dog by lineage—and though most of his ninety-five pounds was solid muscle, Nigel did toss Winchester a sufficient number of bacon, sausage, and black pudding scraps at breakfast each morning to maintain the barest suggestion of a paunch in the dog's middle. On the rare occasions that Justine caught Nigel feeding Winchester at the table, she reprimanded her husband severely, explaining with exasperation how bad it was for both the dog's health and his behavioral conditioning.But those scoldings only served to increase Nigel's cunning at tossing the scraps when Justine's attention was diverted. Winchester, intelligent animal that he was, quickly caught on to the ruse—he figured out how to gulp the tidbits down instantly, without a sound—much to Nigel's delight. And deceiving Justine in this way sparked fond memories for Nigel: the adrenaline surges from his teens, when he used sleight of hand and misdirection to hustle three-card-monte on the streets of Leeds—taking great pride in always operating as the dealer, while his older, more experienced cohorts acted as his shills.

So, as had become his routine each early morning, Nigel threw on a hoodie and jeans, fetched the dog's leash from the kitchen drawer, kissed Justine goodbye where she stood at the stove, and set out with 'Chester at his side.

• • •

The small city of San Rafael, about twenty miles north of San Francisco, certainly had ordinances requiring dogs to be on leash—but at that hour of the morning, and in the relatively remote part of the city where they lived, Nigel saw no need to keep 'Chester tethered. He did, however, always leash the dog before they left the house, releasing him only after they'd turned the first corner—out of sight of Justine, in case she was watching from the window.

Although 'Chester kept pretty much by Nigel's side through most of the walk, he did occasionally dash off to chase a squirrel, or one of the lingering nocturnal raccoons that had scampered out of the forest area to avoid becoming a coyote's nighty repast. Winchester was strong and fast—and though not nearly quick enough to have ever caught a squirrel or raccoon, he had dispatched the odd mouse and gopher hiding just underground on numerous occasions. He could be a cuddly child inside the house playing with his toys or a fearsome protector on a deserted street if he encountered an unsavory stranger.

Their silent forty-five-minute hike traced the identical hilly streets each morning—reached the same sandy mounds in the nearby park—and inevitably crossed paths with the unchanging early dawn denizens of their neighborhood.

There was the angry burly man, bald but for the razor-thin ring of red-tinged hair that circled the back of his head ear to ear. He wore only gym shorts and never a shirt, no matter how cold and foggy it might be. His manner of propulsion was the belligerent amalgam of a jogger and an Olympic speed walker, with his upper frame leaning ominously forward. He was an older man, probably retired, but still quite robust. And although it was very rare to encounter a vagrant in this neighborhood, the burly man seemed to savor doing so, stopping to scream at any sporadic stranger he came upon, warning them to vacate the area. He and Nigel passed each other every morning, on opposite sides of the street, acknowledging each other's presence with the barest nod.Nigel recalled the very first time Winchester had encountered the angry bloke. The dog growled menacingly, stood poised to attack, and glanced up at Nigel for permission. Nigel leaned down, petted the dog, and told him that the man was okay. They passed him without incident from that day on—though on mornings when Nigel was in a foul humor, he'd imagine 'Chester tearing the old tosser's throat out—which always made Nigel feel a bit better, especially when 'Chester picked up on Nigel's energy and responded with a quick bark and aborted lunge in the angry man's direction.

Nigel and Winchester also sometimes encountered an old priest from the tiny local Russian Orthodox church. In a long black robe, with a heavy silver cross dangling from a thick chain about his neck and wearing a black ornamental hat, he made his way slowly, chanting in Russian, tightly clasping an ornate rosary of purple beads. His head always faced down—he did not acknowledge Nigel's or Winchester's presence. Nigel invariably shook his head and chuckled derisively as soon as the priest passed them.

The only other person they encountered on occasion was the lunatic newspaper delivery man, whose old maroon van would veer manically into driveways and up onto sidewalks as he tossed his parcels out his open window. Nigel made a point of never pausing or rerouting to avoid him—he especially enjoyed forcing the frustrated bloke to wait before hurling his paper. Winchester stayed with Nigel when the van was nearby, though the dog always made a point to glare and growl, warning the driver to mind his manners.

Most amusingly to Nigel, every time the paths of the lunatic newspaper delivery person and the shirtless burly man crossed, the two engaged in brief but passionate screaming sessions—encounters which appeared to have no lasting effect whatsoever upon the behavior of either one.

• • •

When Nigel and Winchester returned to the house from their walk this foggy morning, the dog immediately raced to his breakfast bowl in the far corner of the kitchen and began guzzling his meal in huge, barely chewed mouthfuls.

Nigel quickly washed his hands, removed his hoodie, and sat down at the small oak table in the kitchen, salivating as he took in the aromas permeating the room—bacon, sausages, eggs, black pudding, baked beans, tomatoes, and mushrooms—along with toast and brisk tea—a proper full English breakfast as he had enjoyed growing up in Leeds. He was relieved that Justine always included all the traditional elements in the dish, even if she was a bit more scrupulous about calibrating the size of each portion than he would have liked.

He smiled broadly as she set the plate before him. "Thanks, luv," he said in his piquant British accent.

Justine sat down across from him. She was having only a small bowl of granola and yogurt with a few fresh blueberries sprinkled on top.

Nigel looked up with that devious smirk that Justine knew well, and chuckled as he quipped, "I trust that none of the blood in this black pudding is from that minging dismembered corpse you pieced together yesterday."

"Actually, I've been thinking about that poor fellow," Justine said with a heavy sigh. "You know, yesterday, after I finished and all, I really thought he was perfect. I called the directors down—you know, the father and son, and they looked him over. And, oh my god, they thought he looked fantastic too. But his face is still crystal clear in my head, Nigel. It's like I can see him right now. And it's not exactly perfect."

"I'm sure nobody could have made him look any better than you did, honey," Nigel assured her, while chewing a huge mouthful.

"I know—and it's nice of you to say—but that's not what I'm getting at. He needs something more—I realized that—and suddenly it came to me. A casket veil!" Her eyes widened and her voice grew more animated. "The viewing is tomorrow. So,

I'm going to go over there this afternoon—you know, back to the funeral home in Oakland. I called and told them that I'm going to bring a few casket veils with me. That'll do the trick. It'll be perfect."

"Casket veils? What the devil are those? I've never heard you mention them." Nigel flashed that mischievous smile again. "And you're never at a loss for words when you're prattling on about sprucing up some manky cadaver."

"Oh Nigel! Show a little respect, please. He was a good man—caught in a terrible explosion and fire."

"All right. Sorry then." Nigel suppressed a chuckle. "So—what's a casket veil?"

"Oh, right. Well, it's a kind of lacy netting. Fancy. Really pretty. You put it over the body and the casket. You can still see the body through it, but it kind of obscures it—just a bit—just enough, you know, to hide imperfections. I don't use it much—very rarely—but it occurred to me this morning—it will be just perfect for Harold. And I know the father and son at the funeral home are going to love it. I have a few—we could try white, or black, or I even have some bluish colors. Well I have pinkish and red too, but they're not for Harold—too feminine. I'm going to take them all to the funeral home this afternoon, and we'll see which one works best. Oh my god, I'm really excited!"

"Brilliant," Nigel said as he gnawed upon a chunk of blood sausage and scooped up a forkful of baked beans.

6

LEMON AND WATER

THE ALARM CLOCK WAS SET FOR 4:00 A.M. BUT AS was the case every morning, it never actually rang. Craig Schumacher arose, on his own, five or ten minutes prior to the alarm sounding.

The moment he opened his eyes, he glanced at the clock's face. Although he had arisen without fail like this for years, he remained genuinely amazed that his body and mind were somehow able to program his awakening so precisely. In an attempt to understand the phenomenon, he had, at times, tried researching articles about circadian rhythms and sleep cycles and such—but even with that, Craig still did not fully comprehend the mechanism at play. He doubted that even scientists did for certain. But he was grateful for the ability, and never took it for granted—waking this way made him feel so much more present and enmeshed in his silent morning ritual.

Over the years, he'd mentioned to a few people his ability to gauge time with uncanny accuracy despite being asleep. It was interesting to Craig that nearly everyone had suggested that his subliminal motivation might have resulted from not wanting to awaken his wife, Shoshana. Craig would always nod politely and say, "Perhaps . . ." knowing, of course, that this explanation was impossible—Shoshana spent weeknights in her clandestine studio in Los Altos. On the weekends, when she was with him, Craig slept in.

Now, Craig sat up in bed, reached over to the night stand, and switched off the clock's alarm button.

He felt energized.

He did not dress. He walked, naked and barefoot as he was, into the kitchen, displaying an alert but tranquil gait. He filled a glass with a small bit of water, perhaps a third of a cup, and put it in the microwave for a few seconds, just enough to warm it. From the refrigerator he plucked the half-lemon from its porcelain bowl and squeezed a few drops into the glass. Craig drank it standing, unhurriedly, almost as if chewing each mouthful with conscious deliberation. In fifteen minutes, he'd begin his yoga session with Uddiyana Bhanda, Agnisar Kriya, and Nauli Kriya—strenuous abdominal contractions. These scant mouthfuls of warm citrus water would prime his stomach for those exertions.

Craig went next to his small yoga studio in the attic. Its steeply vaulted ceiling was framed by stout rafters of Douglas fir, which sloped down to meet the room's wood-paneled walls. The floor was a thick blue carpet, which served as Craig's enormous yoga mat. There were two skylights built into the roof, but at this hour it was still dark, so he switched on the overhead light and calibrated the dimmer to a low level.

Craig turned on the heater—he liked the room hot when he practiced. When he held a pose and his skin dripped with perspiration, it made him feel as if he were in ancient India, practicing at sunrise, outdoors near the Ganges River. He was aware that during the past few years, "hot yoga" studios had become trendy. He'd been heating his room for his solitary practice for decades. The temperature he sought was a good deal less ferocious than what he understood to be the case at the commercial "hot yoga" studios—though he'd never been to one to validate that presumption.

He lit an incense stick—he used only Chandra Devi imported Tibetan incense, the sandalwood/jasmine combination being his unvarying choice. He let it burn for only a few seconds and then extinguished it. For centuries, this type of incense had been used for yoga and Buddhist meditation, to help focus the mind and calm the body. Craig very much appreciated that aspect of it, but was also aware of scientific studies citing incense's smoke and particulates as a cancer risk quite similar to that of cigarettes. Craig had found that lighting the incense very briefly and letting the tiny amount of smoke dissipate into the air in the otherwise well-ventilated room (aided, perhaps, by the electric heater's fan) fragranced the air quite sufficiently for his purposes, with an amount of smoke so insignificant that it would be harmlessly tolerated, both by himself and by Golda.

The shelf on the wall near the door held an array of hardcover books with worn pages and cracked bindings. They had been amassed over many years—most from second-hand distributors because the texts were long out of print. They were Craig's prized collection of works on the practice of yoga—books that depicted the practice as it had existed in India for centuries, long before it became commercialized and rendered somewhat unrecognizable in trendy classes throughout America and Europe.

As he did each morning, he grabbed the first book on the shelf and left the room, careful to close the door behind him, both to prevent heat from escaping and to enable the vestige of incense smoke to permeate the environs.

Craig went back downstairs, to a rear room of the house, where their rabbit Golda slept in what would customarily be called a hutch, but which Craig often jokingly referred to as Golda's two-bedroom condominium. It was a huge estate, sitting high off the ground, made easily accessible by the carpeted block of four stairs set against its front side. Its main compartment, or the "living room" as Craig called it, was spacious, with a 180-degree view of its surroundings through its wire mesh walls. Carpeted copiously with fresh straw, it held Golda's water bottle, a large pile of hay for munching between meals, and a few toys. Less conspicuous was Golda's "bedroom"—a separate secluded space with solid walls, always dark and protected. Accessible to Golda through a narrow doorway, this was a place where she could be undisturbed, or sleep.

He opened the latch. Golda bounded out and down the four stairs. She, too, embraced their morning ritual.

"Golda" was the rabbit's nickname. Her full name, chosen by Shoshana to honor her favorite Israeli Prime Minister, was "Golda My Hare." She was a dwarf Dutch bunny, with its distinctive black-and-white color pattern.

The hutch was kept latched only at night, when the rabbit slept. Otherwise, Golda was free to wander the house, which she loved doing. She was a well-behaved girl—there was a litter box or two on every floor of the home, and Golda knew their locations and used them religiously. The only other necessary precaution, which Craig had spent hours taking care of the day before they adopted Golda, was to encase every exposed electrical cord in the house in strong plastic tubing. Rabbits, it seemed, liked to chew on wires and could be electrocuted if they bit through the insulation. Craig checked the sheaths every few weeks and replaced any areas where Golda's teeth had begun to make inroads.

The door to the hutch was always left wide open during the day—Golda used it as a comfortable home base—she returned frequently to rest, or to munch on hay before venturing out again.

Golda followed Craig to the marble-tiled bathroom, where Craig sat in silence and allowed his bowels to empty unhurriedly. While he did, he opened the book he'd been toting—*The Yoga Sutras of Patanjali* with commentary by Sri Swami Satchidananda—the same copy he'd owned for over thirty years—and chose, at random, one of the brief aphorisms, with the lengthier accompanying commentary by the Swami, to scrutinize. He'd been through the book many times—and although he did try to come to each Sutra with fresh eyes every time he revisited, he understood fully that this was more a daily sacrament to galvanize his sensibility for yoga practice—rather than an academic endeavor to wring a new scholarly assessment from the passage. He immersed himself in the day's Sutra in that spirit, placid and patient as he pored through it.

Golda was just a step behind Craig as he walked back up the stairs to the attic. She hopped into the yoga room alongside him and immediately positioned herself in the far corner, her familiar vantage point to watch intently as he performed the initial abdominal cleansings.

As traditional practice dictated, he began every morning's routine with Shatkarma, the subset of Hatha Yoga containing sequences designed for internal cleansing of various organs. Shatkarma had been viewed by ancient Yogis as among the most important exercises in the canon of Hatha Yoga—the classic fifteenth-century yoga text, *Hatha Yoga Pradipika* by Swatmarama, called the abdominal cleansings "the crown of Hatha practices"—so it was distressing to Craig that these exercises, which he practiced so zealously each morning, were almost completely absent from the curriculum of most modern American studios. He assumed the movements were considered strange and frightening, likely to dissuade potential customers.

As Craig squatted slightly to initiate the contractions, Golda stood up on her hind legs, facing him, imitating his posture. Craig exhaled forcefully—initially through his nose with a rasping whistle—then expelling any remaining remnants of air through his mouth with a loud hiss. Finally, with his lungs and throat completely devoid of air, he pulled his entire abdomen back and upward, into the vacuum created in his slender naked frame. A casual onlooker, at first glance, might have been shocked—it was almost as if the entire front of Craig's torso had been engulfed by his own body.

He always practiced the three variations in the same order—holding the contraction motionlessly in Uddiyana Bhanda—performing a rapid series of contractions and distensions in Agnisar Kriya, and then executing a circular, washboard-type cleansing by sequentially isolating individual abdominal muscles in Nauli Kriya. Between each variation, he took several slow deep breaths to replenish his oxygen levels, and then embarked upon another stringent exhalation to initiate the next effort.

At the conclusion of Shatkarma, Craig felt invigorated and ready for Asana, or postures.

He began, as always, with convex or backward bends—like Cobra, Locust, and Bow—entered and exited slowly and deliberately, held motionless for two to three minutes, and repeated three times each. These postures elongated the front of his spine while compressing the back of it, massaging his inner organs and glands. The stretches energized and focused Craig. A calm but intent concentration engulfed his being—he forged through their unvarying sequence with a relentless, methodical vigor.

After forty-five minutes he transitioned to concave or

forward stretches, like the Plow, and the many variations of the Westward Bend. These poses didn't just elongate and compress his spine in the opposite direction—they had the powerful psychological effect of calming and relaxing him. Craig's focus remained intent, even sharpened, but it morphed now into a profoundly peaceful, deeply internalized trance. It was full-body meditation—a stillness contained completely unto itself.

Even after all these years of practice, Craig marveled at how manipulating the spine in one direction could be so exhilarating and emancipating, while coiling it in the other turned him inward and quieted him. And Craig remained awestruck at how these ancient movements had been sequenced and calibrated so precisely—to transition eventually to seated breathing exercises and meditation—which then stilled the mind as well as the body, and opened the entire being to be filled, like an empty vessel, with spiritual energy.

During the backward bends, Golda had watched attentively, occasionally stretching her own body in a fragmentary imitation of Craig's posture. But with the forward bends, Golda appeared to sense the peaceful mindset into which Craig now drifted. The rabbit began licking herself slowly and rhythmically, as if in ritual ablution. When Craig lay on his back to prepare for the Plow posture, and then slowly raised his legs up and over his torso until his feet rested on the floor behind his head, Golda wedged herself into the space between his toes and the top of his crown and crouched there, her fur pressed affectionately against the short wiry gray hair atop Craig's scalp. The Plow, in its traditional execution as Craig practiced it, was really three sequential postures, each asserting an increasingly formidable concave bend of the back and neck. Golda understood the succession and the duration of each movement—she adjusted her body slightly to align with each variation, pressing closer against his head with each permutation.

When Craig moved gracefully into the headstand and held that, motionless, for three minutes, Golda rested in front of his face, her body equally tranquil, her nose pressed nearly against his.

And when he finally lowered himself back to the floor, slowly folded his legs into full lotus, stretched his spine to rise erect from his hips, and made a circle of each thumb and forefinger, resting his wrists upon his knees with his palms face up—he paused, giving Golda time to climb up and sit in her accustomed spot, in the valley formed by his left heel, his right thigh, and right knee. The rabbit remained there, unmoving, mesmerized by Craig's abdomen as it alternately distended and contracted with each long, exaggerated breath, his belly just barely touching the fur on Golda's cheek with each extreme distension.

Craig's Pranayama, or breathing exercises, always culminated with the profoundly calming alternate nostril breathing—rhythmic, hypnotic breaths inhaled through one nostril while a finger shut the other, retained for a set time, and then exhaled gently, to a predetermined count, through the nostril previously closed. Called in Sanskrit nadi shodhana, it was, traditionally, the transition from physical Hatha Yoga to Raja Yoga, or meditation.

Craig now began to meditate. He calmly allowed stray thoughts to dissipate, and soon he was submerged in that powerful sensibility he sought so fervently each morning. The trance engulfed him—but it was not a stupor. He was alert and energized—intently focused—yet at the same time emptied of active thought.

His reverie deepened.

His essence seemed to him now a part of all things—a tiny cog in the massive machinery of cosmic consciousness—reveling in its enormous beauty and power—its timelessness and immutability now palpable—its energy overwhelming. He grasped viscerally how this colossal consciousness asserted itself inexorably into every moment of all life.

His immersion into this non-rational state unfettered Craig's habitual emotional reticence, and empowered him now to experience boundless love—for every creature and thing in the universe. The past, present, and future merged into a single timeless entity. Synchronicity and magic asserted their stature, dwarfing cause and effect.

He became one with that consciousness. It swallowed him.

Craig meditated in this manner, each morning, for forty-five minutes. Golda sat upon his leg and experienced it with him—neither one moving—their energy intimately shared.

Craig had long assumed that his meditative state was somewhat akin to Golda's normal sensibility—devoid of constant stray thoughts or worries hammering her mind—a state which she, and other animals took for granted, but which he had worked so hard, over many years, to achieve.

Just as he awoke each morning without an alarm, Craig could sense unerringly when the time to end his meditation session had arrived.

By the time yoga concluded, it was generally close to six-thirty.

As soon as Craig finished, he fed Golda—placing in her hutch a fresh mound of hay, and a bevy of assorted raw vegetables including her favorites: carrot tops, mustard greens, and bok choy. Craig found it comforting and agreeable to have a pet who was a vegetarian as he was.

He showered and shaved quickly, then slipped into a suit and tie. Known at work for being unfailingly dapper, Craig made no secret of the fact that he was mildly colorblind and severely fashion-impaired. Each suit, shirt, tie, and pocket square he owned had a numeric code etched onto its label. He dressed by consulting the online spreadsheet he'd compiled, based upon seemingly endless permutations created and laid out for him over the years by Shoshana.

7

EARL GREY TEA AND SCONES

THURSDAY AFTERNOON, AFTER A BRIEF HELLO TO Carolyn, Craig met first with Geoff, then with Carolyn's other two director-level reports, and finally, in the late afternoon, with Nigel Silver. Carolyn had suggested to Craig that he should consider his meeting with Nigel optional—she reminded Craig that although Nigel led one of the four sub-divisions in her shop, his rank was senior manager, not full director, and she considered him still a bit unpolished, and junior.

Craig took in the general ambiance of Nigel's office as he entered. It was sparsely yet immaculately appointed—a large chessboard with carved traditional pieces sat on a small table in the far corner—a huge, striking world globe, boasting evocative colors and the slightest textural jaggedness in mountainous or hilly areas rested atop a low bookshelf. This décor was in stark contrast to Geoff's office, which had been an egregious mess. Geoff had needed to yank a pile of file folders off his visitor's chair and shove various stacks of paper to the corner of his desk, just to enable the men to have a conversation while making eye contact. The other two offices Craig had visited were tidy, but not distinctive.

"I like your office," Craig said. "I don't think I've been in here before."

"It's cozy for me," Nigel replied with a grin. "And sometimes, even a bit therapeutic."

"That's a beautiful chess set," Craig said. "Chess is interesting, isn't it? It's fierce intellectual combat—yet the pieces on each side have to work together in seamless cooperation to assert their will."

"Sort of what I was getting after by putting it up. Do you play?"

Craig found Nigel's accent beguiling. Prior to working with people who came from Great Britain, Craig had never differentiated much from one British dialect to another. But the distinction between the crisp, almost haughty London speech inflections of Carolyn and Geoff, versus Nigel's earthy, inviting, legato Leeds accent, was quite striking. Craig wondered if Geoff and Carolyn looked down a bit on Nigel because of it—especially when he occasionally slipped back into substituting "f" or "v" for a "th" sound, which Craig noted Nigel wasn't doing now—but he'd overheard Nigel doing it in casual banter with his team members on a few occasions.

"I played a good deal of chess in high school and college," Craig said. "Not much now. In fact, I don't think I've played a game in years."

"We should go at it sometime," Nigel said, with a broad smile. "We'd probably be equally rusty and gormless."

"No doubt," Craig said. He had no idea what "gormless" meant, other than that it was undoubtedly British slang, which Nigel employed liberally, and its meaning could be inferred from context. Craig glanced toward the bookshelf. "And that globe," he said, pointing. "It's quite striking. Does it have significance?"

"I was a geography major in college," Nigel said.

"Geography?"

Nigel laughed heartily. "It usually triggers that reaction! You're probably wondering what the hell we do other than look at maps and memorize nation's capitals."

Craig smiled. "What *do* you do?"

"A lot of it is what they call *human* geography—think of that place where geology meets anthropology—you know, hard science melding with social science. Brilliant!"

Craig nodded, lowered his gaze a moment, then looked back up. "Your team has been very successful," he said. "I've noticed that if there's ever a problem in Carolyn's department, it's never your team. So, congratulations. You've been doing a fine job, Nigel."

"I think people like working for me. I trust them to get on with it, in their own way. I'm not in their face." He paused, looked at Craig, and flashed that impish smile. "You know, unless they require a swift kick in the ass."

Craig chuckled. "Did you pick that management style up from Carolyn?"

"I picked it up from *you*! Carolyn's more micro—she's in your shorts—but I assume you've sussed that out on your own. People enjoy working for you, Craig. They feel respected, empowered."

"That's nice of you to say. Did Carolyn mention anything to you about her future plans?"

"No. But I heard her say a few things to Geoff that made me think she might be moving on to something else. And here you are, visiting, after all."

Craig grinned and nodded. "Just between you and me, she *will* be moving on. We'll be announcing it soon. Please don't say anything till then." Craig looked directly into Nigel's eyes. "And speaking of Geoff, what do you think of him?"

Nigel laughed. "Honestly? You really want me to say?"

"Yes, I'd like to hear."

"Well, he's a bit barmy, don't you think?"

"Barmy? I'm not familiar with the term." Craig assumed that he could deduce the meaning from context, but he wanted to be certain—and to force Nigel to elaborate.

"Ah, yes. Barmy. It's English slang. I think you say 'bonkers' or such, here in the States."

"In what way would you say he's barmy?"

Nigel chuckled. "Sounds strange now, you saying *barmy* with that American 'r' of yours. Uh, well, let's see. Barmy. Well, the man jabbers on and on. He's prissy and particular. He micromanages his staff ridiculously—drives them nuts. It's like Geoff's hopelessly nervous and frightened that the world is crashing down upon him at any moment—and he certainly lets everyone around him know about it." Nigel smiled. "You have to model a sense of confidence and calm if you're leading people, don't you think? I notice *you* do that."

"You don't like Geoff much, do you?" Craig inquired with a grin.

"I think you'd be properly hard-pressed to find anyone who does. Outside of Carolyn, that is. And honestly—I don't quite get that."

Craig dipped his head slightly, raised his eyebrows, and offered Nigel a knowing glance.

"It's been really good talking to you, Nigel," Craig said as he rose from his chair. "I've always liked your style. We'll talk more sometime. I have a meeting I need to run to now."

"Well, then . . ." Nigel said as he stood.

The men shook hands.

Craig nodded, smiled, and took his leave.

• • •

Craig took the night to consider it.

He dutifully laid out the pros and cons in writing—he always did a bit of that—but his purpose was never to glean a logical solution. Rather, it was to get the rational thinking taken care of and out of the way, so that his subconscious fount of intuition could assert itself unfettered, and eventually spurt out the decision that felt right to him.

The next morning, his first stop at work was to see his boss, whose office was at the other end of the hallway. Craig had to wait though, because Bruce, a senior VP, never arrived before nine-thirty (he did tend to hang around until seven or eight each evening). Bruce was a large, perennially cheerful man, with an immaculately bald head, large ears, horn-rimmed glasses, prominent hearing aids, and a mug of hot coffee always close by.

"Ah, Craig!" Bruce exclaimed in his customary resonant baritone when Craig popped his head through the door. Bruce rose and shook Craig's hand energetically, while his left hand grasped Craig's shoulder. "My favorite VP. What can I do for you?"

"Good morning, Bruce. I stopped by to let you know that Carolyn is leaving. She's transferring to our office back east. Family stuff."

"Oh. Too bad. She's a good one." Bruce had released Craig's hand but still held his shoulder affectionately. Bruce, nearly a head taller than Craig, now leaned in and whispered with a grin, "Not bad-looking either, is she?"

Craig nodded politely. "So, I'm thinking about her replacement. Everyone's expecting me to promote Geoff. He's her number two, he's next in line, he's paid his dues. But I wanted you to know that I intend to go with Nigel Silver instead."

"Geoff is a bit odd, isn't he?" Bruce whispered. "I don't know Nigel Silver at all."

"Nigel's only a senior manager, so it's unlikely that you would have run into him. But he's ready for this, and he's the right guy."

"Geoff will probably quit if you pass over him."

"Yes, I expect he will. Frankly, that's not a bad thing."

The senior VP smiled.

Craig paused a moment. "Listen, Bruce, if you don't feel totally right about it, I can give Nigel the position provisionally. And we can reassess after three months, or maybe six."

"No, no, Craig. This is your appointment and I trust you. If you say Nigel's the guy, then he's the guy. I have great confidence in your judgment. Put him in, free and clear. It's better for *him* that way, too."

"Thanks. He's going to be terrific."

"I'm sure you'll see to it that he is!" Bruce said with a hearty laugh. "Good seeing you. Thanks for the heads-up. Take care."

• • •

Craig's next stop was back in his office, with the door shut. He'd decided that a phone call to Carolyn would keep the histrionics somewhat more subdued than would be the case with a personal visit.

When she answered the phone, Craig could tell by the slightly mumbled cadence of her greeting that Carolyn was talking through a mouthful of her usual morning scone and Earl Grey tea with lemon and sugar. But as soon as he told her that he'd chosen Nigel, her tone sharpened.

"I had a feeling you might do this. It's a mistake—I'm not at all certain why you can't see it. It's a huge position, this one. Geoff has far more experience."

"I need someone I'm comfortable working with. Someone who models the values and perspectives I want this department to have. That's Nigel. It's not Geoff."

"You know, Craig, you and I haven't always seen exactly eye-to-eye on all that values and perspectives folderol—but you liked the job I did."

"You're very different from Geoff."

"Well, I suppose. But you need to understand that people in this department will find your choice most unexpected. I think some people may be upset."

"Well, people who actually *like* Geoff may be upset—but aside from you, Carolyn, I honestly don't come across many of those."

"Really? He's a steady leader." She took a moment to search for the optimal wording of her next thought. "Granted, Geoff has his little quirks. But he follows protocol. Nigel can be a bit headstrong—not a terribly obedient chap."

"That doesn't especially bother me. Within reason."

Carolyn sighed sardonically. "There you go, love, being bloody patient with people, again."

"You seem to like it when I'm *bloody* patient with you . . ."

"Oh, I don't mind that a bit," Carolyn replied, and began to giggle. "It's when you're patient with people who annoy me that I'm bothered. And people tend to annoy me rather easily."

Craig chuckled along with her. "There's a unique charm about how you express annoyance, Carolyn."

"Oh, is there? Well, hold onto that thought, dear—I'm quite certain you haven't seen me at my raging worst."

"Something to look forward to, then!" Craig paused, and modulated his tone. "Okay, then, Carolyn. It's done. I'm sorry we disagreed on this, but I'm going with Nigel. I'm about to call him now and tell him."

"Well, good luck. I truly hope he works out for you. He seems to like you, so there's that. I seriously doubt Geoff will stick around once he hears the news. So you'll have *him* to replace now, too."

"No. Actually it'll be *Nigel's* job to replace him. Nigel needs to put someone in there that he trusts, so it's an opportunity for him to do that, early on, and assert his leadership. It'll be good for him."

"I suppose." She paused and spoke softly. "And please, love, forgive me for prattling on about Nigel being a mistake. I'm sure he'll work out. Every decision you make seems to." She chuckled. "People think it's magical—like you're the mystical yogi with spiritual powers—but they don't see how scrappy you really are. I see it, though. Because I know you. I've watched you annihilate enemies—you can be bloody brutal, dear—but you do it so quietly and methodically. Like a sleek, shadowy ninja. I can picture you as a boy, Craig, surviving that way on the gritty streets of New York City. Quite a little sight!"

Craig laughed heartily. "My goodness," he said, "that's flattering. But let's keep it to ourselves. It's probably better if people continue to think of me as a guru and a pacifist."

She giggled. "Certainly gives you the element of surprise, doesn't it!" Carolyn puffed out a soft extended sigh. "Well, sorry I stirred all this up by moving east. Promise me though—you really must come visit me in Maryland. You do need to go there on business now and then, no? I mean, it's one of your regions."

"Oh, I think such a visit could be at least *semi*-plausibly justified."

She laughed. "Cheerio then, love. See you soon."

"Take care, Carolyn."

• • •

Craig took a few minutes to stroll to the break room and fill his mug with hot water. He tossed in a green chai tea bag from the few he always carried in his suit coat pocket, a squirt of honey from the small plastic-bear dispenser in the cupboard, and a narrow wooden stir-stick from the jar on the counter.

He returned to his office and phoned Nigel.

"Hello," Nigel said.

"Hi Nigel. It's Craig. How are you doing this morning?"

"Quite chipper. And you?"

"I'm doing well, Nigel. Do you have a couple of minutes? There's something I'd like to discuss."

"I'm free and clear."

"Well—the reason I'm calling—I'd like to offer you Carolyn's position. Are you interested?"

"I am," Nigel said, matter-of-factly. "Thank you."

Craig waited for Nigel to go on, but nothing more was forthcoming. After a few moments of uneasy silence, Craig said, "Well, that's terrific. I look forward to working with you." He paused. "Um—how should I say this, Nigel—I'm a tad surprised—I thought you'd be a bit more excited when I offered you the position."

"Ah, sorry mate. No. But perhaps you'll take some solace in knowing I would've been seriously pissed off had you given the position to anyone else. Especially that muppet Geoff."

Craig found Nigel's dry sense of humor irresistible. That particular quip sent him into a furious laughing spasm, and it took him nearly half a minute to settle himself and continue the conversation. "We should go to dinner sometime next week, Nigel, after work. Give us a chance to talk things through. How about Tuesday night?"

"I can make that happen."

"Great. Oh—and Nigel—when we're at dinner—please don't make me laugh like that if I have food in my mouth."

"Sorry, boss," Nigel said, "can't commit to that."

8

CLUB SODA

THE TOWNHOUSE SHOSHANA SCHUMACHER RENTED in Los Altos boasted two large bedrooms.

Both were equipped for play.

Most afternoons and evenings, Shoshana worked alone, but Friday and Saturday nights were popular—there was almost always some friend from the BDSM community who would rent the second playroom and do sessions herself as well. The rental terms were straightforward: there was a nominal nightly fee for use of the room and one of the phone lines, and ten percent of the hourly charges for the sessions performed. All ads to solicit business, whether in underground newspapers or elsewhere, had to contain the phrase "NO SEX" in uppercase letters.

It was especially nice for Shoshana when she could get someone to join her on a Tuesday, Wednesday, or Thursday night. Craig wasn't there on those days, and Shoshana very much enjoyed the company.

• • •

On this Friday evening, as Craig did every Friday before driving down to Los Altos, he first stopped at home to make sure that Golda's hutch was clean, and was stocked with sufficient hay and water to last till Saturday noon. Golda was accustomed to being put inside for the night a bit earlier on Fridays and Saturdays, and Craig always placed a couple of extra toys in the front area of the hutch to occupy her. Tonight that included a new one he'd purchased on the way home from work: a set of three small chew balls woven, respectively, from rattan, seagrass, and water hyacinth.

Golda had been sitting nearby, observing the goings-on. When she saw Craig position the chew balls atop the straw that lined the hutch's floor, she climbed up the upholstered stairs and settled inside. He latched the door behind her.

Through the wire mesh, Craig gazed at her for a time. She sniffed the seagrass ball and nudged it a bit with her nose. Then she began chewing on it.

As he watched her gnaw upon her toy, waggling inside the hutch's confines, Craig imagined that Golda felt serene—safe—protected from quandaries and turmoil.

Wistful tears pooled in his eyes.

Craig shook his head and recaptured his focus. He walked to the bedroom, changed into comfortable clothing, and began his leisurely drive down the peninsula.

• • •

It was a bit past seven when he arrived and let himself into the townhouse. He found Shoshana and her friend Lynn huddled around the small Formica table in the curtained-off area just to the left of the foyer entryway. The curtain was open—clearly there were no clients in the house right now. The tiny television that sat at the end of the table was on—its miniature portable antenna was plugged into one of the ports in back of the set. The two women, in tee shirts and jeans, were watching a rerun of Gilligan's Island, with the volume very low.

"Oh, hi, honey!" Shoshana said as her features curled into a broad smile and her large eyes beamed. She rose and greeted him with an exuberant hug and kiss. "You made good time coming down tonight. It's so nice to see you."

In the midst of their embrace, the phone rang. Shoshana glanced at the counter. From the lit button, it was clear to Craig that the line ringing was hers. She broke free and dashed over.

Craig turned to glance at Shoshana's friend Lynn and whispered a polite hello.

Shoshana lifted the phone to her ear. "Good evening," she intoned, affecting a distinctly imperious air, and slipping Craig a sly grin as she did.

She listened for a moment.

"Yes, this is Mistress Delilah. Do I know you?"

Craig grinned. He recalled those words vividly. A palpable chill had encased his body when he heard Shoshana say them, years ago, during his first call to her to schedule an appointment.

Shoshana's eyebrows lifted slightly, and she nodded.

"Oh. Yes, of course. I haven't seen you for quite a few weeks, Jack. Have you been a well-behaved boy—worthy of my attention?"

As she spoke, Shoshana cradled the receiver with her chin and shoulder, and thumbed through the index-card file.

"All right then, Jack, I'll see you at eight. And I needn't tell you to be on time. You wouldn't want to make your Mistress impatient, would you?"

Something on the index-card engendered a blink and a not quite audible sigh.

"Very well," Shoshana said, after a pause. "I'll see you at

eight." She hung up the phone.

She glanced at Lynn. "Jack Security Guard," Shoshana said.

Craig found it interesting that in Shoshana's business, which stressed anonymity, last names were never shared. Shoshana created her own identifiers using either the client's occupation or some unique physical trait.

"Craig, honey," Shoshana said as she finished scanning the index card and slipped it back in the small file box, "fetch me two of the bottles of club soda from the refrigerator and bring them in the back while I change into costume." She turned to Lynn. "I'd totally forgotten—he always likes to end the session with a golden shower. I'm dry as a bone. I need to hydrate." She began walking quickly to the larger of the two bedrooms in the back of the house.

"He'll be here in forty-five minutes, honey," Shoshana shouted.

Craig understood that to mean that she wanted her club sodas immediately. "Excuse me," he said to Lynn, as he nodded sheepishly and rushed to grab the bottles. He twisted one open as he walked to the back of the house.

• • •

What ensued in the master bedroom between the two of them was akin to a spontaneous and impeccably choreographed dance—Shoshana changing clothes and Craig assisting her. Though it looked to be scrupulously rehearsed, it was in actuality the result of years of Craig's careful attention to Shoshana's facial expressions, body language, and other subtle cues. It was something Shoshana had lectured him about, long ago. Craig remembered that discussion vividly, because it came just after Shoshana had stunned him by suggesting that they transition their relationship from one of weekly paid sessions to a personal and intimate liaison. After he told her that he'd love to do so, she said, "Craig, honey, for this to work, you need to understand—a good slave doesn't just obey—he anticipates his Mistress's needs and attends to them before she asks. A Mistress doesn't want to spend her time telling a slave what to do. She wants to be taken care of. Pampered. That needs to be your primary focus of attention, sweetie. You're very smart. I'm sure you can learn to do that."

So, it was in that spirit that he caught her tee shirt as she yanked it free and dropped it toward the floor. And while still holding the crumpled shirt in his hand, he gently grasped her pullover nylon spandex bra on either side just as she raised her arms, and he lifted the bra gracefully over her head.

She unbuckled and unzipped her jeans, and let them fall to the floor. Craig gathered them up the moment she stepped out of them, and he carried the tee shirt, bra, and jeans to the bureau in the corner of the room. As Shoshana gulped down the first bottle of club soda, Craig quickly folded the items and placed them in the bureau's bottom drawer, reserved for items that had been worn but weren't yet ready for laundry—"semi-clean" as Shoshana liked to call them.

Just as Craig closed the bottom drawer, he noticed Shoshana beside him, reaching for a drawer near the top. She held the empty bottle of club soda in her hand—Craig took it from her seamlessly, placed it back on the shelf next to the other bottle, and returned to Shoshana's side as she began rummaging about in the drawer. He watched as she chose a lacy red push-up bra (one of Craig's favorites), a red silver-studded leather corset, fishnet stockings, very high red stiletto heels, and a pair of red satin panties.

As soon as Craig saw her grab the satin panties, he lowered himself to one knee and gently pulled the more voluminous white cotton pair she was wearing down to her feet. Shoshana stepped out of them.

"Laundry hamper?" he whispered.

Shoshana's lips parted as if she were about to issue a perfunctory response, but she stopped, gazed at Craig who was still down on one knee, and smiled affectionately.

"You're being so sweet and attentive, honey. I think you deserve a treat. While I do the session, instead of you sitting out at the table in front, chatting with Lynn—how about I tie you up in the closet—like I used to when you were my brand-new personal slave?"

As Craig gazed up at her, still on one knee, his features softened into an astonished and appreciative twinkle. "Oh, yes, Empress. Thank you."

She reached down and held out her palm. He handed her the worn panties.

He could smell her essence the moment she thrust the wadded panties against his nostrils. Then she squeezed the sides of his jaw between the thumb and fingers of her free hand, forcing his mouth open. "You'll taste me while you're in the closet," she said, as she stuffed the panties into his mouth. He received them willingly. Gratefully.

"I used to do this to you all the time, sweetie. Remember?"

He nodded yes. It had been so long since she'd gagged him with her panties—so long since they'd done anything remotely like this when she wasn't showing off at a play-party.

• • •

Shoshana was nearly Craig's height in stocking feet. Now, fully in costume, balanced regally on her six-inch heels, she was half-a-head taller. Craig's slender physique appeared even more scant when juxtaposed against her voluptuous big-boned frame. As he stared into her eyes, these disparities were prominent in his consciousness—they aroused him, luring him inexorably into an even more compliant and submissive state.

She had him sit cross-legged on the floor in the closet—not at all difficult for a man who practiced full lotus at four each morning. "Be absolutely silent," she reminded him. "My client can't know you're in here." She rolled a bandana, wedged the middle of it between his lips, and tied it behind his head to keep the wadded panties inside his mouth. She secured it only moderately tightly—it was more for effect—he could work it loose if he were about to choke—but that would only happen if he panicked. And as she tied his hands in front of him at chin level with soft hemp rope and secured the end of the rope to a closet beam above his head, he felt as calm and relaxed as when he meditated.

The moment she closed the closet door, an evanescent surge shot through his loins. The closet's shutting had automatically turned off its overhead light. The darkness now was engulfing, yet somehow comforting—it deepened his sensibility of surrender.

• • •

For a short time the room outside was empty—he had heard Shoshana leave when the doorbell rang. She soon returned with her client.

"Strip naked, slave," Shoshana commanded.

"Yes, Mistress Delilah," Craig heard the man whisper.

From the dark closet, through pitched slats that ran horizontally at the base of the door, Craig caught glimpses of Shoshana's feet—first in her high red heels as she positioned her client in the middle of the room. She unfolded her step stool beside him. He heard the man exhale excitedly, and when he saw Shoshana's stiletto heels climb the two stairs on the stepstool, he pictured her stretching the man's manacled hands taut above his head while securing the chain from his cuffs to the ceiling hook directly above him, making sure to leave no slack—just as she had done so many times with Craig, when he was a paying customer.

Then he caught a glimpse of Shoshana's hands, as she bent down and strapped the respective ends of a long spreader bar to each of her client's ankles, rendering the man vulnerable and nearly immobile. She must have blindfolded him then, because a moment later he saw Shoshana moving about the carpet in her stocking feet, pulling the stepstool aside, then reappearing with the tip of a leather whip slithering along beside her, as she positioned herself behind the helpless man. As Craig listened to the lashes being administered, and the man's ecstatic moans, he made a mental note to remember to swab the leather blindfold clean with alcohol when he tidied up the room (which he knew Shoshana would do herself, for purposes of sanitation, were he not there). Craig had never realized, as a client, how much Shoshana hated walking in those heels, and how she removed them secretly as soon as her client was blindfolded and slipped them back on again just before the session ended and she released him.

And it also explained why Shoshana never blindfolded her clients with a scarf—Craig knew from experience that one could see downward through the tiny gaps caused by the bridge of the nose and cheekbones if blindfolded with a scarf. Snug-fitting leather blindfolds, shaped to fit the contours of the face, left no such apertures.

Their effectiveness in concealing Shoshana's stocking feet

was a pragmatic solution to a problem.

But the manner in which they immersed an already bound man into a sensibility of utter powerlessness was delicious, insidious, and relentless.

9

BRUSCHETTA AND GIMLETS

LIKE MOST PEOPLE, ADELLE DORN LOOKED FORWARD to weekends, appreciating the break from work. But for her, other far more important factors came into play.

Her husband's job required that he be on the road, away from home, a great deal of the time. More troubling for her, though, was that it necessitated Byron's being unflaggingly outgoing and collaborative—a pretense that she knew was counter to his nature—the stress of which she suspected took a long-term toll upon his mental and physical well-being.

So weekends were a relief to her. On Saturdays and Sundays she watched as Byron toiled happily, alone and in silence, doing seemingly endless repairs and upgrades on their East Bay home—exhibiting the sort of patience and quiet focus that she believed calmed and centered him.

They could certainly have afforded to pay contractors to do these things. But Byron adamantly refused to do so. He said he resented the outrageous fees contractors charged. But Adelle suspected that the real satisfaction he derived was in proving that he could accomplish exactly what professionals did, just by renting a do-it-yourself video from Blockbuster, reading a couple of articles, and proceeding with great caution and planning.

The fact that it took him months of weekend labor to do what a skilled contractor might have accomplished in a day's time didn't bother him—Byron insisted to her that his scrupulous attention to detail made for a better job in the end. Adelle doubted that was true, but she was happy that the work kept him busy and out of trouble, and contributed to his overall health.

She even pitched in to help a bit on those rare occasions that Byron needed someone to steady a ladder or hold a can of paint. Mostly though, Byron worked by himself. Adelle would make him snacks and bring him bottles of sparkling Pellegrino water—the only brand he'd drink.

On this particular Saturday, Byron had already spent several hours on his hands and knees, laying new tile in their guest bathroom. Months ago, Byron's knees had grown so worn by such work that he was experiencing pain and trouble just standing and walking day-to-day. Adelle had insisted he see a doctor, but predictably, Byron had refused. He did not have a regular doctor—he hated physicians in general and refused to have anything to do with them. Whenever she pressed him on this, he fully acknowledged that his eating and drinking habits, the stress of his job, his being overweight, and the fact that he engaged in no daily exercise had most likely rendered him susceptible to various heinous conditions, some perhaps already incubating inside him. But he insisted he was happier not knowing. If one of these blights someday reared up and struck him dead, he just hoped it would be quick and relatively painless. He saw no point in spending time dwelling on it—he wasn't about to change his ways.

So, Adelle had consulted privately about the pain in Byron's knees, with the local doctor for whom she worked. And now, when Byron laid tile, he dutifully wore the bulky cushioned knee pads the doctor had recommended. They appeared to have resolved the problem—or at least rendered Byron unwilling to mention any further episodes of discomfort.

• • •

It was four in the afternoon.

Byron had been working since morning on the bathroom floor, and was now happy to pause for a few minutes and eat the half dozen pieces of warm bruschetta that Adelle had prepared for him. Byron loved Italian food, and carefully guarded his position as the designated chef in the house—but he permitted Adelle to make the occasional tidbit, as long as she prepared it according to his precise instructions.

Adelle stood in the foyer, just outside the entrance to the bathroom, as Byron munched on her garlic-rubbed toast, which she'd obligingly topped with small chunks of room-temperature San Marzano tomatoes, and drizzled liberally with a fine and fruity extra virgin olive oil. He took a sip of Pellegrino after he swallowed each bite.

"How's the bruschetta?" Adelle asked.

"Good. You made it good."

Adelle wore her platinum-dyed hair in a voluminous pixie cut, which Byron thought worked well for her—longer hair might have called undue attention to Adelle's short, boxy stature. She was slightly overweight, but because she carried most of it in her breasts and hips, Byron liked the result.

"So, what's new, honey?" Adelle asked. "Anything going on at work?"

Byron chewed his mouthful especially slowly, took a swig of the sparkling water, and finally said, "That new guy. The one Craig promoted. Nigel. He seems like a real dipshit."

"What's the matter with him?"

"He's a fucking smart-ass."

"Maybe he's nervous in the new position," Adelle offered.

Byron took a large bite. His eyebrows dipped with disquiet as he chewed. He spoke slowly, his lower teeth growing more prominent as he went on. "I think this Nigel guy is Craig's new favorite. Craig's doing a tour of all the regions—taking Nigel with him like his little lap dog." Byron gulped some Pellegrino. "You know—*I* used to be Craig's favorite."

"I'm sure you're still his favorite, Byron. Nigel's just new. He probably needs some hand-holding."

"Craig never travels with *me*. Never did. Sure—once in a while he happens to be in the same region where I am—so he joins us for dinner. That's different."

"You travel to all the regions yourself, all the time, honey. You wouldn't *want* Craig with you—you know, looking over your shoulder all the time. You were an experienced director when he hired you. So, he didn't need to go with you on trips."

"Well. Yeah. I didn't need him. And he knew that. And he hates big, loud dinners anyway."

"So, what's *really* eating at you, Byron?"

Byron chewed some more, wondering if he should share his thought. He took a long swig of sparkling water. Then he shook his head. "No. Something's different with the two of them." He paused and gazed piercingly into Adelle's eyes. "They're both Jews—Craig and Nigel—did you realize that? I think something's up with that."

Adelle's features tightened, and her lips narrowed. "I knew Craig and Shoshana were. Even when they do Christmas dinner, and invite us over—it's not a real Christmas thing, you know?"

"True."

"Well, honey, you might *have* something there. Those Jews do stick together. You know—do favors for one another—sneaky—the way they do it."

Byron finished the last piece of bruschetta. "That's exactly what I think is going on."

"You know, Byron," Adelle said, "you haven't been out to dinner with Craig for a few weeks. You should set one up, on a night you're in town. You two always go out once a month or so. To that Italian place you like."

"I was waiting, you know, hoping *he'd* set something up."

"Craig's busy, honey. Set it up yourself. Take the initiative. Then you can talk to him. You know—the way you're good at. My guess is, Craig still has your back, honey."

"That's not a bad idea." Byron paused and took two long swigs of the Pellegrino, finishing the bottle. He gazed at Adelle and hesitated for a moment before he spoke. "There's something else I need to tell you."

"What, honey?"

"It's weird. Really weird. I think I discovered something about Shoshana. You know, Craig's wife."

"Sure. We've known Shoshana for years."

"Maybe not as well as we thought. You won't believe this. I saw her one night. Walking. In Los Altos. Alone. With grocery bags."

"What? Why were you in Los Altos?"

"The freeway was jammed up. I was trying to get home. Anyway—she has a place down there. Like a townhouse. I watched it. Men came by. They showed up right on the hour. I checked it out a couple of other nights too. There's always men. Right on the hour."

"My god. You spied on her?"

"Well, just kind of checked it out a few times. I couldn't believe it so I had to see." He shook his head in disbelief. "I think she's some kind of high-end prostitute."

"Jesus! What? Shoshana? A prostitute? How the hell could that be? I find that very hard to believe."

"I do too. But, if it's true—I mean, who knows—maybe I could use it to my advantage."

"What do you mean—to your advantage? Like blackmail? Is that what you mean?"

"I don't know. I haven't thought it through. But don't you think it could be a useful thing? I mean—potentially—in some way or another?"

Adelle said nothing for a moment. Then her eyes narrowed. "Let me give that some thought, honey. This is juicy. And totally bizarre. In the meantime, have that dinner with Craig. See what you can find out about that new guy he promoted. But don't mention anything about Shoshana."

• • •

As was habitual, the email Craig received contained one word:

"Carlucci's?"

The response Craig crafted, as was invariably the case, was a bit more expansive:

"Dinner sounds great, Byron. It's been a while, it will be nice to catch up. How's next Tuesday? Looks like you'll be in town that day."

Byron's reply:

"Good."

The venue for Craig and Byron's periodic dinners never varied. Craig knew that Byron considered Carlucci's the best Italian food in San Francisco, and wouldn't eat anywhere else. It was old-fashioned Italian cuisine—rich sauces and big portions.

And the restaurant sufficed for Craig too—he could get reliable vegetarian fare. At home, during the week, when Craig cooked for himself, he unfailingly made simple but very tasty and well-seasoned vegan stews of beans, organic vegetables, whole grains, and a sprinkling of raw nuts and seeds.

But the traditional diet prescribed by Yogis for centuries to promote spiritual illumination was lacto-vegetarian, not vegan—so Craig had no problem with expanding his choices to include dairy when he dined with friends or on the weekends when he shared meals with Shoshana.

• • •

There was never a need to specify meeting time. Byron had grown accustomed to Craig's making the reservation for 6:00 p.m.—and also to Craig's dependably arriving just prior to that hour.

Byron, however, made certain to leave work early so he could get to Carlucci's right at five. That was when their bar opened, and it filled up quickly—the tall wooden stools were all snatched up long before five-thirty, when the restaurant began serving food.

And Byron loved that Carlucci's wizened old bartender was so familiar with his preferences that he began mixing his drink as soon as he caught a glimpse through the restaurant's large front window of Byron outside, striding toward the entryway. A vodka gimlet with an extra splash of simple syrup was set down the moment Byron claimed his favorite spot, the last stool at the far end of the bar.

Byron was working on his second gimlet when he saw Craig

enter the restaurant.

Craig Schumacher was not an especially tall man, but he was several inches taller than Byron Dorn, palpably evident to Byron as he rose from his bar stool and engaged in a brief perfunctory hug. And though Craig was less than ten years younger, the wrinkles on Byron's forehead and around his eyes, and the sagging skin on Byron's cheeks and chin, made the gap feel far more stark.

As the two men's bodies fused for that cursory hug, Byron was reminded, jarringly and viscerally, of the disparity in their reporting relationship, as well as in their height and age. As the men separated, Byron silently assured himself that he was the far beefier of the two, and because he worked with his hands much more frequently, he could surely dispatch his willowy yoga-obsessed boss quite quickly, were they ever to come to blows.

"Are we ready to claim our table?" Craig inquired cheerfully.

"Yeah. Gimme a minute."

Byron chugged the remainder of his drink and threw a few bills on the bar—enough for his tab, plus a generous tip for the bartender. He noticed Craig signal to the hostess, who grabbed two menus and motioned for them to follow her.

Byron set off as Craig walked behind him.

• • •

Craig wasn't sure exactly how many drinks Byron had already quaffed, but he guessed only one or two, because it was clear that Byron had not yet transmogrified into a communicative, confident, and congenial dinner companion. In fact, Craig's observation was that the first couple of drinks each evening often tended to render Byron resentful and testy—a temporary circumstance additional cocktails would quickly ameliorate.

Their stroll to the usual table in the rear of the large back room took nearly a minute, and as Craig watched Byron saunter before him in his distinctive swiveling shuffle, Craig flashed back to Byron's curious hiring process, several years ago.

Under the vice president who preceded Craig, the position of executive director for interfaces and conversions had been filled, for nearly two years, by a slick, senior-level partner from a large national consulting firm, who'd been steadily building his own little empire inside the department. For reasons that seemed murky at the time, that VP was unexpectedly fired and Craig installed in his place. One of Craig's first assigned priorities was to get a full-time employee in to replace the smooth-tongued consultant, and to begin to dismantle the prodigious pool of entry-level contractors from that same consulting firm, which now comprised over half of the interfaces and conversions team. When, just weeks after Craig had settled into his job, the recently dispatched VP was hired into an executive position by the consulting firm in question, the reasons behind his firing became decidedly less murky.

Craig had no one to promote from within into the executive director spot, so he asked the human resources department to start a nationwide search for an experienced candidate to fill the position.

Byron Dorn, at the time, held a fairly equivalent job at a small firm in Tallahassee. So, Craig expected that for him, this opportunity to join a national corporation based in San Francisco, with a much bigger team and at a significantly higher salary, would be enticing.

Craig had been impressed with Byron's resume and endorsements, and wanted very much to like him. It took half a dozen long phone interviews though, for Craig to warm fully to Byron's strange speaking cadence and laconic nature. But

Byron's experience, track record, and ultimately his lack of pretense—along with the dearth of any other reasonably qualified candidates and a pressing need to fill the position—won Craig over in time.

Once Craig brought Byron on, it then fell to Craig to convince an array of skeptical associates, clients, and superiors that once they gave Byron a chance, they'd come to see his impeccable competence, and perhaps even his subtle charm. But people remained stubbornly reluctant to accept him, until Craig scheduled a major strategy presentation and made Byron one of his featured speakers. Craig coached Byron fastidiously, forcing him to rehearse the PowerPoint slide show and field rapid-fire questions Craig threw at him, ad nauseam.

The meticulous preparation reaped benefits—Byron's presentation was well received, and he was warmly accepted by the enterprise from that point forward.

• • •

As soon as the hostess seated Craig and Byron, the waiter appeared and asked if they wanted drinks. Byron ordered another vodka gimlet with an extra splash of simple syrup. Craig, as always, requested a bottle of O'Doul's, a non-alcoholic beer—and Byron knew Craig would nurse that one bottle through the entire evening. Though Byron never commented on it, he always wondered what the hell was the point of ordering a bottle of beer that contained no alcohol. He assumed it was just part of Craig's yoga vegetarian madness, and he knew better than to question that.

• • •

"So, Byron, how are things going in your department?" Craig asked.

"Good."

"Good?" Craig repeated, hoping for a bit more detail.

"Goin' good."

"So, I assume your team is finishing up unit testing on the interfaces that will be part of what Nigel's group starts integrated testing on, at the end of this month?"

"Right."

Craig was incredibly relieved when the waiter appeared with the drinks and promised to return soon for the food order. Craig was careful to remain silent and give Byron a chance to down his gimlet. When Byron raised his hand to catch the waiter's attention across the room and pointed to his nearly empty glass to signal that he wanted another, Craig grew confident that soon, meaningful conversation would ensue.

Byron's fourth gimlet was delivered when the waiter returned to take their dinner order. They decided to start with a bottle of Pellegrino for the table. For a shared appetizer, they chose bruschetta—made Carlucci-style with chopped tomatoes and fruity olive oil—precisely as Craig and Shoshana had enjoyed it many times when invited to the Dorns' home for dinner.

After a few sips of his fourth cocktail, Byron's demeanor changed markedly. He leaned back comfortably in his chair and his shoulders began heaving rhythmically, up and down, as he chuckled.

"You remember the first time we had dinner together?" Byron asked, still laughing as he spoke. "I saw you were ordering all vegetarian stuff. And I thought, what the hell—is my new boss gonna be insulted and pissed because I'm eating veal and shit?"

"Yes," Craig said, smiling, "I remember. And I remember exactly what I said when you asked about it, because I've said it to so many people, so many times."

"Right," Byron replied, "that hardly anyone you knew was a vegetarian—that even your wife wasn't a vegetarian. And if you only ate with vegetarians, you'd never have anybody to eat with."

"That's exactly right. And I believe I added this: Do I *wish* that all people in the world were vegetarian? And that *nobody* killed animals to eat them? Yes! Of course. And do I believe that will *happen* someday? Yes, absolutely."

"But do you think there's a chance in hell of it happening in your lifetime?"

"Not a chance," Craig said with a grin. "Maybe a thousand years from now, but not in my lifetime. But you know, Byron, my spiritual side has to coexist with the world I live in. I want to be a productive person in this life. So I make do—the best I can."

"You do fine."

After the bruschetta, Byron's first course was prosciutto e melone—cold, thinly sliced Italian ham served with melon. Craig opted for a bowl of the minestrone soup, a hearty vegetable, bean, and pasta concoction. Craig was always comforted by the assurance, right on the menu, that the soup, including the stock, was pure vegetarian. He liked not having to ask. The serving was sizable .

"So," Byron asked, "your new director—Nigel—he's doing okay?"

"Yes, I think so," Craig replied, after swallowing a mouthful of the flavorful minestrone and gauging Byron's nonchalance in posing the question as feigned. "Nigel and I visited the five small regions—well, the five here on the continent. The Hawaii region we'll do by teleconference. And the big Southern California region—that's another trip in itself. But I think he adjusted well. His natural inclination is to be brash, and to think that he's charming enough to get away with anything he says. That didn't work exactly right, and I talked to him about it. And, you know, to his credit, he dialed it back. At first, he overcompensated a bit. But by the third meeting or so, he really had it down. I think he's going to do fine—he made some friends out there already."

"Good. Good to hear." Byron finished his cocktail. "You're right though, he can come on too strong at first."

"That's true, Byron. But, you know, guys like us—we've been doing it for so many years, we take that kind of thing for granted—how to interact with people. But we had to learn it too, way back when. Nigel's still young. And I have to say, he picked up on it pretty quickly. I think you'll enjoy working with him."

The irony of Byron's observations about Nigel's interpersonal style, given Byron's own frequent bumbling in that same arena, was not lost on Craig, who chuckled silently and imperceptibly to himself.

The main courses arrived. Byron's was saltimbocca alla romana—veal with prosciutto and mozzarella, which was served with a side of pasta and marinara.

Craig had a bowl of fettuccine pesto.

Before the waiter departed, Byron ordered a glass of Chianti to drink with his veal.

"So, you think I'll like working with Nigel?" Byron pressed.

"I do. You know, his people have to test all the software that our various departments produce. Integrated testing. Volume testing. It all comes together in his shop. So it's important that we all can work well with him—and I do think that once everyone gets to know each other, that will happen. Nigel has a good heart. People will see that. And he's smart."

"Maybe too smart for his own good, sometimes?" Byron said, his shoulders once again heaving with laughter, as his Chianti was set down.

Craig chuckled. "I think he'll tone that down a little—and everyone will get used to him and tolerate his sarcasm a bit more—so we'll all meet in the middle. His sarcasm is actually pretty funny, sometimes, you know, if you're braced for it."

Byron took a huge gulp of Chianti.

Craig finished a mouthful of his fettuccini and took a small sip of his non-alcoholic beer. "Listen, Byron, I just had an idea. Nigel and his wife Justine are coming over to our house for dinner Sunday night. Why don't you and Adelle join us, and make it a sixsome?"

"A sixsome, eh? Sounds interesting." He paused. "Yeah, I think we'd like that."

The expression on Byron's face, and the uncharacteristically measured cadence in his response, made it immediately clear to Craig that this invitation had struck Byron as an afterthought to a rendezvous from which he had been initially excluded—and that Byron resented not only the impromptu nature of his inclusion, but the very fact that Craig and Shoshana were socializing with Nigel and Justine at all.

Craig was tempted to try to make some comment to mitigate Byron's angst. His skill at ameliorating perceived slights was well honed, and served him admirably, both at work and in his liaison with Shoshana. But right now, nothing came to mind that didn't have the potential to actually prolong and exacerbate the situation. So Craig said nothing.

They finished dinner in silence.

When the waiter came to take away the plates, Byron ordered his usual after dinner cordial. "A double Grand Marnier," he instructed the waiter.

"Nothing for me," Craig added.

The waiter departed.

"So, what will you be serving for this sixsome dinner?" Byron suddenly inquired.

Craig was a bit surprised that Byron had resurrected the topic, but was relieved that he had. "Well, as usual," Craig said with a sheepish smile, "we're going to order from somewhere. You know Shoshana doesn't cook. And I *love* to cook, but I only cook vegetarian, which Shoshana doesn't mind, but I wouldn't foist it on guests." He chuckled. "And certainly not on *you*, Byron, fanatical carnivore that you are. We haven't decided where to order from yet, but if you and Adelle are coming, I suppose we can get takeout from here at Carlucci's—so you two will be sure you'll like the food."

"Carlucci's, eh?"

The waiter set down Byron's double Grand Marnier and departed. Byron lifted the drink and appeared to gaze at it—the sweet golden liqueur glistened at the bottom of its huge ornate glass snifter.

"Oh—and Byron," Craig said, "a thought just occurred to me. If you don't mind, maybe *you* can be the designated bartender that night." Craig grinned apologetically. "Instead of *me*, I mean—I don't drink, so I don't know much about it. I usually try to do the best I can with that little cheat-book I have—you know, the bartender's guide, with all the drink recipes—but it would be really nice to have a pro like you to mix drinks for people."

Byron was silent for a moment. Then his eyebrows heaved upward, and he smiled. "I'll tell you what, buddy," he said, "why don't we move the dinner to *my* house, down in Cupertino. Cooking Italian food is my specialty. I'll make dinner and take care of drinks." He leaned back with his glass of Grand Marnier and curled his paunchy frame against the cushiony seat. His shoulders rose and fell as he chuckled. "And don't worry, man. There'll be a vegetarian version of everything—for you!" He laughed heartily. "Byron Dorn guarantees it." He raised his glass of Grand Marnier in Craig's direction, then reeled it back to his own lips. He took a long swig, and with a sly smirk, he added, "I'll even get you a goddamn bottle of O'Doul's."

10

FETTUCCINE ALFREDO

IT WAS A SUNNY SUNDAY AFTERNOON IN THE SOUTH Bay.

Byron Dorn parked his old, seldom-used black van in what he considered a perfect spot, on that now-familiar street in Los Altos.

Later that evening, at their home in Cupertino just a few miles to the south, he and Adelle would be hosting the dinner for six. Byron already had the menu thoroughly planned, the precise timing for cooking the various courses committed to memory, and the ingredients laid out on the counter in the order he'd need them.

Now, as he sat in the van, Byron did some quick calculations: in less than an hour, Nigel and Justine would start their drive down from Marin County, to pick up Craig and Shoshana at their home in San Francisco. The four of them would then continue down the peninsula for the hour trip to Cupertino, headed for the get-together.

All of which meant that Shoshana couldn't possibly be at the Los Altos house now.

But Byron had spied on the house sufficiently at this point to know she was never there on Sundays in any case.

When he shut off the engine, Byron noted that there was a lamppost at the end of the block—but he suspected that, at night, it would be nearly pitch-black at the spot where he was stationing the van. He'd been circling the block for over half an hour, waiting for a place within camera range of the house.

There weren't all that many cars parked on the block, but Byron needed to secure a space with an unimpeded view of the home's front door—preferably at an angle that would expose at least a sliver of the inside hallway when the door opened just enough to permit a man to enter. Where the van was situated now was perfect.

Byron had approached this foray into reconnaissance with precisely the same sort of patience and methodical organization he brought to the weekend renovation projects at his home, and the plotting of business strategies at work. He was prone to being painfully meticulous—when sober.

He had even taken into account the fact that repeatedly circling the block, searching for this ideal parking space, might have aroused suspicion—so he instead made wider circles, sometimes wandering a quarter or half-mile away from the house, and he chose slightly different routes each time, to minimize the likelihood of drawing attention to his machinations.

He'd started on the project weeks ago, searching intensively to find the most appropriate equipment. He'd familiarized himself thoroughly with how the instruments operated, and he'd made certain, through exhaustive testing, that the infrared camera and the motion sensor attachment would work seamlessly together in this application. Byron had then rigged up brackets to affix the camera inconspicuously, at an adjustable angle, behind the rear side window of the van, and tested it again from that position.

His final tweak just prior to declaring the system operational was to disable the small red light that signaled when the camera was on. In the near total darkness of the street, he didn't want it calling attention to the van.

It was ready to go.

Byron hoped it would produce conclusive evidence.

Admittedly though, at this point, Byron himself hardly needed more convincing. What he'd observed, after a good number of after-work stakeouts, had pretty much confirmed in his mind what was going on.

What *was* vital, though, was that the camera would enable him to record his findings.

Even without the videos he was about to amass, however, pure logic would pretty much have made the case. If Shoshana were a therapist of some sort, the hour-long sessions would have made sense. But she had never mentioned being a therapist. And if she *were* a licensed therapist, there would be some listing for her and her therapeutic specialty. Nothing of the sort existed.

Nor was it at all likely that a female therapist would see only men—men who, in fact, didn't look especially like the type who'd seek therapy—men who did not return regularly for appointments at the same time each week.

In all the conversations he could remember among the four of them, Shoshana had never once referenced an actual job. He knew she did some crafts and sold a bit of that on the internet—she'd always use that as a diversion if questions about a job came up. But mawkish needle-felted animals that took many days to make, and sold for just thirty dollars each if they sold at all, could hardly contribute significantly to the family income. The house Craig and Shoshana lived in was impressive and situated in a remote and exclusive area of San Francisco.

It was possible Shoshana came from wealth, but she didn't seem the type—and when she talked about her childhood in Philadelphia, she always depicted a modest middle-class household.

Byron was absolutely certain that his boss Craig hadn't grown up in a wealthy family—Craig often mentioned how he came from a lower middle-class Jewish neighborhood in Brooklyn. Byron had heard him relate stories, over dinner, about playing stoopball and stickball in the street, while his mother kept an eye on him through the kitchen window of their small, two-bedroom apartment.

Although Craig now made a good deal of money, it still was probably not enough to sustain that home, and the vacations that he and Shoshana regularly took.

There had to be other income.

And if Shoshana earned money in some other way, Byron was determined to ascertain precisely how.

With the camera setup complete, he turned the apparatus on and did a quick test. When he was confident that it was working as planned, he pulled out his cellphone and called his wife.

"Hey, Adelle," he said. "I'm done. It's set. It'll work exactly the way I said. You can come pick me up, now."

• • •

Though he did his best to disguise it, Craig Schumacher found the body language and facial expressions of Justine and Nigel inordinately amusing—the way their bearing shifted so jarringly the moment Adelle opened the front door and greeted them.

It was clear that Justine and Nigel feared that they had upset their host in some way, because Adelle appeared to be grousing and whining at them as soon as they entered the house. But after a few uncomfortable moments, the two at last seemed to realize that Adelle was fine—vocalizing in that manner was evidently her odd, but customary inflection.

Craig wondered, just momentarily, if perhaps he should have warned the two about Adelle's idiosyncratic vocal intonation during the drive down. But he quickly brushed away that concern. Watching the situation unfold was beguiling for him, and he assumed it would also provide for a lighthearted bit of repartee during the ride back.

Adelle suggested a tour of the house, an offer that Justine and Nigel jumped upon. Shoshana quickly opted to join them as well.

Adelle was dwarfed by her three guests as they set off. Shoshana and Justine were both tall women—Justine slender, and Shoshana full-figured—but even in medium heels neither was quite as tall as Nigel, who stood just over six feet. All three women appeared to be directing their comments exclusively Nigel's way, so Craig also surmised that Nigel was, from their perspective at least, quite pleasingly constructed.

Shoshana, of course, had visited the Dorns' home many times and didn't need the tour, but she'd decided to tag along with Justine and Nigel anyway. "Your home is so lovely," she'd exclaimed to Adelle, "I want to see it all again." But Craig was sure that her opting to join was merely a convenient ploy, enabling Shoshana to avoid Byron's company until he'd had sufficient libation to render himself bearable.

All of which left Craig in the kitchen, alone with Byron, who was now thoroughly immersed in intensive chef mode, uttering nary a word as he labored methodically to churn out his meal. Craig took a small sip from the heavy glass mug into which Byron had emptied that promised bottle of chilled O'Doul's.

Byron worked in silence. As he did, Craig grew bored. He had assumed that Nigel would keep him company in the kitchen, and was surprised when Nigel had announced he'd take the tour with the women. In Craig's experience, men generally had little interest in house furnishings—so Craig's immediate inference was that Nigel, like Shoshana, was simply looking for an excuse to avoid Byron's churlish company. But Craig had been forced to reconsider that assumption when he heard Nigel comment that he was truly fascinated with how homes were laid out—and again when the three walked off, and Justine mentioned that Nigel had been intimately involved in every decorating decision they'd made for their house in San Rafael.

After mulling all that over for a minute or two, Craig ultimately concluded that a combination of both considerations probably caused Nigel to make the decision he did—after all, if Nigel had opted to major in geography, he probably did care at least a bit about how things around him were laid out—and Nigel's office, with its globe and chess set, had indeed seemed calculatedly striking.

Craig took another leisurely sip of the O'Doul's. Knowing it would be a while before Byron's surly edge softened and conversation ensued, he decided he had time to conjure up one of the aphorisms he'd examined recently from *The Yoga Sutras of Patanjali*, and ponder some personal additions to the commentary of Sri Swami Satchidananda.

But Craig's silent rumination didn't yield anything especially new or interesting, and he soon found his attention turning back to Byron, who had mixed himself a second gimlet and downed at least half of it, and who was now tossing a bowl of chilled greens he'd retrieved from the refrigerator. From what Craig could discern, Byron had whisked a dressing together on the fly, blending extra virgin olive oil, balsamic vinegar, salt, pepper, and the tiniest touch of Dijon mustard.

As he watched Byron guzzle some more of his gimlet, Craig recalled the times while on business travel that he'd found himself in the same corporate region as Byron. He had been able, on those occasions, to observe firsthand the unique manner in which Byron attacked his responsibilities.

Byron's department built and installed interfaces and conversions—software that enabled old computer systems to talk to new ones. Especially now, with Y2K just a year and a half away, and the company using that deadline to try to standardize and unify the processes of the various regions via a new national suite of computer systems—Byron was on the road more than ever.

Craig found the inherent nature of Byron's job fascinating. Both interfaces and conversions—the two software products Byron's team produced—needed to be designed with great precision. And although both required exhaustive testing—the two entities differed from each other fundamentally in a manner which engendered entirely disparate levels of anxiety in the regional people with whom Byron interacted.

Interfaces were built to enable real-time sharing of data between old regional legacy systems that were remaining in place, and new national systems that would exist alongside them. So, interface software would be up and running twenty-four hours a day, seven days a week, for years to come. Thus, the regional technicians who maintained the old legacy systems would keep their jobs.

Conversions, on the other hand, were software packages built to work once and once only. They sucked the data out of an old, now obsolete regional system just prior to its demise, and then converted that data into formats that could be fed into the new, national replacement system just before it went live. When the old system was gone, the need for the regional technicians who maintained it also disappeared.

The dilemma for Byron, though, was that despite the different human impacts of the two, both interfaces and conversions required the same exacting technical precision to build. And there was only one way to do it—through open, thorough, and seemingly endless personal conversations between the regional people working on the old systems, and people from Byron's national team working on the new ones—to painstakingly identify and map the format and purpose of every individual data element that the products utilized.

Predictably, regional staff, fearful of losing their autonomy and, in some cases, their livelihoods, were reluctant to communicate openly and constructively with people they viewed as marauding usurpers from the national office.

So, coordinating such discussions took great skill and tact.

But Byron Dorn, whose job responsibilities included overseeing, scheduling, and moderating endless numbers of such conversations, was by nature neither gregarious nor ingratiating. As a man of few words, which he sputtered out in a curt, clipped cadence, Byron often appeared to people first meeting him as sullen and gruff.

Craig had observed however that, over time, people realized that Byron carefully considered everything said to him—that he was pragmatic and reasonable in every suggestion he offered—and that, true to his word, he invariably tried to identify new job responsibilities that could provide opportunities for any displaced regional technical staff.

But the most outrageous trick in his arsenal was that every evening, without fail, Byron took the people with whom he was working, both regional folks and members of his own national team, out for dinner and drinks at some local Italian restaurant.

Once there, after three or four cocktails, Byron magically morphed into a jovial wag—the shoulders of his short paunchy frame heaving with constant laughter, as he related humorous tales amidst burgeoning revelry.

Craig had partaken personally in only a few of those rowdy dinners, but he had clearly witnessed their therapeutic long-term effects on cooperation and communication. For this reason, Craig never argued with Byron's colossal expense account reimbursement tallies. That was how Byron did business, and his results were impeccable. Craig simply incorporated the numbers into his budget for Byron's department—classifying the expenditures as customer engagement costs.

• • •

Byron prosecuted his formula for dinner preparation with maniacal focus, which in turn, now slowed his drinking a bit. There was still some of his second gimlet remaining in his glass as he put the final touches on his wide assortment of appetizers. Byron desperately wanted people to love his food—and he knew that people clung stubbornly to first impressions—so his appetizers needed to be especially dazzling visually as well as gastronomically.

Green and black olives of various shapes and sizes were piled fastidiously into a hand-painted ceramic bowl Byron had purchased in Deruta, Italy. The bowl had a smaller matching receptacle attached to it for depositing pits.

Hefty wedges of Italian cheeses, ranging from creamy gorgonzola, to young and mild provolone, and finally to firm and sharp pecorino, were set out agreeably on a small cutting board with a cheese knife and crackers.

Pieces of sourdough toast for Byron's signature bruschetta

had just been snatched from the oven, and were now being quickly rubbed with a raw garlic clove, prior to being topped with chopped San Marzano tomatoes and extra virgin olive oil.

And an array of thinly sliced Italian meats—salty prosciutto, spicy Calabrese salame, and savory finocchiona—had all been rolled appealingly and placed carefully on their own ornately rimmed stainless steel platter, which was now positioned at a sizable distance from the other offerings. Byron had learned, from sour experience, that Craig was so fanatical in his vegetarianism that he'd avoid cheese, crackers, bread, or anything else that had come into even incidental contact with meat. Craig wouldn't never complain about it or even mention it—he just wouldn't eat the food.

Satisfied now with his appetizers, Byron continued to work his way conscientiously down the kitchen counter, coming next upon a casserole dish containing his homemade veal parmigiana. He'd assembled and baked the whole thing yesterday—battering, breading, and lightly frying his pounded veal cutlets before layering them with cheese and tomato sauce, along with sprinklings of basil, oregano, salt, pepper, and garlic powder—and baking the casserole until the cheese was melted and the sauce bubbling. He'd let it cool, and then refrigerated it overnight. Byron now put the casserole dish back in the oven and set the timer for forty minutes, giving it time to reheat and then cool just a bit before serving. Byron had, on several prior occasions, explained to dinner guests that casseroles such as this were always better the next day. The overnight chilling gave the flavors an opportunity to gel, and rendered the texture of the finished product more savory and chewy.

Byron assumed that the final two recipes lined up on the counter would be of particular interest to Craig, one being a meatless pasta course and the other a vegetable. Byron glanced at Craig to see if he appeared especially interested in the preparation now commencing, but Craig's features were expressionless and gave him no clue.

The ingredients for Byron's fettuccine Alfredo were neatly laid out. He slid the noodles into the large pasta pot on the stove in which the water was now boiling. When perfectly al dente, they'd be tossed with cream, butter, pecorino and parmesan cheeses just prior to plating. The pasta would serve as Craig's main course and as a side for the other diners. Near the edge of the counter was a large nutmeg seed with a tiny grater beside it—Byron considered the grating of fresh nutmeg atop the pasta just as it was presented to be not just an authentic addition but also a personal touch of panache.

Byron dumped a package of frozen peas into a smaller pot and began seasoning them. He usually cooked peas with butter and chicken broth along with salt and pepper, but tonight he was substituting vegetable broth—which he personally found flavorless and unappealing—but Craig wouldn't eat it otherwise, and what would be the point of making a vegetable if the one vegetarian in the room wouldn't eat it?

Byron turned the heat up on the peas and took a quick break from his work, downing the rest of his second gimlet and quickly mixing himself a third.

• • •

As Craig watched Byron mix his third gimlet, he anticipated that Byron would become conversant within the next few minutes.

Byron now tested the texture of his boiling fettuccine noodles by snatching one out of the water with tongs and tasting it. Craig recalled the many times before that he'd seen Bryon preparing that dish. In truth, Craig would have greatly preferred a tomato or pesto sauce rather than something so absurdly dairy heavy. But he knew that he was already a burden to cook for as a vegetarian, and if he'd assured his host that he ate dairy, then it would be poor form to complain later about being given too much of it.

The observation that crept next into Craig's mind was a familiar one—it manifested every time he kept Byron company in the kitchen. Byron was exquisitely efficient and meticulous—but went about his efforts much like an automaton making his way down an assembly line. There seemed to be no passion or creativity.

When Craig cooked his vegan stews on the nights he spent alone, the experience was never exactly the same. So much depended upon what was fresh at the natural foods store where he shopped—how the raw ingredients smelled and looked, what spices seemed right for the day's temperature and humidity, and whatever nuanced sensibility had seized Craig's mood that evening.

But Byron's ingredients, proportions, and cooking methods never varied by even an iota. Which, Craig imagined, was probably fitting, because Byron often talked about opening a small Italian trattoria when he retired—a place with a full bar, which Byron would tend, and which would serve simple pastas, pizzas, breads, and salads. Byron had shared how he'd picture himself, sipping Grand Marnier and cappuccino with Adelle and the owners of other nearby eateries after closing. He habitually divulged such personal musings as he nursed an after-dinner drink, sitting across from Craig, at the conclusion of a satisfying Italian restaurant feast.

And Craig assumed that if Byron someday owned a restaurant and had people cooking for him, he'd want them to execute a given recipe precisely the same way every time.

It was at that moment that he heard the women and Nigel returning. Byron immediately chugged down the gimlet in his glass and poured another, as if to psyche himself for conversation.

• • •

The returnees were concluding the remnants of whatever conversations they'd been engaged in, as they now gathered round the kitchen counter and began sampling the appetizers.

"What a beautiful spread!" exclaimed Justine as she reached for a slice of bruschetta. Compliments began flowing, all uttered enthusiastically from mouths zealously chewing upon Byron's tidbits.

Byron bowed graciously and asked, "What does everyone want to drink? I have chilled prosecco to start, or I can mix pretty much any cocktail you'd like."

The three women all opted for the sparkling wine.

"I fancy a stiff gin martini, if you can manage it," Nigel said.

"I just happen to have a big bottle of Beefeater's Dry London Gin in the cabinet," Byron said. "Right up your alley, eh?"

"Thank you. It's a fine British gin, I'll enjoy it," Nigel said, flashing a roguish smile, which the three women seemed to find beguiling. "I'll forgive the fact that it's whipped up in bloody London, though. I'm from Leeds you know—a good ways north of all that London madness."

"Leeds?" asked Shoshana. "Isn't that near Liverpool, where the Beatles were from?"

"About an hour and a half by car," Nigel said.

"Oh, by car?" Byron exclaimed, seizing upon that remark with an uncharacteristic gusto that caused Craig and Shoshana to shoot each other veiled glances lasting no more than an instant—their two expressions identical—eyebrows dipping down, narrowing their respective eyes into incredulous squints.

"Do you like to drive?" Byron pressed, his inflection excruciatingly cheerful.

"I suppose," Nigel stammered, appearing nonplussed by Byron's suddenly enthusiastic line of questioning.

"That's an understatement if I ever heard one!" Justine proclaimed, breaking into laughter as she did. "Nigel loves cars and he loves driving. Oh my god—he has a ridiculously expensive banana-colored Lotus convertible in our garage—it's his weekend toy!"

"Sounds like a beautiful car," Byron said. "I'd love to go driving with you sometime."

"That might be arranged," Nigel said, smiling now.

"Do you like car racing?" Byron asked, as he poured sparkling wine for the women.

"As a matter of fact, I do," Nigel responded. "I love watching the races up at Sears Point, in Napa. I've even traveled about, to watch other races at times."

"Well, it looks like the boys are talking cars," Adelle whined. "Why don't us ladies take our proseccos and go into the living room? I'll pile some of the appetizers on a platter to take with us."

"That sounds nice," Justine said.

Shoshana nodded, and she and Justine headed into the living room. Adelle followed soon after with a heaping plate of food.

Back in the kitchen, Byron said to Nigel, "You know, up at Sears Point, they give racing lessons some weekends. You get to drive the real cars. You're alone on the track, of course. They don't want lawsuits up the ass." He chuckled. "But you *can* drive incredibly fast. I mean, like getting up to a hundred and fifty miles an hour. It must be a damn powerful rush."

"You know," Nigel said, "I've always wanted to do that—never have though—sounds as if you haven't either."

"No. I was looking for someone to do it with."

"Well, perhaps we ought to try it together some weekend," Nigel offered.

Craig interrupted. "You know, gentlemen, as you're both undoubtedly aware, I happen to be that annoying guy who crawls along in the right-hand lane at fifty-five miles an hour—and I drive a twelve-year-old Corolla. So, I think I'll mosey off and join the ladies. I'm actually overjoyed that you two are bonding, even if it's over something I can't possibly relate to."

Nigel and Byron laughed. Craig momentarily trained his barely quaffed mug of O'Doul's in their direction, then nodded politely and headed out of the kitchen, grabbing a couple of pieces of Byron's bruschetta as he did. Craig had noticed that when Adelle piled up the platter of food for the living room, she'd thrown the cold cuts on top of everything else. There'd be nothing edible for him on that plate.

• • •

Once Craig left the kitchen, Byron leaned closer to Nigel and whispered, "You must have been in a bunch of rental cars with Craig when the two of you were touring the small regions. Were you able to stand the way he drove?"

"He does proceed at an unbearably snail-like pace," Nigel agreed, chortling heartily now with his new cohort. He instinctively glanced in the direction of the living room, to make absolutely sure their boss was out of earshot.

"I'll get that martini going for you, bro," Byron said.

• • •

When Craig joined the women in the living room, Adelle was

querying Justine about what she did for a living. Craig sat down next to Shoshana on the couch.

"Yeah, I know it sounds strange to people," Justine said. "But I really have to say, the death care industry, and funeral cosmetics in particular—that's like a really special calling for me. These poor people need someone to help them—there's nothing as final as death—and, like, so many friends and family members are affected."

"How on earth did you get into it?" Shoshana asked.

"You know, I had this strange experience when I was eight years old. My grandmother died. I was really close to my grandmother."

"Did you go to the funeral?" Shoshana inquired.

"That's where it happened!" Justine said. "I had a bunch of cousins, all around my age. Girls—every one of us. So, we were all there, in our little black dresses. We must have looked so cute. I remember one of my uncles kept calling us the 'vee-jits'—you know, V-G-I-T's—valley girls in training." Justine laughed uncontrollably at this recollection, then gazed at the faces of her audience and laughed some more. Adelle, Shoshana, and Craig all smiled politely.

Justine continued: "So, all my cousins found the dead body totally spooky and gross—they were, like, super frightened of it, you know?—they'd only go over when they had to—and they'd hold their parents' hands really tight when they were forced to say those quick goodbyes. But I was fascinated by the body. I mean, it was my grandma! Just lying in this box. And the grownups kept telling me she wasn't really there—but she was right there!—looking really pretty and happy—I remember her nails, they were so perfectly polished—and her hair, it looked so beautiful and perfectly done. So, I kept asking myself, was she there, or wasn't she? And then I tried to touch her hands—they were resting on her tummy, you know? And that *really* got me. They were so cold. And waxy. It was, like, totally weird. I couldn't stop brushing my fingers over the backs of her hands. My mother had to call me away. But I kept sneaking back to touch her hands again. If you've never touched a dead body, you can't understand what it's like. It's kind of like going to another world."

Shoshana and Craig stared at Justine with rapt fascination.

Shoshana squeezed Craig's hand and flashed him an evil grin. Craig recalled that she had spoken of a particular client with fantasies of being slowly tortured to death by his mistress, as punishment for severe misbehavior. He wondered if his wife planned to mine some of Justine's know-how for such a roleplay.

Meanwhile, Craig's mind wandered to a BDSM play party a couple of years back, to which Shoshana had taken him. A good friend of theirs, a surgeon by profession, had always nurtured a number of vivid fantasies, one of them involving cannibalism. The surgeon, very stoned after smoking a couple of joints, had been wheeled naked into the main playroom of the party, lying still on a metal table—his entire body painted with tanning lotion so that he looked as if he'd been roasted—with slices of baked carrots, celery, onion, and tomatoes, brushed with olive oil and still hot from the oven, layered upon his torso. The women at the party, all Dommes in leather outfits, pretended to eat him. They poked at the vegetables with sharp-pronged forks that pricked the man's body as the women plucked off the vegetables and consumed them. It was a special treat for the surgeon's birthday, dreamt up by his girlfriend.

• • •

As she watched Shoshana and Craig grinning and nodding at

each other, Adelle's reaction to Justine's childhood recollection was radically different. Adelle struggled to keep her features placid in the face of the ghastliness of Justine's anecdote—and of her own awareness of Byron's intent to cultivate a friendship with this couple.

Adelle opted to pivot.

"And what about you, Shoshana," she inquired, "in all the time we've known you and Craig, I never really asked what *you* do for a living."

• • •

Craig eased his hand onto Shoshana's thigh. He was tempted to say something to divert the conversation—to come to his wife's aid. But it was more complicated for him than that. He was her bottom. She was his top. And though that aspect of their relationship was unknown to these people, such behavior would, in that context, be seen by his mistress as disrespectful and inappropriate. And he knew Shoshana could handle it—her fictitious backstory was fully devised. It just bothered him because he understood how going through these duplicitous motions was unpleasant for her.

"Have you seen the latest additions to my craft pages on Amazon?" Shoshana asked brightly. "My needle-felting is selling extremely well." This was invariably her first line of deflection, and generally sufficed.

But this time, Adelle probed more sharply. "No, I don't mean your hobby, Shoshana. I mean what you do to bring in money. I mean, the home you guys have, and the vacations you take. What do you do, honey?"

Craig looked to Shoshana, wondering if she'd offer some unspoken sign that she'd appreciate his intervention. Instead, she looked directly at Adelle and smiled warmly.

"Oh, you know dear, it isn't something I usually choose to talk about."

"Well, we've known each other so long. I'm just curious. Can't you tell me anything?"

Justine squirmed in her chair. "I can go join the boys in the kitchen—if you guys want some privacy."

"No," Shoshana assured her, gesturing with her palms that Justine should stay where she was. "It's fine. It's just that there's not much to say. You see, I do investigative work, but I can't reveal anything about my employer or what it is I investigate. You understand—it's part of my job agreement."

"You're a private eye?" Adelle exclaimed.

"No. Hardly!" Shoshana chuckled. "No. I work for a company. A private company. Not the government. And I signed an agreement that I wouldn't talk about it. And so, I don't. I'm sorry. You know, to be honest, it really isn't all that interesting or exciting—but anyway, I can't talk about it."

Adelle's lips parted as if she had a follow-up question, but instead, her eyes narrowed and her lips pursed. An awkward silence filled the room for the next few moments.

The stillness was shattered by Byron's unexpected call: "Dinner's ready!"

Craig turned his head, and was surprised to see that Byron had not yelled from the kitchen. Rather he was in the doorway of the living room, just a few feet away. Craig wasn't sure how long Byron had been there—but Craig doubted that the timing of Byron's announcement could, by pure chance, have landed so perfectly in the belly of the conversation's awkward lull.

Craig sensed something odd.

For as long as he could remember, Craig had relied heavily upon his intuition, both at work and elsewhere, to form judgments. Perhaps his power of intuition had been staunch from birth—but Craig was convinced that decades of yoga and meditation had honed it preternaturally, well beyond any congenitally endowed level of efficacy. As he sat beside Shoshana, he glanced quickly at Adelle on one side of them, then back to Byron on the other. The energy was amiss. But he didn't know what it translated to. Only that he needed to be on guard.

• • •

Dinner was done.

Shoshana, Craig, Justine, and Nigel were gone now, having started their drive north toward San Francisco.

The hearty, multicourse dinner had garnered much praise and appreciation. The conversation throughout the meal had remained cordial and lively. Byron had pulled a few cartons of delectable imported Italian gelato out of the freezer for a surprise dessert.

But now, all had given way to a quiet house, a bare kitchen table, and a sink full of dishes being tackled by Adelle, as Byron sat in a chair turned toward her. He sipped upon a hefty snifter of Grand Marnier.

Byron's lips curled into a contented smile and he nodded confidently as he spoke. "I guess my homework paid off," he said. "Once I picked up on Nigel loving cars—that was at work last week, from somebody who knew him—that gave me the idea. And it all went just like I figured." Byron took another few sips. "And I heard your interrogation of Shoshana," he said. "Good job, babe. So, what d'ya think?"

"Well, it went just like you planned it," Adelle said. "And like you predicted, honey—what I got was a total cock-and-bull story." Adelle chuckled, stopped loading the dishwasher, and shut the sink's faucet off for a moment. She turned to look at him. "An investigator? But she can't talk about it? Right. Total bullshit!"

"Yeah, total." Byron smirked. "But now, with the car races, and the driving lessons up at Sears Point—I'm going to bond with that twerp Nigel. And when Craig is forced to go, and they give me his VP spot, Nigel will be my biggest supporter."

"But why does that even matter?" Adelle asked. "I mean, Nigel's the new guy. He doesn't have any say. So why is it so important to get him on your side?" Her features tightened. "And, honey, if you're going to become friends with Nigel, then I have to be friends with Justine. You know, tonight, I asked Justine about *her* job first, just like you mapped it out. And that chick is weird. I mean, really super weird—dead bodies—touching dead bodies—like it's a sexual rush for her. Jesus!"

"Like I told you," Byron said, "something's going on between Craig and Nigel. They're getting really tight. It's never any good when the boss gets super tight with one guy. Believe me, I've been through this before—at other places. But if you can get in tight with the guy your boss is tight with, then you stay in the circle. You keep your influence."

"But if you're going to get Craig kicked out, and get his job, what's the difference? Why do you need influence with a guy who's getting kicked out?"

Byron pondered that as he took a long hearty swig of Grand Marnier. His eyebrows dipped. "It may take some time, babe," he said slowly, cobbling his words together as he spoke. "And in the meantime, I just have this feeling about Nigel. Like he's capable of real damage. He could fuck things up for me before I even get a chance to spring my shit on Craig. Trust me on this. He's dangerous. Potentially. I've seen guys like this before—at other jobs. I gotta be able to know what he's up to. That keeps me in control."

Adelle reached for another plate in the sink but aborted that maneuver and instead walked closer to where Byron had turned his chair to face her. She gazed at him intently as she spoke. Her tone was tentative. "You know, honey, the more I think about this, the more I'm not sure about the way you're approaching the whole thing. I mean, this isn't Tampa, babe. Back there, we were dealing with normal people."

"Normal people?"

"This is San Francisco, honey." Adelle's tone grew more assured now. "We talk about this all the time—the people out here are all left-wing crazies. You know that. I mean—will anyone out here even care if Shoshana's a sex worker? These lunatics don't think the way we do. Political correctness out here is like some kind of insane religion. These people at work may consider it just fine."

Byron lowered his snifter and rested it on his knee. He gaped at her. "What? No. That can't be. You mean, you think corporate executives out here wouldn't give a shit if one of their VPs was married to a prostitute? I can't believe that."

"Well, it's not like she's working the streets, honey. Who knows what she does in that house? It's high-end stuff, whatever it is. Who the hell knows what people out here think? What if what she's doing is medical—like a surrogate?"

"So, you're saying that even if they found out, you don't think they'd give Craig the boot?"

Adelle raised her head, and pursed her lips. "You know, honey, I'm not sure what the hell they'd do. But I think you should go about it a different way."

"Like what?"

"Well, you were thinking about leaking the evidence to the bigwigs. I mean anonymously. Right?"

"Right."

"See, honey, I think you should focus on Craig himself. Don't you always tell me how he's always trying to be Mr. Perfect? You know, always dressing to the nines, never saying the wrong thing, never losing his temper? Never talking politics or religion? Always soft-soaping the right people? Believe me, if he's really like that, he couldn't stand to be outed. Even if nobody else cared that his wife was turning tricks. He'd be mortified if it came out. He'd walk away on his own before he'd let you do that."

Byron's head lowered and his eyes reflexively peered leftward as he considered what Adelle just said. Then he let out the barest chuckle and took a big swig of Grand Marnier. "And, if I promise Craig that I'd keep my mouth shut about the whole damn thing if he recommended me for his position . . ."

"He sure as hell would."

Byron finished what was left of the Grand Marnier and set the snifter down on the table behind him. He leaned back and laughed mischievously, his shoulders heaving up and down. "Jesus Christ, Adelle, you're right! That's the exact way to play it. You hit it on the head. Damn!"

Adelle snickered. "I guess you had good taste when you fell in love with me—way back when." She walked back to the sink, turned on the water, and resumed her work, giving each dish a cursory rinse before loading it into the dishwasher. "My man's gonna be a VP," she said.

He watched her from behind. Adelle's wide hips and sumptuous buttocks gyrated as she toiled. Byron grew aroused.

11

BRIE AND CUCUMBER

SHOSHANA SCHUMACHER NEVER SAW CLIENTS ON Sundays or Mondays.

Having Mondays off worked well logistically. It enabled her to tend to personal chores and private assignations—Craig was at work, and businesses were open.

She'd found that Mondays were slow for sessions anyway.

Sundays, though, were quite different. Shoshana insisted that she and Craig reserve Sundays for time together. Long drives culminating in picnics or in restaurant lunches on outdoor patios—lovely spots down the coast—these were her frequent choices.

And a Sunday picnic was indeed on the calendar for today, but Shoshana arose earlier than necessary and roused Craig too, so that there would be time to design, print, and mail party invitations prior to setting off.

Craig wasn't a trained artist, but he'd always displayed a playful flair for cartoons and caricatures. Shoshana found his style perfect for the invitations she produced every month or two for the La Maîtresse Society parties.

Craig sat now at the dining room table in their large San Francisco home. With swift, bold strokes of his black drawing pencil amidst sweeping interjections with his soft triangular eraser, he did his best to set down the scene exactly as Shoshana dictated. She stood directly behind him, her left hand leaning lightly on his upper back, her right hand gesticulating spiritedly so that he could detect her movements out of the corner of his eye, as she issued her frenetic, nonstop directives.

"Make the woman bigger . . . taller and bosomy . . . no! . . . bigger tits and a full ass . . . bigger!"

Craig sketched frantically.

"Yes . . . Good! Good! Long wavy hair . . . really long . . . longer! . . . and that's supposed to be a leather corset she's in, can you make it look more like leather? . . . and put, like, silver studs on it . . . Yes! Beautiful! . . . And the expression on her face . . . I like that it's stern, but lighten it just a tad . . . like it's sort of *playfully* stern . . . like she's smirking."

Shoshana paused a few moments to allow him to catch up to her, then started up again. "You got the expression perfect now, honey. That's great. But that riding crop you have her holding is puny . . . make it a big bull whip . . . make it outrageous! . . . you know, like nothing any of us would ever actually use."

Craig erased and resketched several times, until he received Shoshana's approval.

"Great! Okay, now, honey, draw her slave. Have him strung up behind her. No! No! Over here . . . Right! . . . No, no! Make him much smaller!" She laughed now as she spoke. "Make him really short and skinny . . . like totally pathetic and emaciated!"

Craig chuckled, erased his lines, and laid out a revised figure.

"Yes! Yes! Now you got it! Oh, that's precious . . . precious! . . .

the woman looks so fearsome and overpowering—but cool . . . and he's such a pitiful little schlump, but so earnest . . . Oh! I love it! I love it!" She giggled heartily. "Okay, ink it now! You can letter in the time, place, and party-theme underneath when you're done with the picture. The details are on this paper, over here."

Shoshana strolled to the other end of the table. The glass of red-tinged juice from the fresh blood oranges Craig had squeezed earlier in the morning still had a couple of sips left. She finished it off and returned to check Craig's progress, handing him the page of information.

"Oh, it's looking so good, honey! Before we leave, will you do that thingy you do with the mailing labels on the computer? And make the copies, and stuff the envelopes?" She leaned down and kissed him lovingly on the cheek. "After that, get the picnic food ready and we'll be able to go. We can mail the envelopes on the way. We're going to have such a lovely day. I'm really looking forward to it."

A barely discernible blur materialized for an instant in the foyer and then was gone, jerking Shoshana's head in its direction. "Oh!" she exclaimed with a quick laugh. "That was Golda. I'm going to go try to find her and snuggle a little. You keep working, honey."

• • •

The La Maîtresse Society, a convivial play group for dominant women and their submissives, had remained small and self-contained, despite being in existence for several years. It was originally the slapdash brainchild of a few of the more socially outgoing professional Dommes in the Bay Area, but they soon cajoled Shoshana into heading it.

Socially reticent by nature, Shoshana was initially reluctant to take on that responsibility. But her cohorts insisted that because she was one of the "madams" among them, in that she ran a house that employed other Dommes—and because her house was always so impeccably organized and smoothly functioning—and because she always seemed to them so imposingly articulate (she was one of the few pros with a master's degree, hers in psychology)—that only she could adequately take the helm.

What they hadn't mentioned, but what they had certainly discussed privately, was that Shoshana and her husband Craig were quite wealthy in comparison to the other couples in the mix. Should the relatively modest party dues ever fail to cover unexpected costs, Shoshana was far better positioned to make up any unforeseen shortfalls.

Over time though, Shoshana came to view the role as an honor. And, pragmatically, it helped her meet other women in the community—and because of the stature the position afforded her, to more easily find dominatrices to staff her house, and keep her company on lonely weekday evenings.

• • •

Their leisurely drive to reach the picnic area in Butano State Park, about fifty miles south of San Francisco, took them down Highway 1, an old two-lane state road that hugged the Pacific coast. Craig had made Shoshana's favorite brie-and-cucumber sandwiches, which he'd garnished with wispy slivers of red onion, vegan mayonnaise, and an herbed butter he'd concocted with hints of garlic and parsley. He'd thrown together a three-bean salad to accompany the sandwiches.

Craig had also packed a bag of the organic potato chips

Shoshana found irresistible—the thick-cut sea salt and vinegar variety. He wasn't much for deep-fried food, but he always shared a couple of chips to be polite and demonstrate solidarity—as Shoshana scarfed down the rest while histrionically lambasting their insidiously addictive qualities.

They had reached a portion of narrow road perched high upon a rocky cliff. As Craig unhurriedly negotiated a bend, Shoshana glanced around for police cars and, seeing none, pulled a joint and a lighter from her purse. She lowered her window halfway and paused a moment to gaze down to the ocean, far below on her right. The waves were high today. Shoshana smiled, lit the joint, and took two long pulls. She reached outside the window and gently extinguished the joint's lit end against its bottom edge, before returning what was left to her purse and closing the pane.

Craig steered gently through another curve, and for just a moment, the vista of the vast ocean flashed in front of him. He inhaled thoughtfully. Craig always found it interesting when Shoshana got stoned on these long drives. She knew not to offer him any—he'd never take it—but even so, it seemed to Craig that despite her opening the car window and blowing the fumes outside, a tiny bit of residual smoke nonetheless lingered inside the vehicle when she was done. It appeared to have a psychological effect upon him, not unlike the barely discernible scent of incense in the air each weekday morning when he and Golda practiced yoga together. The cannabis smoke seemed to relax both Shoshana and himself, and open them to more probing and meaningful conversation.

"Thank you, sweetie, for everything you did this morning," Shoshana cooed. "The picnic food looks yummy. And the invitations are adorable. I'm so glad they're out and in the mail. It's a weight off my mind, you know? I can relax more, and enjoy the day."

"I love making you happy."

"The party is in two weeks, honey. Are you looking forward to it?"

Craig paused a moment, making certain to word his response carefully.

"Very much so, Empress. You know I love the parties. They're really the only time that everybody's just completely in the fetish head—I can just drop everything else and be a sex slave." He chuckled. "Yes. I'm looking forward to it." He hesitated, then continued. "Um . . . Empress . . . you didn't mention if you were planning to bring anybody else . . . or just me."

"I was thinking of bringing the hauler guy, honey."

"Joe Hauler Guy?"

Shoshana grinned. "Right. That's exactly what it says on his index card. You've been paying attention when you visit! He's a good customer. And a very well-behaved boy. It's such a rare treat for him to go to a party like this. He's not lucky, like you. You get to go to all of them."

Craig had met Joe Hauler Guy just once, at the one other party to which Shoshana had invited him. Joe was not a scintillating conversationalist. Nor was he particularly well-off financially—he made what living he did by moving furniture, painting rooms, or hauling junk from people's garages to the dump. But Craig knew that to Shoshana, Joe was a tall, dazzlingly handsome, and well-muscled plaything who could be paraded about at parties—proclaiming Shoshana's power and stature via the submissives in her stable.

Craig also understood that although Shoshana (and all the women who worked for her) had a strict no-sex policy with clients, Joe had become one of those rare customers who now inhabited that strange netherworld which hovered between a personal and professional relationship. Shoshana occasionally allowed Joe to make love to her if there were no other women in the house, and she had no sessions scheduled for a time after.

Craig was quite familiar with that status. It had been his for several months, years ago, before Shoshana suggested that they live together.

"That's fine," Craig said.

His inflection was just a bit hesitant—not something most people would have picked up on—but Shoshana knew him too well.

"I know you'd rather I just take you," she said. "But you'll play with lots of women at the party. You won't be neglected."

"It's always fun to play with other women." He smiled quickly and glanced at her. "But I'd be just as happy playing only with you. Anyway, it's fine. I love you, Empress. It's all fine."

Even after years of marriage, Craig remained cautious. His relationship with Shoshana afforded him privileges rare for a submissive man in the Bay Area's BDSM community. There were probably a hundred submissive men for every dominant woman in the scene. Most men paid for sessions or fantasized alone. Being Shoshana's husband provided him entrée into all sorts of groups and parties. Without her, he'd again be one of the nameless wretched masses. He didn't think he could bear to return to that.

• • •

Craig pulled into the small gravel lot near the picnic tables. From the back of their black SUV he retrieved their well-worn picnic backpack stocked with plates, silverware, plastic wine glasses, linen napkins, and a large colorful tablecloth, all ingeniously secured in assigned compartments with elastic straps.

He hoisted that onto his back and also grabbed the cooler, along with a large brown-paper grocery bag that currently held the chips and a roll of paper towels, but which would soon become their portable garbage receptacle. A far table sitting in the shade of two large trees looked perfect, and he set out toward it. While he laid the tablecloth atop the rough wood, Shoshana stole another couple of tokes on the joint in her purse, then scurried to join him.

Craig set the table and put out the food. He uncorked a bottle of chardonnay that had been chilling in the cooler and filled a glass nearly to the top, which he set down in front of Shoshana. For himself, he opened a quart bottle of sparkling water and poured a glass of that.

They sat side by side.

"The food is really yummy!" Shoshana exclaimed. She leaned into him, put her arm around his shoulders, and kissed him on the cheek. "You're so sweet to me," she whispered in his ear.

Craig said nothing. He closed his eyes. The barest hint of a smile formed on his lips. He luxuriated in her gentle touch.A moment later, Craig leaned his head down and pressed it softly against her, just above the tops of her breasts. He unobtrusively sniffed the cleavage rising from the low neckline of her sweater.

She had dabbed a touch of perfume there. Its scent aroused him.

Shoshana took a long sip of chardonnay. When she put down the glass, Craig lifted his head and slowly sat upright. He took a bite of his brie and cucumber sandwich.

"It's a beautiful day, isn't it, sweetie?" Shoshana observed softly.

"Very beautiful, Empress."

Craig drank some water, but soon fidgeted just a bit, and breathed hard. It was inconspicuous, but Shoshana picked up on it right away.

"It's still hard for you, isn't it sweetie?" she said. "To share affection like this—without you being locked up in some sort of symbolic artifact—like handcuffs or a collar."

"I'm okay."

"Be honest, honey. You're not."

"All right. I guess so. It's just . . . we've been through this, Empress . . . you know, if we just played once in a while like we used to. That's all I'd need—to fuel me and keep me going. Just once in a while."

"We play at parties."

"I know. And I love that. But you're already in character at a party—for everybody there—you know, like you're performing for a crowd. I just would love it if we could do it once in a while when we're alone, just you and me. Like we used to when we first got together."

"I've told you. I don't see you that way anymore, honey. You're my husband. And I love you for that. I don't need to string you up and whip you."

"Just now and then."

"I do it all day at my job. I really don't want to do it at home."

"You do it all day—yes—but the thing is, Empress, I *never* get to do it. Just at parties, and mostly not with you." He paused. "I realize we're coming at this from totally different places. I get that. But it would be nice. Just once in a rare while."

"Oh, honey," she purred, "you're such a sweet thing." Shoshana kissed him on the forehead, then eased his head down gently so that it rested on her ample breasts. She spoke softly. "This is exactly why—why every couple in our community has play-partners outside the marriage. You see that, honey. I know you do. After a while, people who love each other just can't play together anymore, except at parties when—like you said—everyone gets into a group illusion of owners and slaves.

Because psychologically—people can't just slip in and out of those heads—like automatically—while they're negotiating a real-life relationship with someone they love. Craig, honey, there are women in the community who think you're cute. And they know how intelligent and sweet you are. You really should get something going with one of them. I can help you arrange it."

"We've talked about this. I feel funny doing that. Like I'm betraying you."

"But I *want* you to do it. How can you be betraying me if it makes me happy to know you're playing with someone?"

Craig lifted his head. He smiled and gazed at her, and then kissed her gently. "I love you, Empress." He took another bite of his sandwich, and began musing: "It's such a strange thing, isn't it, Empress? Needing to play with other people. And nobody outside the community gets it. They really don't. I mean, how could they?" He thought for a moment and sighed. "People always talk about—you know, how there are all these huge social obstacles and stigmas for *gay* people. And there *are*—I don't in any way mean to minimize that. But nobody gets the issues that people like us—heteros in the BDSM community—deal with."

"It *is* hard for gay people, honey," Shoshana said. "We get spoiled, living here in the Bay Area bubble. We forget how difficult it can be for gay people in other parts of the country. Not to mention other parts of the world."

"Absolutely. Like I said—I in no way want to diminish that. But the point I'm making is that—especially in places like here in the Bay Area where being gay isn't such a big deal to most people anymore—sure, there are still some social and legal obstacles—but ultimately, gay people can have healthy and happy relationships—almost exactly like a conventional male/female couple—just same-gender—and not officially married. In San Francisco they can even be domestic partners. You see what I mean? They can be *themselves*. They have a logical progression from love to sexual monogamy. And I'm sure California will legalize gay marriage at some point. It's inevitable."

Craig drank some more water, and then continued, his cadence soft and thoughtful. "What I'm trying to say, Empress—is if gay people do encounter obstacles here—they tend to be visible ones. External ones. But for folks like us—the problem is the thing *itself*—the fantasy aspect of a dominant/submissive relationship—which is intrinsic to what it is, and who we are—it doesn't let us make that leap into a day-to-day loving relationship. You know—it forces our relationship to change—like you said—to morph into a kind of hybrid where your primary relationship turns vanilla—and then you have fantasy interludes with people outside your marriage. And that's sad. Well, at least it's sad to me. And worse, it's invisible. Nobody outside the community understands how hard it can be. To be unable to be your real sexual self with the one person you love."

"You're such a sweet, sensitive boy. I really do adore you, honey."

Shoshana finished the wine in her glass, and Craig immediately poured her another. He opened the bag of potato chips and set it before her. He dished a spoonful of the three-bean salad onto her plate, alongside her half-eaten brie and cucumber sandwich.

These little gestures of servitude made him feel comfortable and momentarily joyful. He took one potato chip and slipped it into his mouth as a show of support—and as he chewed it, he gazed at her and wondered why he found it so difficult to be happy and satisfied just serving her this way—the way she wanted. Isn't that what a truly submissive man would enjoy? Indeed, if she were to play with him as an obligation, just because he insisted upon it, that would surely destroy all the joy in it for him.

Even so, Craig's mind then began to embrace the incipient thought that as two people in the real world, each with needs—there could be some compromise, some accommodation.

But he knew that harping aloud upon such a thought would be damaging right now.

He turned his mind off, and reached for one more potato chip.

• • •

When they finished eating, they cuddled and traced the shapes of animals in the cumulus clouds above them. Before Craig packed the back of the SUV for the ride home, Shoshana had him temporarily store the cooler and other paraphernalia atop the front seats.

In the back of the vehicle, where the rear seats had been lowered and laid back flat to the floor, she told him to roll out the mattress pad they kept there, and to pull down the car's window shades.

"Make love to me," she whispered.

He complied. He did it the way she liked. First, he took her breasts into his mouth and aroused her. Finally, she laughed and said, "Enough of that!" This was her familiar signal to him to turn his oral attentions to her nether regions, to which he now attended assiduously.

After he'd induced several orgasms, she smiled and sighed. "Thank you, honey. You may fuck me now."

He did so, consciously using his member as a tool to please her rather than himself. As he thrust softly, he fantasized about the early days, when, prior to sex, she would string him up and clamp his nipples, buckle on a ball-gag, and beat him sensually with a cat-o'-nine-tails.

That image kept him excited.

Finally, when he felt he could no longer contain himself, he whispered, "May I come, Empress?"

His thrusts grew momentarily more powerful and spasmodic as he waited for her response.

Just before he exploded into her, she said, "Yes, slave." It was an artifact from their early days. He was grateful it had somehow remained part of their ritual.

12

OSSO BUCO AND POLENTA

CRAIG WAS THE FIRST PATRON TO BE SEATED IN THE small Vietnamese restaurant when it opened its doors a couple of minutes after eleven. He had arrived a bit early, having taken a leisurely stroll from his office. As he waited on the street to be permitted in, he focused consciously upon downtown San Francisco's late-morning sunshine and gentle breezes.

It was more than ten minutes later when Nigel Silver dashed through the restaurant's front door and joined him at the table. It was not a surprise—Craig had become accustomed to Nigel's being a far less punctual lunch partner than Carolyn had been.

Despite that, Craig found himself developing a personal connection with Nigel that was closer than he'd expected. Over the past few months, their formal weekly one-on-one status meetings in Craig's office had morphed into a facsimile of the periodic Vietnamese lunches he'd shared for so long with Carolyn.

As Nigel plopped hastily into his chair, he glimpsed the young Asian waitress a few feet away and called in her direction,

"Spicy beef curry!" He glanced at the menu and pondered for an instant, before adding, "Extra spicy, very hot."

Nigel was out of breath. The combination of his throaty, panting shout and his mellifluous Leeds accent made Craig grin.

The waitress ambled over and nodded at Nigel as she noted his order on her pad.

She turned to Craig.

He said, "Tofu and vegetables in lemongrass soy sauce," then paused for a moment to give her time to write.

He was about to say something more when the waitress interjected in her heavily accented English: "Brown rice. No fish sauce. Vegetarian." Her eyes gleamed as she finished writing, and she then fixed her gaze upon Craig with a broad endearing smile.

Craig bowed slightly in her direction and laughed.

As the waitress headed back into the kitchen, Nigel leaned in and whispered, "Well, she's flirting with you now, boss. You'll need to up her tip going forward. Significantly, I'd reckon." He flashed his impish grin.

So stark was the difference in sound and insinuation of the word "reckon" in Nigel's Leeds intonation, compared to the customary lilt of an American southerner, that it made Craig stop and think about it for a moment. He leaned his head imperceptibly and then reached for the steaming pot of jasmine tea he'd been enjoying since his arrival. He poured a cup for Nigel, and topped off his own.

"It's so nice to see you, Nigel. How are things going in your department?"

"Hunky-dory. Blinding in fact."

"And Stacey, the woman you promoted into Geoff's spot?"

"Brilliant. Stacey's been absolutely brilliant."

"You made a good choice with her. You know, I ran into her a couple of times lately—just chance meetings in the hallway—we had brief chats. I was very impressed. Sometimes the quiet ones have more leadership ability than people assume. You were able to see that in her."

"Nobody could tell how good she was before, because that wanker Geoff and his bloody insanity gobbled up all the air in the room."

Craig chuckled. "Interesting way to put it. Very true, though. Incompetence coupled with neurosis can have quite an impact on the people forced to abide it. Anyway, I'm glad to hear Stacey's doing so well."

"Hard to fathom how Carolyn put up with that prat Geoff for so long," Nigel said with a suggestive smile. He took a long and piercingly sibilant swig of the hot tea. "Oh, before I forget, boss—I need to request travel clearance. Here—I wrote the dates down for you." Nigel fished around in the breast pocket of his suit coat and handed Craig a piece of paper.

"Let's see," Craig said, scanning the note. "You want to do it at the end of this month—the Ohio region on Thursday and Friday—and then the Colorado region through Wednesday of the next week." Craig thought for a moment and looked up. "Did you know that Byron's going to be in those regions at the same time?"

"Right. We're transitioning his unit-testing in those regions into my team's integrated-test program. So, we're coordinating it."

"Ah, coordinating with Byron. That's good, I'm glad to hear it."

"Didn't Byron mention it?"

"No. No he didn't." Craig examined the dates on the paper again, and looked at Nigel. "So, if I'm interpreting this right, you'll get home late Friday and fly out again Sunday night? Makes for a short weekend. I mean, Byron lives that way. But maybe Justine would appreciate a bit more of your time that weekend."

"No, it's all cleared. Actually, I didn't note it there, but that Monday is Memorial Day—so it's a long weekend. And—in truth—Byron and I aren't flying home at all between stops. We timed it that way so we can spend the weekend together in Indianapolis. We have tickets to the Indianapolis 500."

Craig stared blankly for an instant, then made the connection. "Ah. That's a car race, isn't it? So, you and Byron are still into your vehicular bonding. Excellent. That should be fun. Enjoy."

"It's actually the biggest race of the year. Even *you* might like it." Nigel's grin, as he concluded that remark, was prodigious—it hovered somewhere between ingratiating and mocking.

Craig laughed loudly. "I don't think so, my friend. But if you were offering to include me at the race, I certainly appreciate the gesture. It's just not for me."

The waitress arrived and set down the hot dishes of food. She shot Craig a quick wink and a grin before she scooted off.

"Yes. A substantial tip, indeed!" Nigel snickered without looking up. He plunged his chopsticks into the spicy mélange of beef and vegetables in front of him and scooped up a mound of white rice atop it. He yanked the aggregation unceremoniously to his lips.

Craig took a slow, quiet sip of tea, admired the simple yet artful presentation of food on his plate, and reached gingerly for his chopsticks. As he did, his mind returned for just an instant to his last lunch here with Carolyn—and that clingy red top she'd worn.

• • •

Nigel winced, but continued to scamper. He took tiny frantic steps, balanced precariously on his toes, as he followed Byron round and round, inside the revolving doors that led from the hotel lobby to the street. He'd never seen Byron laugh this hysterically, and had certainly never witnessed Byron's short paunchy frame gambol quite so farcically as it did now, with Byron's stubby arms pushing the revolving doors as fast as he could make them go. They'd already circled three times, with Nigel dutifully scurrying along, one section behind, wondering how long this would go on.

And even more puzzling for Nigel—why were they exiting the hotel at all?

They'd had a long, late dinner in the big Italian restaurant attached to their hotel's lobby. "Best Italian food in Indianapolis," Byron had assured him earlier, when they were having drinks at the hotel bar. "I ate here the last two times I came in for the race," he'd said, "really good."

There had been lots more drinking and merriment as they dined. They'd had osso buco on Byron's recommendation, which Nigel found abundant and tasty atop its huge bed of creamy polenta—though the restaurant's ornate wood panels, gold-plated chandeliers, bright red tablecloths, and plushily upholstered chairs were just a bit gaudy for Nigel's taste. He'd lost count of how many gimlets Byron had downed between the bar and the restaurant, but as Nigel finished his dessert of chocolate cake and espresso and watched Byron take his last sip of his double Grand Marnier, he assumed they'd leave the restaurant shortly and head back up to their rooms.

So, when Byron told him he had a surprise, and to just follow him through the revolving doors, Nigel was taken aback. But he complied.

The two men had just gyrated through their fifth breakneck rotation when Nigel spotted an elderly couple emerge from a taxi and walk slowly toward the hotel's entrance. He was relieved to see that Byron noticed them too—he slowed his pace and exited sedately onto the street. Nigel joined him there, wondering what was next.

Byron glared up at Nigel with a ferocious grin.

Nigel waited a moment, until the elderly couple walked past them and entered the lobby. "You're really drunk," Nigel teased. "I mean, not just happy and relaxed like usual—I mean seriously pissed. Quite pleasantly so, though, mate."

Byron emitted a loud, frenetic laugh, his shoulders heaving. "Could be," he said. "Could well be, bro. It's just so damn nice to be away from home—but not actually at work—you know. And with a new friend."

Nigel smiled. It seemed to him that Byron was about to share something more. Nigel took a moment to observe how warm and humid the evening was as he waited.

"I have a plan," Byron finally said.

"What the hell are you up to? That's an evil smirk across your gob!"

Byron lowered his voice and leaned in closer. He peered up at Nigel, who towered affably above him. "I know a place," Byron said. "Been there half-a-dozen times. High-class hookers. Gorgeous. Super clean and discreet. On me. You up for it?"

Nigel's eyes ballooned and his lips curled in a mix of uncertainty and wantonness. His expression morphed into a broad smile. "Let's grab that cab, mate. He's about to drive off."

They ran over and hopped in for what turned out to be just a five-minute ride. The taxi pulled up to a nondescript house.

Byron whispered, "This stays in Indianapolis."

"Of course," Nigel replied, as he watched Byron slip the driver a twenty-dollar bill.

"Keep the change," Byron said, as Nigel followed him out of the cab.

• • •

It was a bit past eleven when Nigel and Byron got back to the hotel.

"The bar's still open," Byron said. "Join me for a nightcap?"

"Sorry, mate, I'm knackered. I gotta get up to my room and collapse. Great night though." He grinned and lowered his voice. "And thanks for that little *do* to top it off—those birds were hot."

"You gonna call Justine tonight?"

"Well, sure. It's still early back in California. A bloke's gotta check in."

"Focus when you do it, bro. Women pick up on the tiniest thing in your voice. We were just at the bar, drinking. Nothing else."

Nigel laughed. "One of these days, mate, I need to tell you about my growin'-up years in Leeds. Believe me, I've told my share of porkies—and nobody's been the wiser."

"Okay. Cool."

Their hug was brief, consummated with mutual back slaps. Nigel trudged off to the elevator.

Byron slipped into the bar and ordered a double Grand Marnier. He noticed the bartender was closing down and said, "Don't worry. I'll drink it quick." He left a generous tip and took the elevator up to his room. He stripped down to his undershirt and boxers and called Adelle.

"Hello?" she said.

"Hi, babe. It's me."

"It's nice to hear from you, honey. How's it going out there? It's late for you, isn't it?"

"Yeah. Me and Nigel were hanging out. Drinking."

"That's nice. How's it going with Nigel?"

"It's funny—I'm actually starting to like the guy."

"I kinda expected that. You know, after the second time you two drove those race cars up at Sears Point—you were warming up to him even then. I could tell."

"Yeah, I think you're right. And, you know, he hasn't actually said it, but it seems like Nigel's starting to see Craig more like you and me do. I mean everything Craig says and does seems cool on the outside, you know—supportive—if you don't really know him. But then there's that smugness—that kind of arrogance that you can sense underneath after a while—you know, it doesn't show, but it's always sorta there. I think maybe Nigel's starting to see it too."

"I'm happy you guys are getting friendly. And I'm even happier that it's been all guy stuff and not foursomes. That Justine bitch is creepy, with all that dead body stuff. And the politics she always loves talking about—like every other bleeding-heart liberal whack job out here in California—but worse with her—sickening."

"Not sure about Nigel that way. He may be a little closer to *us*. Just doesn't want to say it. Gotta be careful in the Bay Area with what you say to people. Anyway, I think you're off the hook with Justine. Nigel says she's getting really chummy with Shoshana. So, you can leave the girl stuff to the two of them."

"That's a relief."

"You know, it doesn't seem like Nigel and Craig have anything in common outside of work—that kind of leaves things wide open—for me."

"Listen, honey. Take it slow with Nigel. I mean, don't even go near sharing anything about Shoshana's secret whorehouse or how you're spying on her. Hell, even *you* don't know what you might wind up doing with all that. You can't trust him with anything like that. I mean it. It's important."

"Agreed. Too soon."

"Maybe never. Like I said. You don't even know what *you're* gonna do with all that. Just let it lie. At least for now."

"Yeah. That's smart."

"Right. Gotta be smart about it."

"Well, gettin' sleepy, babe. Gonna sign off. Love you."

"Okay. Love you too, honey. Have a good time out there. Sweet dreams."

• • •

As soon as he hung up, a sense of closure and satisfaction saturated Byron's psyche. Everything had gone so well. Adelle didn't suspect a thing. The night with Nigel had proceeded flawlessly. And, at the house, Byron had landed a girl with whom he'd been before—it had been a year or two ago—she remembered him, and she made their session especially intimate and personal.

As he sat on the edge of the bed, he looked in the direction of the bathroom and took an abrupt breath. He needed to wash his face and brush his teeth. But he was tired. And he was here, alone in a hotel room, spared of Adelle's inconspicuous yet persistent surveillance. He felt free of obligation or encumbrance.

He decided he'd wash in the morning—a tiny assertion of volition, which in itself, felt like a small triumph.

The top sheet and papery blanket peeled up easily in his grasp, and Byron squeezed in.

He reached over and turned off the lamp, then relaxed on his back. The slightest hint of a grin formed upon his lips as he shut his eyes and began to consciously slow his breathing into a slow rhythmic cadence.

But then, without warning, his head and shoulders spasmed and his torso bolted upright. He tried to stifle the groan stampeding upward from his convulsing larynx, but it reverberated loudly in the small hotel room.

It was another of the torturous memories that seized him, unannounced—and always when he was alone.

The genesis of this one was invariably a word—the same word—a word he wished he had never come upon. *Lieder*. German, for a poem set to music. He'd discovered the word in a book when he was barely twelve. And although he had never heard even a single example of actual classical Lieder, the idea of it inspired him.

Byron was an ungainly self-absorbed loner as a boy—short, chubby, and socially maladroit. But he found solace in the inexpensive nylon string guitar his mother had claimed as a gift from the S&H Green Stamps she collected at the grocery checkout. She had presented it to him for Christmas when he was eleven.

His singing voice was awful, but he became adept at plucking out tunes—and though his talent was rudimentary, its spark was fiery and it sustained him in his loneliness. He fiddled with his guitar for hours each evening, at first croaking out songs he'd heard and pieced together, and later composing original melodies with basic accompanying chords. He wanted to write lyrics for his songs, but devising anything even remotely unembarrassing proved to be an effort well beyond his reach—he'd never been verbally gifted—English was consistently his worst subject in school.

So, when he came upon the concept of Lieder—taking a poem that already existed and setting it to music—he felt inspired to try. Soon he had produced dozens—none earth-shatteringly brilliant—but each with a discernible melody and simple but harmonious chords.

By the time he reached high school, it had become his secret and solitary passion. And in his junior year, when he discovered that the girl in the third seat of the first row in his history class was named Hallie Lieder, he became obsessed.

He was convinced that destiny was at play.

She was impossible for him to get a clear read on. He imagined her to be wildly popular—someone who might laugh or ignore him if he approached her—but he couldn't be sure. She looked pretty to him, though her face was very round, and her hips and shoulders were wider than those of most girls, and her waist not markedly small—traits that might make her somewhat more accepting of him. She always carried the day's edition of the St. Petersburg Times folded neatly atop her binder and textbooks, something no other student did. She seemed aloof—he took that to suggest she was quite sure of herself.

It took him two months to work up the courage to ask her out, endlessly rehearsing what he might say. When he finally caught her alone, he beseeched her haltingly, barely able to keep eye contact, stammering through his much-practiced script.

He was relieved but stunned when she immediately smiled and said yes.

He took her to a movie—so he wouldn't need to talk too much—and when he escorted her home and they stood facing each other awkwardly at her front door, he wanted to kiss her, but he couldn't summon the courage. He said goodnight and walked off, but after just a few steps he raced back and pecked at her cheek, then dashed off wordlessly in a muddled mix of euphoria and humiliation.

For the next few days it was difficult for Byron to recall much of what had actually transpired during the date—it was all a blur—but he was convinced that he had made a sufficient fool of himself such that there was no point in ever trying to ask Hallie Lieder out again.

So, when she approached him before class a week later, with

a warm, excited smile, and handed him a printed invitation to her sweet sixteen party, he was too flummoxed to do anything but take it and nod sheepishly.

He had never been to a sweet sixteen party, but the very idea of it filled him with dread. Popular kids—people whose world was totally separate from his—dancing and laughing and making jokes. He tried to picture himself at such a thing, and it was excruciating. He couldn't possibly go. It would be an embarrassing debacle. But wasn't he obligated to tell her he wasn't going? She'd ask him why—what on earth would he say? That alone would be mortifying.

So, he did nothing. He avoided Hallie scrupulously for the next three weeks. Not a word between them was shared.

The party was scheduled on a Saturday night, at a Tampa hotel and restaurant just blocks from where Byron lived. The afternoon prior to the party, Hallie caught Byron in the hall, emerging from his biology class.

"Are you coming tomorrow night?" she asked with a sweet grin.

"Sure," Byron whispered, and immediately ran off.

But he never showed up at the party.

As that Saturday evening wore on, he paced alone in his room and watched the clock. He agonized every moment over whether to throw on a tie and his one tattered sport coat and dash over. But each time he pictured the scene in his head—the cool kids dancing and laughing while he made a fool of himself—he became paralyzed.

He heard about it through word-of-mouth days later. His empty seat had been right beside hers, and she'd kept gazing at it all night. She'd considered him her boyfriend! How on earth would he have known that? He'd ruined her special night.

As more people learned about what happened, Byron became

a pariah. Prior to this incident they had just ignored him—now he had morphed into an object of disdain and ridicule.

These harrowing recollections now raced inexorably through his mind, as he sat alone in the dark Indianapolis hotel room. "Stop!" he screamed. But Hallie Lieder's despondent face was the only response his mind conjured. She stared at him, unblinking, her eyes welling up with tears.

"I'm sorry!" he cried. "I've been sorry since the day it happened. Why can't you leave me alone? Jesus. Why the hell should I still give a shit. You're probably a fat old ugly bitch by now. Why the fuck can't you just stop? I'm sorry, for god's sake. I had no one to help me—no one to tell me what to do—no one to teach me how to dance."

He began to hyperventilate. Hallie Lieder's beautiful face grew in size and filled the room, her sad eyes fixed upon his. "I couldn't dance!" he pleaded. "I didn't know how. For god's sake, I would have made a fool out of both of us. People would have laughed at us for weeks—months. For god's fucking sake, I'm sorry! How long will ya keep haunting me? Why can't you just forgive me and leave me alone! I'm fucking sorry."

13

OYSTERS

ON THE HALF SHELLTHE SUN WAS HIGH IN Sausalito's midday sky. The fog had dissipated and the air grown warm. From the restaurant, the view, which spanned the shimmering water to Belvedere and Tiburon, was mesmerizing.

Shoshana and Justine sat at a small outdoor table, sharing a half bottle of Vernaccia, a white wine Shoshana had fallen in love with years ago when she and Craig dined at a café in the hill town of San Gimignano in Tuscany. Shoshana often wondered whether it was the actual taste of the wine, or rather the heady mix of memories associated with that night—new love, unabated sensual passion, dazzlingly nuanced infliction of pain, and an ingenious bondage configuration leveraging the small hotel room's wooden ceiling rafters and bedposts—that rendered the wine, forever after, so silky and lustrous on her tongue.

For the two women, lunch together had become a weekly ritual, always on Mondays—their husbands, Craig and Nigel, at work—Shoshana concluding her makeshift weekend—and Justine almost always free because funeral-related activities had culminated by Sunday evenings.

The waiter arrived with their order—a double platter of

oysters on the half shell with rosé mignonette: fresh raw oysters assembled on a bed of crushed ice with lemon wedges, accompanied by a bowl of absolutely perfect sauce comprised of nothing more than sparkling rosé, minced shallots, a splash of white wine vinegar, and a few turns of freshly ground peppercorns.

"These Monday lunches are so nice," Justine said, as she dolloped a bit of sauce on an oyster and lifted it to her lips.

"They are," Shoshana replied. "When we started, I was afraid you might be working most of these Mondays, but it's so nice you've been free."

"I have so much more control over my schedule now. People don't usually need anything finished till later in the week. I really worked a lot more hours when I was a full-time funeral director. Oh my god, I'm so glad I don't do that anymore. Now that I specialize in, you know, the extreme restorations, it's a lot less. I have tons more time to myself, for sure." She sipped a bit of wine before continuing. "And it's really super nice that Nigel's doing so well now, too." Justine looked up and smiled broadly. "And who do we have to thank for that?" She reached for her wine glass and held it up to toast with Shoshana. "To your husband! Oh my god—Craig is just so sweet—what a great boss—I mean he and Nigel are totally different people, but Nigel has a lot of respect for him."

"I hear Nigel's doing very well. What's it been, about six months now since he's taken charge of the testing team?"

"Just about, yes. I'm really happy for him. But he's traveling so much more now—he's away for days at a time—it does get lonely, especially with me not working so much anymore."

Shoshana slurped up an oyster with sauce and took a long slow sip of wine. She gazed into Justine's eyes and weighed the situation carefully before speaking. "Can you keep a secret, honey? I mean really keep it? Like, *you* keep it from Nigel, and

I'll keep it from Craig. If not, that's okay. We'll just skip it. No big deal."

"I have lots of secrets from Nigel—I'm sure he has lots from me—especially now that he's on the road so much. So, yes—like totally. What's the secret?"

"Well, let me start with a question. How do you feel about kinky sex?" Shoshana leaned in. Her eyes widened as she awaited a response.

Justine's features crinkled as she pondered. "Kinky? I'm not exactly sure what you mean by that. I'm not *bi*, if that's what you're getting at—I mean if you're coming on to me, Shoshana, I'm flattered—you're a gorgeous woman—but I'm totally hetero."

Shoshana chuckled. "You're a gorgeous woman, too. But no. I'm not bi either. When I said kinky, I meant, like creative. *Sexually* creative. Role playing."

Justine giggled. "I had this boyfriend—it was a while ago—and he liked to pretend I was, like eleven or twelve. When he first suggested it, I thought it was creepy—like grody to the total max—but he said he'd never really do it with a little girl—he just liked to pretend. We had some fun, I guess. We broke up for a whole bunch of other reasons—but that little-girl stuff was kinda fun—like once in a while—if I didn't think about it too much."

Shoshana took a long sip of wine. "Do you remember when we were all at Byron and Adelle's place, and she kept asking me what I do for a living? And I said I was an investigator but I couldn't talk about it? That wasn't the truth."

"Yeah. I didn't think so," Justine said, raising her hand to her mouth to suppress a giggle. "It didn't, like, really ring true. I'm not a good liar either. Now, Nigel . . . he's a master at it. Anyway . . . go on."

"I'm going to tell you what I do. It needs to stay secret. But

I think you'll get it. And I trust you."

Justine leaned toward her. "I appreciate that. You can trust me."

"I have a townhouse down in Los Altos. I see men. They're submissive men—sexually, I mean—they may be completely controlling or strong outside of that. But they like to do sexual role play. I help them with that."

Justine's eyes widened and her lips parted mischievously. "You're a dominatrix?"

Shoshana smiled. "You're familiar with the term!"

"I had a girlfriend in art school who did it, like a couple nights a week to help pay tuition."

"I don't do sex. I'm not a prostitute."

"Yeah, yeah, same with my girlfriend. It's almost like being a therapist. But, like, with kinky benefits!" Justine laughed.

Shoshana smiled and reached across the table to gently take Justine's hand. "I knew you'd get it. And now I have a question. I know this might sound like a lot. So, don't feel like you have to give me an answer right now. You can think about it."

"Are you, like, asking me to do sessions with you?"

Shoshana blinked purposefully. Her lips pursed into what looked almost like a kiss. "Yes, sweetie. That's exactly what I'm asking. Well—at first—if you want—you can just come and keep me company. You can watch what I do. You could even sleep over—I get lonely on weeknights. But . . . I was thinking. You kinda seem like a natural. And, I mean, especially with your skills—you know, prettying up corpses and such—I have clients who have all kinds of death fantasies. Like being cooked and eaten—being tortured to death—being, like, mummified and used as a statue in their mistress's house. Crazy stuff! I mean, harmless. Fun even—if it's just play. I was thinking—you could make it seem so real. And you could make a few extra bucks too.

And like I said—I'd really love your company."

Justine's features flashed a cunning, disobedient smirk. She raised her glass of Vernaccia to toast. As the women's vessels clinked, Justine leaned her head toward Shoshana and purred, "Oh my god! This is going to be so fun!"

• • •

It had been a cold and foggy Sunday morning in San Francisco, but as Craig and Shoshana drove south along the coast, the sun began to show itself, and the clouds ultimately ceded to a warm sky of crisp deep blue.

They'd left early, having planned a long drive. They were looking forward to sharing lunch on the outdoor patio of Brahma's, a quaint fast-food place they'd discovered in a town just south of Santa Cruz, nearly two hours away. Shoshana had taken a half-dozen tokes on a joint as Craig had navigated the cliffs overlooking the ocean twenty minutes earlier, and now she was mellow and relaxed.

"You know," Craig said, "I looked up the history of Brahma's the other day. It's quite a story. It opened years ago, as a natural, vegetarian alternative to McDonald's. So, they originally called it McBrahma's. The logo had a little circle in the upper left with the letters 'Mc,' then the word 'Brahma's' in big capital letters."

"That's cute," Shoshana said with a coy smile.

"Well, evidently, McDonald's didn't think so. They sued the little vegetarian restaurant."

"No!"

"Actually, from what I've read, they've sued over fifty companies for using 'Mc' as a prefix."

"How can somebody own a prefix?"

"Well, they have a big team of lawyers, so I guess they think they can. But wait, the story gets better. So McBrahma's agreed to drop the 'Mc' from its name. But I suppose just to be snarky, what they actually did was put the circle-slash thing over the 'Mc,' so it read like No-Mc-Brahma's."

Shoshana laughed. "Priceless. Very clever. I guess that showed 'em."

"No, McDonalds sued them again."

"Wow." Her eyes widened and her head snapped in Craig's direction. "Oh! So, that's why now their sign has a circle-slash thing with that adorable little cow's head smiling inside it. The cow replaced the 'Mc'!"

"Exactly."

Shoshana lovingly stroked the back of Craig's head. "You tell the sweetest stories, honey."

"Speaking of stories, how have your Monday lunches with Justine been going? Any good stories to tell from those?"

"Well, according to Justine, Byron and Nigel have been getting pretty chummy."

"Yes, I suspected that. The two of them did a long weekend together to watch some car race a while back."

"Right, the Indianapolis 500. And they've raced cars together up at Sears Point. And just tooled around Marin and Sonoma in Nigel's Lotus with the top down a few Saturdays."

"I really didn't think they'd wind up getting so close. They're very different. I think Nigel has a lot more going on intellectually than Byron. But it's nice that they are. And it's great that you and Justine are becoming such good friends. I honestly believe it's healthy for you to have some lady friends outside the BDSM community—you know—people who don't know anything about it, or how you're involved in it."

Shoshana's lips struggled to curl into a smirk, but she was successful in keeping her features emotionless. She sought to change the subject. "You know," she said, "Justine and I shared a half bottle of Vernaccia with lunch the other day—and it made me think of *you*, honey—and that amazing time we had in San Gimignano, in Tuscany. Do you remember that?"

"Yes, of course. I remember it so fondly. We were somehow able to juggle the roles then. I mean I was your submissive—and we were lovers and real people—but it didn't clash—we just were *us*—and we made it work."

Shoshana flashed a wistful smile. "Not really, honey. You were my slave then. Pure and simple. We raced around Italy with our backpacks stuffed full of ropes and sex-toys. We weren't husband and wife. We'd just recently become intimate. We didn't have a home—or a living trust—or a tax attorney—or years and years of seeing each other as people with real-life challenges and responsibilities. It was a fantasy, honey. We lived it out, day to day on the trip. But it wasn't real. It was a total fantasy."

Craig was quiet for a moment; then he spoke softly. "You know, we've barely made love lately—I mean even vanilla love with no play—even after the last play-party you said you weren't in the mood. I miss being intimate with you. I miss it a lot, Empress."

"I'm sorry, baby. But it's cyclical. You know that. We've been through it before. I'll be back into you. It's just when something new comes up, it occupies me for a while. But I love *you*."

"How many times a week are you doing it with the Hauler Guy now?"

"Darling, that's an impolite question to pose to your mistress."

"But that's kind of *it* now, isn't it. I mean, you're my mistress for the things that suit you—when I'm drawing party invitations—or cooking dinner for you—or asking uncomfortable questions—but not for all the other things—the things that *I* really want and need."

Shoshana leaned toward him and massaged his shoulders gently as he drove. "Oh—my dear darling boy—I love you so much, but I keep trying to tell you—navigating life when you're wired for SM isn't easy, it's very hard. But the answer everyone in the community seems to come up with is out there for you too—you need to find women in the community to play with and to be intimate with—women you can be totally in a fantasy with. And I can help you with that. You try every now and then—but nothing ever seems to come of it—I'm not sure why—but you need to keep trying. You know I *do* love you very much. I can help you make it work."

Craig smiled and rested his right hand on her thigh. "I love you too, Empress. I suppose you're right—it's just been hard for me. But I'll have to try to figure it out." He paused. "Let's talk about something else."

Shoshana lovingly stroked his cheek. She fully understood that Craig had terminated this thread of conversation because he'd concluded that taking it further would be counterproductive. She knew he didn't actually believe that by trying harder he could make it work. She loved him very much, but she was certain that the extracurricular activities she proposed were the only way to sustain their union. She regretted that it hurt him, but she was sure that compromising on that now, to spare his feelings, would ultimately be disastrous for them both.

They engaged in some vapid small talk for a while, which served as a benign transition to a long stint of peaceful silence as they drove together down the coast highway toward Santa Cruz.

Shoshana thought back to Craig's indelicate probing into the frequency with which she and the Hauler Guy were seeing each other. It caused her now to soundlessly compare the two men.

Hauler Guy's submission was playful and perfunctory—it was really the intense sensation of pain that seemed to motivate him. He had nothing remotely approaching the deep psychological manifestation of submission that Craig felt toward her—and which Craig was somehow able to sustain. That made Craig her preeminent choice for a partner.

And it probably meant that she should be more willing to be intimate with him.

But what she knew she could never voice to Craig, was how much it thrilled her when the big hulky Hauler Guy neared orgasm—dropping all pretense of submission—growling and groaning and morphing into a primitive convulsing animal—hurled into that unreined feral state solely by her allure.

Craig, dear, sweet, loyal man that he was, was not capable of sinking into such an unbridled state. Craig orgasmed inside her dutifully—lovingly—his cerebral disposition deeply and unerringly submissive—his entire being calibrated precisely to act as a tool for her joy and satisfaction.

• • •

It invariably made Shoshana laugh when she answered the condo door to find Justine standing in cloak-and-dagger attire on the top step—Justine's long loose black coat buttoned up to her chin—the enormous front brim of her wool fedora drooping just low enough to obscure her eyes and nose. When Shoshana had stressed that everything about the work needed to be kept secret and confidential, she didn't expect Justine to take it quite this far. But it was preferable to her taking it too lightly, so Shoshana always chuckled, and never complained.

"Oh! I have a gift!" Justine exclaimed as soon as she passed through the curtained area, and presented a small colorful shopping bag with tissue paper jutting from its top. She dug into it and placed on the table a kettle-shaped wooden bowl and lid, and five tiny, sealed bottles of liquid. "It's aromatherapy! Oh my god, I really want you to try it. You know, not for when clients are here—but after—when we relax and have a late supper and go to bed. It'll be so relaxing for us. You know, kind of get us to shed it all and bliss out."

Shoshana examined the items and smiled. "They're lovely. Thank you, Justine. I can't wait to try it."

"You're so welcome," Justine said, as she removed her outer garments and the two women sat down.

It was 7:00 p.m.

Shoshana had not scheduled an early appointment, so that she and Justine would have an hour now to review and finalize the choreography for their 8:00 p.m. rendezvous with Pete Tax Accountant. He had agreed to a two-hour session, with a premium charge for having two women work on him, so Shoshana wanted to make sure that the psychodrama played out vividly and effectively.

"So, are you ready?" Shoshana asked.

"I think so."

"Okay. Let's go through it, one last time, to be sure."

"Right. So, like, we're pretending that we kidnapped him."

"Yes. Exactly. He swindled me—as my accountant. So now we're going to make him pay. First, we'll strip him, and tie him up, and make him sit on the exam table. I have a toy gun you can point at him while I tell him what a shit he was for stealing from me when he did my taxes. He'll plead, but I'll ball-gag him to shut him up."

"And I'm just holding the gun, right? I'm not saying anything yet."

"Correct. And right about then, I'll tell him that he's a typical male piece of shit, and he doesn't deserve to live. And that, now, we're going to kill him. So, after I say that, we need to give him time to react—he'll struggle with his bonds and the gag—he'll try to scream for help but nothing much will come out. We'll just watch him and laugh. Finally, he'll accept that he's totally helpless."

"Okay. Got it."

"Be really haughty, honey."

"Oh my god! We're such a couple of bitches!"

Shoshana chuckled. "Right about then, I'll introduce you as the undertaker who's going to prepare him for his showing. You know, in his coffin. And you're going to erase all clues that might implicate us in his murder. Okay?"

"Right."

"Did you bring the stuff you're going to wear?"

"I did." Justine opened her black leather satchel and pulled out a pair of goggles, a face mask, and latex gloves. Then she produced a long plastic robe and modeled it by pressing it against the front of her body and pivoting slightly, side to side.

Shoshana's eyebrows lowered and her lips curled into the suggestion of a frown.

"You know, honey, I love the goggles, and the mask, and gloves. But now, on second thought, I think the robe is too much—it's too bland—and it's not sexy at all. I have a beautiful black corset that will fit you—I wore it years ago but it's too tight on me now." She touched Justine's arm, and they both giggled. "It'll look really hot on you with some black fishnets and black stiletto boots."

"Thank god our shoe sizes are the same!"

Shoshana smiled. "That'll be the right balance for how you should look," she said. "I know it's not totally realistic, but the goggles and stuff look authentic, and then the rest makes it hot. It's a fantasy, after all. It actually shouldn't be completely authentic."

"Sounds good to me."

"Okay, so then I'll insult him while I strangle him. You still hold the gun on him at that point. I'll use a stocking to choke him. It's soft and stretchy, so I can pull it tight enough around his neck so it feels real to him, but it doesn't actually cut his air off enough to hurt him."

"Cool."

"Then after I've squeezed for a minute or two, I'll say, 'You'll be dead in thirty seconds, you worthless worm,' and he'll pretend to die and lie back on the table."

"And that's when I come in?"

"Yes. I've done that much with him a lot of times—you know, got up to that point—but now you take over. God, he was so excited when I suggested this extended addition to the session with him. So, now, you put down the gun and come over with all your embalming stuff and makeup."

"Right. So, first, I'll pretend to embalm him. And then I'll wrap him."

"Just keep talking while you do it—describe what you're doing, so he can hear it."

Justine laughed. "Talking while I work is not a problem for me!"

"I'll help you dress him, honey. He said he'll bring a suit and tie. He'll try to act like dead weight, but he's a really sweet guy so he'll help us little—you know, inconspicuously, when we need to lift him to get his shirt and pants on—but you can say something like, 'Jesus, for a scrawny guy he's hard to lift!' Then go into the makeup—you brought it, right?"

"Well, some is real funereal makeup—but a lot is just regular makeup—I kind of disguised the bottles and tubes. You know, funereal makeup doesn't really take on living bodies sometimes."

"Good thinking, honey. That'll work. So, you keep doing the

makeup—I figure it'll take a while. And again, keep talking about what you're doing. And I'll keep an eye on the clock so we can end on time."

"And we'll leave him dressed and made up like that?"

Shoshana chuckled. "Oh yeah, he'll wear it home. And when he lies down on his bed and jerks off, he'll watch himself in his ceiling mirror. I guarantee you he'll explode."

"So, we won't put a condom on him—and do him with a vibrator at the end—you know, like you did with the other clients in the sessions we did together?"

"No, honey, not him. He's really private that way—he likes to go home—you know, he has a long drive—and he keeps replaying the session in his head. Like I told you, he's a super sweet guy. He's just so lonely. It's really sad."

14

GOUDA AND WATER BISCUITS

IT WAS A BALMY EVENING ON THE PENINSULA.

As soon as Craig spotted him, he adjudged the large man's ludicrously snug jeans and torso-hugging polo shirt to have been chosen for no reason other than to call attention to his imposing physique—a vapid, hackneyed ploy—and one to which only a person with little to contribute intellectually would stoop.

Craig pulled over and waited as the Hauler Guy eased into the back seat of the SUV.

Craig had reconciled himself, some time ago, to the fact that Shoshana would take them both to this La Maîtresse play-party. Craig also knew, from sour experience, that Shoshana's persistent assurances that he'd be well taken care of meant that she'd make certain that other women played with him—but that she wouldn't be paying much attention to him herself.

But just yesterday, Shoshana had also posited the unconvincing argument that Hauler Guy's house was roughly on their way to where the party was being hosted—or that it was at least not that far *out* of their way—and that they should pick him up, and that the three of them should arrive together.

As Craig pulled away from the curb, he noticed the Hauler Guy produce a small, wrapped package—evidently a gift for Shoshana—which he now passed to her with exaggerated deference.

She turned slightly toward him from where she sat in the front passenger seat. "Thank you, slave," she said in a haughty whisper. "I'll open it another time."

As Craig made his way back to the freeway and continued down the peninsula, he was silent. He felt far more like a chauffeur for Shoshana and her favorite new submissive—rather than her husband and party companion.

• • •

Casual observers, from nearby windows, would have thought only that a small group of entirely unremarkable people were arriving for a sedate weekend party. Closer observers might have noticed that the women appeared to carry oversized purses, and many of the men had backpacks or gym bags. But otherwise, they would barely have given anyone a second glance.

Craig found a space just a block away.

Keeping with protocol, they entered the home in normal attire. Once inside the house—with its shades drawn and its curtains closed—they went immediately into the back bedroom to change into costume.

A few minutes later, Shoshana sashayed into the main room with a comically pompous smirk and an affected swagger—a naked slave on either side of her. She wore a silver leather corset studded with rhinestones, along with a black, lacy plunge bra and sheer silver panties. The corset had long garters of silky gold ribbon—they clasped the tops of black fishnet stockings, which emerged from slinky stiletto-heeled metallic boots.

The men were nude but for locked leather collars. The taller man carried Shoshana's bag of toys and restraints.

There had been many parties in the past when Craig was Shoshana's lone slave. It always seemed to him, then, that when they made their entrance, the women in the room admired his slender, wiry yoga physique—particularly in comparison to the many soft, paunchy male slaves in attendance who had sedentary office jobs and seldom exercised. Tonight, though, paraded along with the huge, burly Hauler Guy, he was certain that nobody was paying much attention to him at all.

Shoshana ordered the Hauler Guy to get her some white wine, and pointed him to the table where paper cups and bottles of beverages were set out. All were clear liquids—white wine, vodka, gin, club soda, and 7UP. Craig had always been fascinated with this mandate—how it irrefutably indicated a female-controlled party—prioritizing stain-prevention over beverage indulgence. And, as it always did, that tiny, redundant psychological observation about the presence of female power induced a twinge of excitement in his nether regions.

Shoshana grabbed Craig's hand and walked him over to Mistress Olga, a very tall and full-figured Swedish woman. Her straight blond hair broke on her shoulders and played seductively off her black rubber dress.

"Good evening, Mistress Olga," Shoshana said, as the two women hugged and kissed politely on the cheek. "I'm going to be occupied with my new plaything tonight, but adorable Craig here needs to be bound and punished for all sorts of transgressions. And nobody does that more expertly than you, dear."

Olga smiled. "Your boy is a favorite of mine," she said in her heavy Swedish accent. "My own slave is off playing with Lady Thorn right now, so I have lots of time to administer the discipline your boy needs. Slowly—the way I prefer." She looked at Craig and narrowed her gaze. "The pain of rope creeps up on you little by little—not like the sharp strike of a whip. You're familiar with it. You like it—I know. You're such a naughty boy."

Craig had always enjoyed playing with Mistress Olga. He knew that she was fascinated with rope play, and viewed the act of tying up a man much as one would an engineering problem. And Craig was confident that he kept Mistress Olga amused as well, which was important to him.

Shoshana smiled and stroked Olga's shoulder, then walked off.

Tonight, as was often Mistress Olga's preference, she began with Craig's wrists. She had him intertwine his fingers behind his back, the heels of his hands pressed tightly against one another. Once she had his wrists snugly bound, she selected a slightly longer length of rope from her bag, anchored the center of it to the wrist tie, and then began weaving the opposing strands up his arms, just a few inches at a time, cinching his arms together tightly at each increment, and securing the segment with a knot. Soon she had worked her way up to his elbows, which were now squeezed securely together behind him, his arms, from there down, a single immovable mass.

Olga admired her work and smiled broadly. "Ah, you are such a dear slave! I know of no other man . . ." she pondered a moment, " . . . and really only a small handful of very young slender women . . . whose arms I can tie together like this. Elbows touching! And, for you my darling, it seems effortless!"

"Thank you, ma'am," Craig whispered.

"Ah! I'm only getting started! You will suffer greatly, my love."

Craig recalled that she'd asked him, the first time they played, how he'd become so flexible. When he'd revealed to her that he had practiced yoga for decades, she'd told him how much she admired him for that.

"Kneel, and then lie on the floor, face down," she said. She supported him as he complied, to compensate for his inability to employ his hands. "On your belly. Good. Now, bend your knees and raise your legs up." When he did, she bound his legs together, first at the ankles, and then where the calves met the knee joints.

With another rope she tugged his feet and hands toward each other and secured them so that they were just inches apart.

Finally, she tossed a long rope up so that it looped around a ceiling rafter. She weaved one end of it through the tiny gap between his hands and feet, and pulled it up to meet the other end of the rope. She first created a sort of slip knot to enable her to increase the tension slowly. When she had it quite taut, she gave it a final yank, eliciting a moan from Craig, and fixed it in place with a square knot.

Olga took a step back, admired her work, and smiled. "You're quite helpless now, my dear. And isn't it wonderful that this house has ceiling rafters? What kind of house has that? It's my favorite party space—for that reason."

Craig gazed at her silently. She looked beautiful standing above him, her hands on her hips. And he found her accent beguiling.

The way she'd configured him was much like yoga positions he practiced each morning—Cobra and Bow—except that now, it wasn't his own strength that held him taut—it was *Olga's* power—expressed through her skill in wrapping, pulling, and knotting her ropes. It rendered him helpless—utterly hers—so long as she deemed it pleasing to own him.

"I need some food," she said with a chuckle, "but I can't very well ask you now, can I?" She raised a hand and flagged down the itinerant server.

He was a small, slight man, a regular client of many of the professional Dommes at the party. Always convincingly cross-dressed as a French maid with a short, flared black dress and a white apron, he was a perennial fixture at these get-togethers—not exactly a personal submissive for any of the women—instead, a servant who worked the entire night as waitress, maid, janitor, and gofer. He was usually rewarded at the party's end by one or two of the women who'd strip him and then string him up and subject him to a brief beating with a riding crop—his choice of punishment device.

The maid now stood before Mistress Olga. "How may I serve you, ma'am?" he asked, in a jarringly realistic falsetto.

"I want you to bring me some food," Olga demanded, "but first, get me that chair over there. I was sitting in it before. I want it over here now, so I can be comfortable while I watch this poor bound boy suffer."

It was a heavy, upholstered chair. The maid dragged it over gingerly, so as not to damage the chair legs or the carpet. He was nimble in his high heels.

"Good. Now, I want Gouda cheese and water biscuits, and some of whatever fruit they have out. I want a good-sized plate, so I have enough to eat while I watch the boy writhe in pain. But please, it has to be the Gouda, not some other cheese. And only water biscuits. No other kind of cracker. If you don't know which is which, ask somebody who knows." She paused a moment. "Oh, and some wine, too."

"Yes ma'am," he said with a slight curtsy, and was off.

Olga sat down and fished around in her bag. "I'm looking for my most painful titty clamps," she said, smiling. "You're entirely too comfortable there, my love."

Craig watched her. His erection grew larger.

"Ah, here they are." Olga leaned down. "Roll over a little, please."

He could roll only slightly onto his side—the bonds were too constrictive to permit more—but he arched his back upward to accommodate her.

As soon as his nipples became accessible, Olga snapped one of the small merciless clamps onto each of them.

The searing pain registered immediately. Craig groaned and hyperventilated for a few moments, before reconciling himself with the sensation. He lowered himself back onto his belly.

Olga batted her eyelashes at him and grinned.

Soon her food and wine were delivered. Olga reclined on the soft chair, her plate on her lap. She ate slowly—small tidbits of food snatched from her right hand and leisurely sips of wine from her left. "You must watch me eat while you suffer," she said to Craig. "See how I enjoy myself, while you are helpless and in pain. You are such a dear boy."

He gazed at her. He observed her as she commanded.

It was sad, he thought, that as much as he enjoyed playing with Olga at these parties—a more intimate, personal connection with her had never materialized. Shoshana had urged them to form a sexual liaison, and at her insistence they'd made several attempts.

He was quite certain that after tonight, Shoshana would urge him to try again.

But it wasn't that straightforward. Here, at parties, the theatrics, costumes, and communal energy made the play seem real and vibrant. But one-on-one, in a more intimate situation, the personalities of the individuals themselves became paramount.

This was especially true for Craig, who was intrinsically so unlike many of the other men. For them, the sensation of the pain itself—usually from a whip or crop, along with the visual image of the dominatrix in costume—provided all the excitement they needed.

Not for Craig. He didn't even especially love pain or discomfort for its own sake. For him it was the psychological power play—the ceding of control on his part—his submission to a woman's dominance—her seizing sovereignty—*that* was what excited him.

But without the trappings of a party—just one-on-one with a woman, often without toys, restraints, or exotic dress—in ordinary, real-life situations, perhaps eating in a restaurant, or naked in bed—Craig needed to see the woman, inherently, as someone to whom he could truly submit. Someone to whom he could convincingly subjugate himself.

And, for him, that came down to her intellect.

As sweet and strong a woman as Olga was, as beautiful as she was in the tall, big-boned way he loved, when he tried spending extended time with her, her intellect always disappointed him. It broke the spell, and left him feeling not at all sexual.

Olga was the kind of person who needed to be out doing something. She was a professional dominatrix and did sessions for a living, but other than that, she seemed to Craig to require constant outside stimulation. For her, sitting and having a quiet conversation meant missing out on all sorts of events going on in the city.

And even if Craig, being dutifully submissive, accompanied her as she gallivanted about, there was never anything to talk about other than the action going on in front of them. Olga did not read anything other than magazines about gossip and popular culture. She didn't follow politics and had no interest in science or serious art. She did lots of shopping, drank lots of wine, and loved trendy, indulgent food. There was nothing meaningful to discuss.

It infuriated Shoshana that Craig short-circuited this way whenever she arranged liaisons for him. Craig had assumed that Shoshana would be flattered that he found *her* intellect worth submitting to—but if she did, any resulting gratification was obliterated by her frustration that he could not find other sexual outlets.

A sharp voice shattered his reverie.

"You're entirely too calm!" Olga exclaimed. "Are you watching me enjoy my food, as I commanded? Or are you lost in overthinking everything, as usual?" She leaned down, careful not to topple the paper plate on her lap or spill the wine she held in her left hand. "Raise up, again, dear," she said, "this will help." When he complied, she grasped one of his nipple clamps, and squeezed and jiggled it violently.

Craig squirmed and tried to suppress a scream, but it spewed out despite his efforts. "Ah, that's better, love." She waited until he finished hyperventilating. "Here," she said, "let me do the other." This time Craig was expecting the surge of pain and was able to tolerate it with a bit less writhing—though his features contorted and he emitted a prolonged groan.

"You may lie down on your belly, again, dear. And now, please obey me, and just watch me eat. Stop thinking about all your nonsense. Or, I'll have to keep torturing you until you do."

They were quiet for a time, Olga enjoying her food, and Craig watching her. He endeavored to focus solely on her eating, as she had demanded, but found it difficult to keep his mind from wandering. It perplexed him. He was so adept at sustaining his focus and clearing his mind during his morning yoga and meditation sessions. That capability, however, did not seem to translate to situations such as these.

A sudden, hazy motion, glimpsed from the corner of his eye, jolted Craig from his musings. There were people passing just inches from his feet. He craned his head to look.

It was Shoshana and the Hauler Guy.

Shoshana had cuffed the large man's hands in front of him and laced a snug leather hood around his head. She was leading him on a leash. It wasn't until Craig noticed Shoshana place her hand lightly upon the man's chest to signal him to stop, that he realized that she'd slipped the blindfold attachment onto the Hauler Guy's hood, rendering him sightless.

Shoshana glanced at Craig, then turned back to Mistress Olga. "Ah," Shoshana said, "I see you have my boy in all sorts of trouble!"

"I love playing with your boy. He's so sweet. And it's amazing how he can get his elbows to touch behind him like that. Very remarkable."

"Well," said Shoshana with a snide laugh, "that's because he has no muscle to get in the way!" She tugged gently upon her slave's leash and led him away.

Craig strained to watch them for a moment as they walked off, then uncoiled his neck—he appeared to be staring forward, but it was clear his gaze was undirected. His features tightened and his face grew red. There was the slightest quivering of his lower lip.

"I see your face, my love," Mistress Olga said, as she leaned over him. Her tone now dropped its frivolous pretense—it was serious and compassionate. "But it isn't pain you're feeling, is it? It's anger."

Craig grimaced—he started to speak—but shut his lips and retreated into silence.

She spoke softly. "She should not have said that to us, my

dear. It was cruel. Yes, it's common for Mistresses to insult their slaves—but in fun. This crossed a line. She, of all people, knows your dedication to yoga, how hard you work at it, how much it means to you. Yes—it does make you so wonderfully flexible—but it also makes you a very special person. In your spirit. Even I see that." Olga stroked Craig's cheek, and gently rubbed his hair. "And there is muscle there, my love. In your arms, and shoulders, and your whole body. I feel it when I touch you. Strong muscles. Subtle. But hard and strong."

Craig's face slowly reclaimed its accustomed hue. His features relaxed.

Olga chuckled. "Just imagine," she purred, "how pathetic it would be if I tried to pry together the elbows of that primitive beast she's leading around tonight."

"Thank you, Mistress Olga," Craig whispered. "You're wonderful. I'm so grateful for the time you spend with me."

Olga grinned broadly. "Now you're getting maudlin, dear." She gestured for him to raise up, then reached for one of his nipple clamps and twisted it ferociously.

The scream Craig emitted was infused far more with vehement unburdening than it was with pain.

15

SALAMI, PROVOLONE, MUSHROOMS & ROASTED PEPPERS

AS SHE FINISHED PUTTING THE FINAL TOUCHES ON her hair and makeup, Adelle Dorn glanced at the clock perched above the bathroom medicine cabinet.

She was on time, but it was tight.

She dashed into the bedroom.

Adelle removed her terrycloth robe and could feel that it was still slightly damp from lingering bath water. She tossed it on the bed and began to dress.

It was a couple of minutes later when Byron traipsed in, sipping on a snifter of Grand Marnier. Adelle was standing near the chest of drawers, in a lacy white bra and matching half-slip.

"It's pretty early on a Sunday morning for Grand Marnier," she said. Her habitual whining cadence was a bit testier than usual.

"Well, me and Nigel are going wine tasting. So, I need a head start. It's like torture—you know, taking those tiny sips—if you don't have something in you already."

"Well, thank god you're not dragging *me* up there with you. I don't need to spend a day with that whack job Justine—listening to her go on and on about the latest dead bodies she's gussied up."

Byron said nothing.

But Adelle could see that he'd begun leering at her. His gaze now appeared to move from her breasts to her hips and back. She knew what was coming and didn't have to wait long before he said it.

"You look hot, babe. Let's fuck."

"God! Byron! You promised to drop me off at church. If we fuck, I'll be late for the service. And I need to get there early enough to find Janet—we're going to sit together. And go out for lunch after."

"Service is at ten-thirty. We have time."

"I already did my hair!" Her platinum pixie cut had grown out, and the copious hairspray she'd applied that morning now had it bordering on a fragile beehive. "You'll crush it!"

"I'll be careful."

"God!"

Adelle tugged off her slip and panties, and threw herself onto the bed such that she lay crosswise to their normal sleeping direction. She wriggled backward so that her head hung over the side, keeping her hair safe.

"Just do it fast," she howled. "Wham, bam, thank you ma'am. No extracurriculars!" She blinked and scowled. "Well, come on! Get to it."

Byron carefully put the snifter of Grand Marnier down on his nightstand and unzipped his pants.

• • •

There was something about tooling around in Nigel's banana-yellow Lotus that always made Byron relax and unshackle his stress. He leaned back in the passenger seat now and took in the scenery.

It was an unseasonably cool and foggy day in the Napa Valley.

The men wore heavy sweaters, and Nigel had on driving gloves—reasonable concessions, they'd agreed, for it enabled them to keep the convertible's top down.

Byron and Nigel had already tasted the full palette at three different wineries, making the progression from lightest white to heaviest red at each stop. Both men had purchased a number of bottles.

Now, they were back in the car, Nigel whizzing north on the Silverado trail. "Where to?" he asked.

"I'm getting hungry," Byron said. "Wanna stop for lunch?"

"I had a massive fry-up for breakfast." Nigel turned his head for just an instant, and offered Byron one of his mischievous grins. "But—I could certainly do with a munch. What did you have in mind?"

"Turn right at the little crossroad coming up in a mile or so. There's an Italian delicatessen. Been there for years. Great little place. We can get sandwiches."

"And what do you recommend?"

"Oh bro, you gotta get their Salami, Provolone, Mushrooms & Roasted Pepper sub—it's on a huge, long sourdough roll. Amazing shit. You'll love it."

"Brilliant!"

Nigel took the turn hard—his tires squealed just enough to be audible—but not enough to be ostentatious.

• • •

With their wrapped sandwiches secured in a bag on his lap, Byron directed them to one of his favorite wineries, perched atop a tall, grassy hill. The place boasted lovely picnic tables and a majestic view of the Napa Valley.

Inside the winery's tasting room, the men sampled a few more reds and selected a smoky Cabernet Sauvignon to enjoy with their lunch. The pourer obliged by uncorking the bottle and supplying them with two stemmed glasses for the meal.

At the picnic table, Byron and Nigel gnawed ferociously upon their sandwiches, accompanying each mouthful with robust gulps of wine. Byron had also purchased a big bag of potato chips, which he now tore open and placed on the table for them to share.

They gazed out at countless rows of grape vines.

"Beautiful view, mate," Nigel said. "Brilliant choice."

"Thanks. You like the sandwich?"

"Reem!" Nigel exclaimed as he chewed.

"Does that mean good?"

Nigel laughed. "It does, sir."

They finished the sandwiches and chips and were working on the last drops of wine.

"So," Byron said, "have you seen for yourself, now, what I've been tellin' you about Craig Schumacher? How he's dangerous?"

"Hard to say. He seems like a decent enough bloke."

Byron lowered his head and swiveled it left and right before looking up again. "You're missing what's really going on, bro. Craig is all about Craig. He's using all of us just to advance himself. He'll leave us all wallowin' in the mud before he's done."

"Can't say I see that. He's always giving credit to people on the team. Not himself."

"Because he knows that makes him look better! Like some kind of fucking saint."

"Could be. Too early for me to tell."

"Listen, bro. I have a plan. I don't wanna get into it right now—all the details, I mean—but let's just say I know some shit. Some shit that can bring Craig down. Bring him down hard."

Nigel's features stiffened as he gazed intently into Byron's eyes. There was an uncomfortable silence for a few moments. Then Nigel responded. "You know, mate, these sorta shenanigans can get dodgy. You got to be dead cert if you're set on trying it."

Byron took a long gulp, pondered, and moderated his tone. "We'll talk about it more, bro. No rush. Just give it some time. Think about it . . . But, look—if Craig goes, I'm next in line to take charge. And you'll be my right-hand man—second in command."

"Well, that's enticing."

"Just keep it secret. For now. Even from Justine." He raised his arm and pointed at Nigel for emphasis. "I guarantee you this, though—if I decide to do it, it'll work. Byron Dorn doesn't go into shit half-assed."

"I'll keep an open mind, then, mate."

16

GREEN CHAI TEA

THOUGH HE WENT ABOUT IT UNOBTRUSIVELY, CRAIG Schumacher was a keen observer of the clandestine and conspiratorial goings-on in the corporate enterprise, both in the main office where he worked, as well as in the various regional outposts. Executive suite stratagems, mid-level powerplays, desperate rank-and-file ploys, along with plain old tawdry gossip, were garnered regularly through friendly, informal conversations with trusted allies of all ranks. And though he certainly subjected the raw data he accrued to meticulous cerebral analysis, he inevitably found that his most consequential deductions and suspicions always spewed out, enigmatically, from his preternatural fount of intuition.

And he always shared such pertinent premonitions with his boss Bruce, who had on numerous occasions improved his own political standing—or at least avoided mortifying calamity—based upon Craig's forewarnings.

It was late afternoon on this Monday, as Craig exited

Bruce's office. He'd offered Bruce an extended—and evidently much appreciated—consultation about current hazards poised to blindside him, along with possible strategies for their neutralization.

As he left Bruce's office and closed the door behind him, Craig was immediately confronted with the precise circumstance he'd noted a number of times prior—Nigel sitting in the guest chair of Bruce's administrative assistant, Leah, flirting with her unabashedly.

Craig offered a cheerful nod. "Hey Nigel," he said, "nice to run into you. Do you have a minute to stop by my office for a quick chat—when you're done here?"

Craig discerned the tiniest flash of panic seize Nigel's lips and eyebrows. He found this mildly amusing, though he took pains to conceal any evidence of having observed it.

He did find it fascinating, however, that the tightening of Nigel's features vanished almost instantaneously—replaced with a sheepish grin, an endearing well-practiced shoulder shrug, and an enthusiastic, "I'll come with you right now, boss."

• • •

Craig settled in behind his desk, and motioned for Nigel to sit in the guest chair facing him.

The dregs of green chai tea with a splash of honey were cold, having sat at the bottom of Craig's large mug all the while he'd been in Bruce's office. But he took a sip anyway. He smiled at Nigel. "Bruce's parade of administrative assistants is intriguing, don't you think? Bruce seems to hire them totally based on their pulchritude."

"Pulchritude?"

"Pulchritude. How good-looking they are. And each one

certainly is. He hires them and hopes they'll work out for him. And when they don't, he just fires them and tries another—always equally young and gorgeous—their competence to be determined. Leah's his latest."

"Yes. She's a hot bit of tottie all right."

"I've seen you sitting and chatting . . ." Craig chuckled. "I should more accurately say . . . *flirting* . . . with Leah on more than one occasion. And I've heard others mention that they've seen you, too. It's not a great look for you, Nigel."

"In my defense, boss—it's all rather harmless. I'm not sleeping with the girl."

Craig nodded. "Well, then, you're absolutely getting the worst of this in *two* ways, aren't you? Think about it, Nigel. It *looks* as if you're sleeping with her, so everybody *assumes* you are—and you therefore suffer all the subtle consequences of indiscreet office behavior." Craig smiled and emitted the barest snigger, before he continued. "But you say you're not actually sleeping with her—and I believe you when you say that—so, clearly, you're not even reaping the benefit of a little naughty clandestine sex. So, you lose on *both* fronts."

Nigel lowered his head and pondered for a moment, then raised it with a broad grin. "God, boss, it's brilliant that you'd put it that way—I mean like one bloke to another—pragmatic—with no high and mighty moral judgment. You're bloody ace."

"Thank you. So, what do you plan to do about it?"

"You think if I cool it now, I'll undo the damage?"

Craig grinned. "People have short memories. Stop now and in a couple of weeks everyone will be on to some new, meaningless scandal."

"I'll do that, boss. Thanks for the tip."

"You're very welcome." Craig lifted his mug for another sip of cold tea.

Nigel scooted forward in his chair as if to get up, but Craig raised his hand, signaling that he stay a moment longer.

"Hey, by the way, Nigel, I want you to come with me to a meeting next week. I just cleared it with Bruce. It's with the company's CEO and a few of his C-level guys. So, it's a big deal. But it's about quality assurance for the Y2K project, so Bruce and I got invited. And I told Bruce that you're the subject matter expert, so you should come too."

That same tiny flash of panic that Craig had noted on Nigel's face a few minutes prior, now returned—but this time it lingered. "I don't know if I'm quite ready for something like that, boss."

"You know the stuff inside and out. I think you'll be fine."

• • •

A week later, at the conclusion of the C-level meeting in the boardroom, the participants exited and made their way down the long corridor to the elevator. They spontaneously broke into small subgroups as they walked. Near the back, Craig and Bruce walked side by side—while a few feet behind them, Nigel trudged silently, his head down and his shoulders slumped.

He watched as Bruce, who was much taller than Craig, placed his arm on Craig's shoulder, and lowered his head to say something.

Nigel wasn't certain whether Bruce was intentionally speaking loud enough to be heard several feet away, or if Bruce's use of hearing aids made it difficult for him to modulate his volume appropriately. But either way, Nigel caught every word.

"Good save in there, Craig. But you need to coach your boy—no one wants to pay good money for someone who's afraid to say anything. You bailed him out—and you did a smooth job, so I don't think the people in there necessarily noticed—but I sure as hell did."

Nigel allowed himself to fall further behind and out of earshot. He watched as the elevator door closed with Craig and Bruce inside. When they were safely gone, he found the men's room and scrubbed his face over and over with very hot water. Then, he reluctantly made his way back to the elevator and down to Craig's office, assuming that by then, Craig and Bruce would have finished their venomous postmortem.

• • •

Craig had left the door to his large corner-office open, and was now glancing up periodically—waiting for Nigel to appear. Finally, he caught a glimpse of him just outside, peering in, slumped forlornly.

"Come over and sit down," Craig said. "We'll talk."

Nigel took a seat. "God, boss, I was a total plank in there. I just froze. I'm really sorry. You must be bloody miffed. You have every right to be. Can't tell you how sorry I am."

"I understand. But, it's actually *my* fault, Nigel. And don't worry. You'll have lots of future opportunities to impress these people. They won't even remember you from this one."

"What do you mean it's *your* fault? It's not your fault. It's mine. I was a bloody pillock. I mean, I just couldn't keep up. Everything seemed to go so fast."

"I never realized it, Nigel. I mean you're so outgoing and charming. But you're actually an introvert, aren't you?"

"I am?"

"People misunderstand. You don't have to be shy to be an introvert. Of course, many introverts are reticent by nature. I certainly am. But that's not really it. What it really has to do with is needing to recharge—alone—think things through by yourself—before you're ready to expound upon them with other people. That's what introverts need to do."

Nigel's eyebrows crept upward and his lips pursed. "Hmm . . . I actually do need to do precisely that. I never really thought about it, though." He leaned forward in his chair. "How the bloody hell did you know that about me, boss?"

Craig smiled. "That's why it was my fault. I didn't pick up on it till now. So, I couldn't prepare you. I'm very introverted, Nigel. And I've learned—over the years—that almost every other executive I run into—here or anywhere else—is extroverted. *Very* extroverted. And extroverts thrive by bouncing ideas off one another spontaneously—thinking out loud—drumming up that kind of communal input."

"You seem to do that very well."

Craig chuckled. "Thank you. But I'm totally faking it. Look, introverts like us can't respond on our feet as quickly as extroverts—so if we just go in there and hope to play their game right along with them, we'll never get a word in. We can't think fast enough. But when introverts have a chance to ponder the question—time to mull it over and figure out possibilities—I guarantee you, we come up with better, more fully thought-out answers."

"So, how do *you* do it, then?"

"It was difficult at first. You know—in management and executive level positions, pretty much everything gets figured out in meetings. So, I had to come up with a way to get around that. And there's only one way I've found to do it, Nigel . . . you have to *rehearse*. And I've learned that you don't even need to make extra time for it. When you walk your dog in the morning—when you shave—shower—drive to work. There's actually lots of time."

"What do you mean, rehearse? What are you rehearsing?

How do you have any idea what's coming?"

"Nigel, you're more than smart enough to anticipate the questions that are going to come up. So, ask yourself—what meetings do you have on your calendar tomorrow? Are any of those especially out of your comfort zone? Look at the agendas—they usually come out in advance. Or, if they don't, you can anticipate what's going to be discussed. What are the problems they're trying to solve? So, then, you think it all through and rehearse good answers. Talk out loud. Go through it over and over. Say it just like you're going to say it in the meeting. Pretend you're another person—think of what they might say to trip you up, catch you off guard. You'll come up with great shit—because you're smart—as long as you take the time to figure it out. You'll dazzle people with what you have to say. And they'll never guess it's not spontaneous."

For a moment, Nigel looked dumbfounded. Then he nodded, and the hint of a smile began to curl his lip. "Thank you, boss. This is more helpful than you can imagine."

Craig continued. "In our department, we all have each other's backs. We lean on each other's strengths—compensate for each other's weaknesses. That's why we have the most consistently high-performing teams in the enterprise. And I know that *you* run your teams that way too."

"Yes, I try to." Nigel pondered for a moment. He looked away, and then back. "That brings up an interesting question, boss. I'm just curious. Stop me if I'm out of line. But all this about teams and trust—this seems dead important to you—running things this way. But before me—Carolyn didn't run things that way. I mean—not at all. She and that bloviate Geoff were like the exact opposite. Why did you keep those two around so long?"

Craig's face froze for a moment before he responded. "Well—Carolyn had other strengths." He paused again. "She's a good person, deep down."

Nigel leaned back. His lips fluttered—the grin germinated slowly at first—but soon it exploded and overwhelmed his features. "Oh blimey! You *fancy* her! You do fancy her, don't you—Carolyn, I mean. I never realized it. My god, you're discreet. I need to learn that."

Craig's lips pursed mischievously, and he cocked his head in a consciously ambiguous fashion. "Speaking of Carolyn, I'll be making a trip to the Maryland region soon. Would you like to come, say hi to her? Mend some fences? Maybe have dinner with us?"

Nigel laughed. "No interest whatsoever, boss, I've really had my fill of Carolyn." He lowered his head and gazed at Craig roguishly. "And it sounds as if you might appreciate some alone time with her."

"I don't know about that. But in any case, let's keep that thought between you and me."

"Sure thing, boss. So, tell me, how did a nice bloke like you get into management anyway?"

Craig's gaze drifted upward as he conjured up the recollection. "Years ago, I was working at a trust company—here in San Francisco. I was writing code. And every Monday morning I'd walk by this huge conference room. It was the weekly managers' meeting. The room had a big glass window, so you could see the whole thing. But you couldn't hear what they were saying. It was the same every week—the director, sitting at the head of the table, and the eight managers in the other seats. And one day—I guess I was feeling pretty shitty about how I was being treated there in general—and I walked by the meeting—really slowly—and I just looked at them—I mean from one to another to another. And, as I walked away, I said to myself—I'm smarter than every fucking person in that room—but more importantly, they're all a bunch of assholes. There's not a single person in there who gives a shit about honesty, or integrity, or treating people with respect and compassion. Someone with *my* values needs to be at that table. And it has to be *me*—because no one else is gonna fucking do it."

"Damn good story, that. I've never worked for someone like you."

"That's nice of you to say, Nigel. So, are you going to start rehearsing now, for big meetings, like I suggested?"

"That's a dead cert, boss. But, do you *really* still do it—I mean rehearsing—after all this time?"

"I need to. I'm an introvert. That's never going to change."

"No one could bloody suspect that it's all canned blather when you talk in meetings, boss. You sound like the smartest person in the room."

"And you will, too. Just put in the time."

"Brilliant!"

Nigel edged forward in his chair as if to rise.

"Oh," Craig said, "one other thing I've been meaning to ask you."

Nigel leaned back and smirked. "Whenever you say you have something to ask me, boss, I know I've mucked up in some way."

Craig grinned. "No, I'm just curious. All this incessant British slang you use. Do people from Leeds really pepper their speech with it as much as you seem to?"

Nigel laughed uncontrollably and had to pause and take a long breath before he could respond. "Well, you've found me out. The answer is no—I mean you hear a word of it here and there—but not the way I toss it about."

"Then, why on earth do you do it?"

"Oh, just to annoy you Yanks. It seems to work. You know, all of you immediately ascribe an extra ten or twenty IQ points to any bloke with an English accent. I just want to make you stop and think about the absurdity of it."

Craig lips narrowed and his eyebrows squeezed into a puzzled scowl. He gazed wordlessly at Nigel.

"Time to tone it down, boss?

"I'd say, time to cut it out. Do you think you can do it?"

"Actually, it will be a relief."

"Good. You can start right now."

Nigel pondered a moment. "If you don't mind though, boss, I think I'll keep it on at home with Justine. It tends to keep her on her toes. And a man does need something to counteract all that valley girl prattle."

17
PEPPERONI

SHE HAD LONG AGO ACKNOWLEDGED AND ACCEPTED that her nature was to please him.

But over time, Justine Silver had also grown frustrated—because she knew that it was precisely that predilection which had allowed Nigel's fondness for fatty meats, rich sauces, and refined carbohydrates to grow into an unhealthy obsession. The visible ramifications were starting to become plainly evident, particularly around his abdomen and hips.

So now, one evening each week, she prepared a plant-based dinner for Nigel and herself.

That one plant-based meal per week was actually her final salvo, having been preceded by a gradual but carefully planned transition to more main courses of chicken and fish—all nicely seasoned, but with lighter sauces, concocted without cream or butter.

Nigel wasn't thrilled with these changes, especially the once-weekly wholly vegan offering, but he begrudgingly accepted them. Justine correctly surmised that he'd never choose to cook for himself—nor would he dare order something for takeout if she had a meal already prepared.

And he still got his proper English breakfasts most mornings (though she had started to reduce the portions on those as well, hopefully imperceptibly).

Tonight, as was always the case for the week's plant-based selection, Justine tried especially hard to render a dish that was eye-pleasing, tasty, inventive, and filling. She knew Nigel wouldn't relish it (or at least never admit to it if he did) but if he ingested a reasonable serving, she'd consider it a victory.

This evening she'd started with a wakame seaweed salad, sprinkled with black and white sesame seeds, and dressed with rice vinegar, mirin, and a splash of toasted sesame oil. The main dish was stir-fried broccoli and black mushrooms with marinated tempeh over brown rice. For dessert, a delightful pear-and-berry compote sweetened with orange juice and a bit of raw sugar. She was very proud of what she'd put together.

Conversation during dinner had been spare, but polite. Nigel had consumed just enough to maintain tranquility in the homestead—though he hadn't commented on whether he liked the food.

After the meal, Nigel took 'Chester on their short nightly walk.

• • •

Justine had heard the two of them return nearly an hour ago but hadn't seen either one since.

Now, she began searching the house.

She soon located Nigel in the den, with 'Chester dozing at his feet. Nigel appeared quite calm and relaxed, slouched in an easy chair, polishing and lubricating his prized Winchester rifles with Ballistol gun oil. Justine also noticed the crusts of two slices of cold pepperoni pizza lying in a plate on the desk, with a crumpled paper napkin atop them. The pizza was left over from a hasty takeout dinner they'd shared earlier in the week, when she'd gotten a last-minute call from a funeral home in Sonoma, asking her to prepare a badly damaged body for viewing the next morning.

Justine strolled over to where he sat. Her hands curled into fists and rested on her hips. "I guess dinner wasn't satisfying enough for you, eh Nigel?"

"Oh, it was reem, hun, absolutely mint. A bloke just needs a little snack sometimes after a brisk walk with the dog." His features scrunched into an ingratiating grin.

"I saw you through the window out there with 'Chester, honey. That was hardly a *brisk* walk!"

Nigel chuckled and took a moment to respond. He glanced at the pizza crusts, and back to Justine. "Well then," he said, "I guess I'm in need of some additional exercise." He gazed up at her and his guise turned mischievous. Putting down the rifle and oil-soaked rag, he straightened in his chair and grinned. "I must confess, babe—you look hot—granted, a bit miffed—but proper dishy nonetheless. Fancy a shag? I'll be good and thorough. That ought to burn some calories— maybe you'll even shed your frown, and get all nice and melty for us."

Despite her best efforts to hold strong, her stern expression soon collapsed into sheepish laughter. "Oh my god," she sputtered. "You're so crude!" Still giggling, she began unbuttoning her blouse. "I can't help it. I guess I've always liked that about you."

He bounded up and grabbed her—and spent a few moments licking, pawing, and manically squeezing any slab of anatomy he managed to encounter. Then, he lifted her in his arms, slung her unceremoniously over a shoulder, and carried her up the staircase and into the bedroom.

The commotion woke 'Chester, who now followed close

behind them.

Nigel tossed Justine onto the bed.

A moment later Nigel leaped up and joined her, clawing at her buttons and clasps, passionately stripping off her clothes—and then his own as well—all the while kissing and suckling.

Soon, 'Chester jumped up on the bed along with them, poking his snout wherever he could wedge it, exploring the sultry aromas and hints of excretions, as the three thrashed about.

Justine panted and screamed in delight as Nigel worked his way through their panoply of favored positions—yanked from her back, to her side, to her belly, and then pulled up on all fours. She loved being flung about by him. It was that luscious contradiction of being so roughly manhandled—while always knowing that she was safe in his arms—that she found so beguiling.

When they were finally done, they lay still—he on his back, she with her head cradled in his arm—both of them warm and breathless from exertion. A patina of sweet-smelling perspiration glazed their flesh.

'Chester plonked down, peaceful and still, at the foot of the bed.

They were all quiet for a time.

Justine's breathing finally slowed a bit. "So, honey," she whispered, "what's been going on at work?"

"Actually, I've had a number of interesting chats with Byron Dorn. You know, we've knocked about together a lot lately. So, lots of time for chinwag."

"And what's up with him?"

"It's strange, you know? He's been going on and on about Craig Schumacher—how Craig's in it all for himself—that he'll bring us down—how I'd do better if Byron was in charge of everything. But, you know, I'm not at all sure. Byron won't stop yakking on about it, but the more I see all the sides of Craig, the more I think he's a solid bloke."

Justine pulled closer and kissed him gently on the shoulder. "Well, whose side are you on?"

Nigel chuckled. "Growing up with sketchy tossers like I did, babe—it makes one good at playing both ends against the middle."

"What does *that* mean exactly?"

"I suppose it means I'll string both of them along—until I see which way winds up doing me the most good. And in the meantime, I'll get as much as I can out of both of them."

"Just be careful, honey. Like really, you're not in the grody parts of Leeds anymore. This is your career." She propped herself up on one arm and gazed at him. "Frankly, babe, it seems to me that Craig is a much more reliable bet than Byron. I mean, like—it's cruel to say—but, oh my god—Byron can't even blurt out a coherent sentence until he's had five drinks in him. You know it's true."

Nigel laughed. "He is a bit of a nutter—I'll certainly grant you that. But, don't worry, babe, I'm a master at playing my cards close to my chest." He licked his lips delicately. "And dealing seconds or bottoms when I need to."

Nigel gently tugged her back down toward him.

She rested her head on his chest and closed her eyes.

18

RED THAI CURRY

CRAIG SCHUMACHER ENTERED THE ROOM HAVING no doubt that something consequential was afoot.

The meeting time was especially early on a Monday morning. But more significantly: at the same moment that Craig's senior VP, Bruce, was hosting this meeting for the six national VPs who headed up the back-office functions of technology, finance, compliance, human resources, facilities, and security—the other six VPs in the corporate office, who handled production, sales, marketing, and all other client-facing services, were meeting just a few doors down with *their* respective senior VP.

And with appropriate care having been taken into account for time-zone disparities, each regional VP outside of San Francisco was meeting locally with their own senior staff at that precise moment as well.

It was obvious that senior management wanted whatever was being disseminated to be heard by all necessary parties simultaneously—to limit leaks, speculation, and gossip—and to control and synchronize management's message.

Craig was also reasonably certain that he and the others would be admonished to keep much of what they were told today secret from their staffs, at least for now—a scenario which had never sat quite right with him.

When everyone settled in, Bruce immediately started reading, in stilted cadence, from a lengthy prepared script. This was in such distinct contrast to his usual informal and folksy style of conducting a meeting that Craig didn't need to wait for the full text of the announcement to know that the news was going to be bad—or at the very least, inconvenient and disagreeable.

• • •

Carolyn Winthrop slipped out of work an hour early, hoping to avoid the worst of DC's rush hour traffic and get to Dulles Airport in time to park and make her way to the baggage area prior to Craig's plane touching down.

Her timing proved impeccable—just as she arrived at the luggage carousel assigned to his flight, she glimpsed Craig in the distance, descending on an escalator with a briefcase in one hand and a small black satchel in the other.

She edged over to a somewhat less congested spot and waved until she caught his eye. When he had nearly reached her, she took a step closer and embraced him warmly. It vexed her that his reciprocal hug was more polite than affectionate, but it was precisely what she'd come to expect, and she let it pass. "Good to see you, love," she said in her crisp London accent as she took a couple of steps back, raising and lowering her eyes to scrutinize his outfit. She shook her head playfully and chuckled. "Not accustomed to seeing you in jeans and a hoodie, love. Did it make for a comfortable flight?"

Craig offered a self-deprecating snicker and a weary sigh. "Well, you've done it yourself, many times, Carolyn—flying cross-country—you know the deal."

"I do indeed. There's the hours in the air to begin with—and there's getting through security before that—and then, of course, there's the time-zone difference. By the time you're done, if you're coming east, it amounts to—I'd say—pretty much the whole bloody day. Did you at least have time to do your yoga before you left?"

Craig smiled and nodded. "Yes, I made sure I did. Golda and I had an especially intense session. It's as if she understood I'd be away—that we wouldn't be doing it together for a while. She's really amazing like that. She always knows when I'm about to leave—but this time it seemed even stronger for some reason."

He looked away for a moment and held his gaze motionless. He appeared to her to be losing himself in thought.

"So, was it a relaxing trip then?" she asked, trying to draw him back. "Were you able to upgrade to business?"

He shook his head. "I have miles saved up, but Shoshana gets annoyed if I use them for work trips. She likes me to keep them for our vacations." He blinked his eyes, and narrowed his lips. "But the airline folks did seem to recognize me as a frequent flyer—they put me in an exit row—the leg space was good. I caught up on some work. Read a bit. I even managed to sleep for an hour or so. All in all, it was fine." He smiled. "I'm hungry though—all I took with me was a banana and a few raw nuts."

"I thought you'd be hungry. I brought a menu. It's in the car. Thai food. Take-out. Very good." Carolyn grinned sardonically. "And they'll leave out your bloody fish sauce. I checked."

Craig laughed. "You make it sound like checking was an odious task."

"I don't know about odious—but certainly annoying. And

speaking of annoying, I'm sure you were in national's version of that horrible meeting we all went through yesterday. You know, the one they so carefully orchestrated so everyone met at the same time."

Just as Craig was about to respond, the luggage carousel roared on and started turning. "Oh, let me get my bag. It's a garment thing—my suits are in it. We can talk about the meeting later. Just more corporate crap. But something dawned on me about it during the flight."

• • •

Inside the massive parking structure, Craig followed Carolyn, who had confidently taken the elevator to her designated floor, but who now appeared quite bewildered as she tried to navigate to the car's precise location. Her pace slowed noticeably. Finally, after a prolonged bout of circuitous and seemingly indecisive wandering, she thrust her finger excitedly in the direction of a large black SUV about twenty feet ahead. "Ah, thank god! Here we are." She scampered toward it and opened the trunk.

Craig scanned the vehicle as he approached it. Its shiny finish and unblemished exterior suggested that it was brand-new. He surmised that Carolyn had sold her old, reasonably sized car before she left the Bay Area and bought this behemoth out here. Why, he wondered, did a single woman feel the need for so large a vehicle—one with a fuel consumption rate unhealthy for the planet?

He decided it was best not to mention it.

Craig loaded his bags into the trunk. As he did, he noticed Carolyn remove her light jacket and toss it onto the SUV's back seat. Underneath, she was wearing that clingy red top he liked so much—the one he always pictured her in when he fantasized about her. He wondered if the choice was intentional on her part—what might she know or suspect? She couldn't possibly have guessed how he imagined it—the way she would force him to pleasure her orally for hours—then leave him bound and gagged in the bed as she donned that red top and jeans to dash out and run errands.

• • •

It took a while for Carolyn to wind through the narrow, curving lanes and reach the garage's pay station. Craig used the delay to fish for his credit card, which he thrust at her when they arrived at the booth.

"Oh, no," Carolyn said. "It's just a few dollars."

"Please. I insist."

"All right. But I'm giving you the receipt. And you must promise me you'll put it on your expense account."

Craig laughed softly. "All right."

The evening sky was beginning to turn dark when they reached the highway. Despite the traffic and the rolled-up windows of the vehicle, Craig felt good just to be outside of a plane or an airport.

"So," Craig said, "about that horrid meeting."

"No, love. Food first. Open the glove box. There's a menu for the Thai place. We can order by phone while we're driving—and by the time we get there it will be ready. I'm getting the red curry. My usual. Really delicious. I highly recommend it. I get mine with shrimp, but you can get it veggie. With tofu."

Craig replied in a mumbly whisper, perusing the menu as he spoke. "Red curry, eh? I'm a bit skeptical about that—you know, they make the curries ahead of time—they simmer for hours—so if there's fish sauce or chicken broth in it, they can't take it out."

"They said they could make it without bloody fish sauce!"

He turned toward her and spoke more clearly. "Sometimes places say that just to please you or maybe there's a language barrier. But I'm going to be safe and get the tofu and vegetable stir fry. We can tell them just soy sauce." He paused as he reexamined the menu. "Do they have brown rice? I don't see it here."

"They don't have bloody brown rice—I asked. Jesus, Craig, eat white rice for one night." She raised her head and emitted a loud, inordinately histrionic sigh. "I can see that I'm going to need a good dose of wine this evening."

Craig grinned, suppressing a chuckle. "It's really not a problem, Carolyn. Actually, I can work it to my advantage. If I'm going to be eating a refined carb tonight anyway, I'll get the stir fry with noodles, instead of rice. I love noodles. And the rice paper spring rolls look really nice for a starter. I just won't dip them in the sauce they give you with it. Never know what's in that sauce. If you have some soy sauce and rice wine vinegar at home, I can make a quick dipping sauce out of that. And a splash of toasted sesame oil, if you stock that."

Carolyn shook her head and giggled. "I do love you, dear. But you really are a royal pain. You realize that, don't you?"

"As I believe I've mentioned, a vegetarian can never be too careful."

A brief silence ensued. Then, a fit of laughter slowly crept upon them both. It began tentatively with aborted sniggers—but the hesitant guffaws of one fed off the other, and soon the two were howling and shaking in unison.

Eventually, their fading paroxysms gave way to a restful lull, which lasted a couple of minutes.

Craig smiled and said, "Anyway, about that meeting yesterday . . ."

"Let's wait till I've had a glass or two of wine," Carolyn said. "It's all a bit too dreadful, you know."

• • •

They sat a couple of feet apart on the living room couch. Ceramic plates and cardboard food containers were situated haphazardly on the coffee table in front of them.

Craig leaned down and poked his chopsticks at the mélange in his dish, seizing a small wad of noodles, a carrot slab, and a saucy chunk of tofu. The chopsticks supplied by the restaurant were the cheap wooden sort—the kind that needed to be snapped apart on top before you could use them. But he maneuvered them adeptly.

"This food is very good," Craig said. "Thank you for choosing it. It's exactly what I needed after a long day."

Carolyn gulped the wine remaining in her glass. As soon as she put it down, Craig reached for the bottle and poured her a refill. "All right," she said. "So, about that dreadful meeting. I'm sure they told you the same thing at national that they told us out here—but let's compare notes to be certain."

Craig put his chopsticks on his plate and spoke softly. "Bruce started by reading a script that basically said that over the past eight months the entire company had made impressive progress on the Y2K rollout. You know—the new suite of Y2K-compliant computer systems—and the processes and procedures that go along with them. And, then he went on to say that now, the enterprise no longer views this whole thing as some sort of potential debacle—or even as an obstacle. Now, it's more of a sure thing that's definitely going to get done. Probably in the next six to nine months. And when it's finally finished—as a bonus—we'll all have a more sophisticated suite of systems to rely on in general."

"Yes. Exactly how they got it started out here, too. Pretty much word for word."

Craig chuckled. "Oh, I have to tell you. Right after that opening, Bruce went off-script, just very briefly, but you could see it—because he put down the paper he was reading from—and his cadence got more folksy and spontaneous, the way he usually talks. So, he said, 'I especially want to recognize Craig's teams for their truly outstanding work in getting this put in and accepted by the people in the regions.'" Craig laughed sheepishly. "I can tell you that the five other VPs in the room did not appreciate that at all!"

Carolyn smiled. "Oh, I'm sure they didn't. Good for you, though. And well deserved. And then did he go on to say that, in fact, because the Y2K effort was going so smoothly, that the big staff ramp-up we did a couple of years ago—you know, to do the design, and the coding, and then the implementation with all the training—that all those people from the ramp-up will no longer be justified in next year's budget? So, in nine months' time, when the new budgets take effect, we'll all have to make big staff cuts—you know—massive layoffs."

"Yes. That's exactly what he said."

"Ugh! I really hate doing things like that."

"I agree. It's horrible. And it was so obvious. The bad news about the layoffs was the real point of the whole thing. That sweet introduction about how well things were going was just their corporate window dressing—their pathetic attempt at softening the blow."

"Clearly. And, of course, they warned us to keep it secret. *Top secret*, they said—just to emphasize it. To use that stupid jargon as if it's a bloody spy movie—it sounded ludicrous."

Craig grinned. "Yes. *Top secret*. Same cheesy term they

used with us."

"And then at the end of the meeting out here, they gave each one of us our numbers—you know, the staff count we'll have to get down to when the new fiscal year starts. I assume you got those too."

"Yes," Craig said. "We got those as well. And after that—just to finish up—they went out of their way to try to justify the secrecy—to try to make the dishonesty appear compassionate. 'There's nothing worse for morale,' Bruce said—you know, reading from the script—'than knowing that layoffs are coming. So, it's kinder to just spring it on them next year—when the time comes—do the whole thing quickly—like pulling off a band-aid. So, nine months from today . . .'"

"Right!" she interrupted. "Pulling off a band-aid! We heard exactly the same thing. Such bloody hogwash! It's really dreadful, don't you think?"

"Absolutely. But on the plane ride over I kept thinking about it. Thinking that there has to be a better way. These are human beings we're dealing with. Not pawns on a chess board."

"So, I'm dying to hear. What brilliant ninja scheme did you come up with?"

Craig chuckled. "Well, I don't know if it's necessarily brilliant or ninja, but I definitely can make it work. The whole idea is just to get to my number gradually—you know, painlessly—over the course of the next nine months—and not have any kind of sudden layoffs at all when the new fiscal year starts."

"Well, that would be brilliant. But how would you bloody do it?"

"When they put me in as vice president, one of the things we made a top priority was dismantling that vast empire of consultants that the evil infiltrators had installed. And—well, you were there, so you know this—I got rid of the main bad guys—and a whole bunch of the henchmen. But—you know—underneath that layer—there were a lot of rank-and-file contractors—the guys who do the day-to-day stuff. Decent people. So—I kept a lot of *them*. I knew these kinds of staff cuts were coming—they come eventually on every big project—so—all along, I've maintained at least a third of my total staff as low-level contractors. And all the contracts are manageable—you know, six months at a time. So, as those come due, we just won't renew them. These people expect it, that's how they choose to work—and they find new gigs pretty quickly. And then there's attrition. You know—over a course of nine months, just normal resignations—people move, find other jobs, take leaves to have babies. So, we don't replace those people either. It's a huge division I run. There are enough people with enough skill-sets to shift around and fill voids. So—if you take the expected rate of attrition—and the known rate of contractors ending their gigs—you're right at the number I need to hit. With no mass layoffs. No trauma."

"That's brilliant, love. Will senior management buy it?"

"Bruce will buy it. He'll know I can pull it off. I suspect he'll feel the need to keep it secret from his superiors. But I can live with that."

"And how exactly will you explain it to your teams? Given that the whole impending layoff thing is," and she smirked, "*top secret*?"

"Right. I thought about that, too. It's maybe a bit of a white lie—but I'll just say that I've worked on enough big projects to know that once everything's in, there are always massive staff cuts that follow. And they hurt. Real people suffer. So, if we approach it the way I suggest—sure, there may be just a little discomfort along the way as we shift around to cover empty spots—but we can make this work. And this is the kind of division we are. We support each other as a team. As people."

He paused, and thought for a moment. "And—you know—everything I've just said is true. It's not really even a lie. Just a little omission."

"Utterly brilliant. As I knew it would be."

"Thank you," Craig said, as he lifted his chopsticks and resumed eating.

"I'm sure we won't be doing anything quite so graceful out here in *this* region," Carolyn said with a snigger. "But we're a small shop to begin with. The impact won't be as huge."

• • •

Sated, Craig put down his chopsticks. He finished what was left in the bottle of sparkling water he'd been nursing and wiped a paper napkin across his lips.

Carolyn swigged the wine remaining in her glass. Craig reflexively reached for the bottle to refill it, but as soon as she placed the glass down, Carolyn hovered her palm over the top of the rim and grinned at him. "I've had more than my fill, love."

"Then, let me help you clean up," he said, rising and gathering up as much as he could from the coffee table. Carolyn followed his lead, and the two traipsed off into the kitchen, arms full.

"A couple of these containers still have a little food left in them," Craig said. "I'll put them in the fridge. The rest we can toss out."

"Thank you, dear." Carolyn put the two plates in the sink, along with her wine glass.

"I'll wash those," Craig said.

"No, just leave them. We'll deal with it in the morning."

Craig glanced about to make sure there was nothing else to help with. "Well," he said, "it's getting late. I guess I'll head off to the guest room and see you in the morning. I believe our first meeting tomorrow is at . . ."

But before Craig could finish that sentence, she was upon him, his head grasped between her hands. She squeezed tightly, and she pulled him to her. She kissed him on the mouth—pressing hard—using her lips to separate his.

Craig was stunned. He stood frozen, neither resisting nor actively reciprocating.

What was happening?

How to respond?

Thoughts flashed through his mind with lightning speed: he liked Carolyn—he'd been fantasizing about her since the day they met—she no longer worked for him—not even in the same region—a dalliance might be viewed by some as untoward or inappropriate—but it was not something HR would have an issue with—Bruce wouldn't care—he might joke that he was a bit jealous.

But even as he tried to make sense of it, their kisses grew more passionate. He realized he had his hands on her shoulder blades now, and he could feel his tongue becoming more active against hers. As he drew her closer, he ruminated on the fact that she knew nothing of his sexual proclivities—nothing of his secret life.

Did he need to tell her?

If he did, there was a good chance the whole thing would short-circuit instantaneously.

But if he didn't—and if they proceeded with what the BDSM community referred to as "vanilla sex"—he might not become aroused.

Or his excitement might ebb at a crucial juncture.

When she stepped back for a moment it startled him—but then he saw her grab for her clingy red top—the one that had become so fetishized in his imaginings. Its sheer material puckered in her ferocious grip as she tugged it over her head and hurled it across the kitchen. Now, she seized his hands and pressed them against her lacy red bra cups. Just before his palms completely covered them, he noted how delicate the fabric was—how intricately decorated. It was clearly not an everyday undergarment.

This assault had been planned.

As he kneaded her breasts, the bra's silky material felt reassuring. He located her nipples and squeezed them through the soft cups. When he did, something triggered.

He found himself aroused.

It must have been obvious because she now stroked his erect penis through his jeans.

She glanced up at him and giggled.

Carolyn turned and started for the bedroom. When she glanced back at him, he hadn't budged. "Well, come on!" she cried. She dashed over and snatched one of his hands. The two now scampered toward the bedroom, Carolyn hauling Craig close behind.

Once there, they tore at each other's clothes.

Naked, she leaped upon the bed and pulled him atop her.

As he fondled and kissed her, Craig grew suddenly unbridled—engulfed in a completely alien mindset—ragingly instinctual and animalistic. As they made love with wild abandon, his ferocity persisted—he did not retreat into his accustomed compliant, cerebral state. Even more remarkable was the fact that as he thrust into her, over and over, he occasionally found that he was outside himself, observing his own mad, feral frenzy—but even *that* didn't wrench him out of it—though he fully expected it to.

What *was* this?

How was it possible that even his own awareness of being

immersed in this bestial trance could not undo it? This was magical—primevally chemical.

Yet pristinely non-cerebral. And seemingly impervious and indestructible.

He had never experienced anything akin to this in his life.

• • •

She had been asleep for hours, but his rustling awakened her. He was on the edge of the bed, gingerly trying to extricate himself from the sheets and blanket without rousing her. She glanced at the digital clock on the bureau across the room. The clock read exactly 4:00 a.m.

"What on earth are you doing, love?" she asked.

"I was going to do my yoga," he whispered.

"My god—even the time-zone change and all the lovely excitement last night hasn't disrupted your internal clock—has it?"

"It's kind of remarkable. But I suppose it's a message. I need to do my yoga."

"Do me first."

"Really, at this hour?"

"Just make it fast." She giggled, repositioning herself higher on her pillow. "But not *too* fast, love." She pulled him closer.

• • •

The guest room was small. Its space was insufficient for yoga, but Craig stopped there for a moment to dig into his briefcase and extract his book *The Yoga Sutras of Patanjali* with commentary by Sri Swami Satchidananda. He always carried it with him when he traveled.

He had noted that there was a large plush rug in the living room—that would suffice as his yoga mat this morning.

Before he began his session, he sat for a short time on the toilet in the guest bathroom, pondering one of the brief aphorisms and the lengthier accompanying commentary in his book, calming his mind. He imagined that Golda was there with him, sitting at his feet, waiting.

When he was done, he returned to the guest room and deposited the book safely in his briefcase. He then made his way slowly into the living room, where he positioned himself for his abdominal contractions. He gazed at the corner of the rug and pictured Golda in her accustomed squat. But he couldn't focus immediately upon his exercise—his mind wandered for an instant to the sex he and Carolyn had enjoyed just minutes ago. This encounter had been much briefer than the night prior—more direct—more comfortable for him to launch. But that same magic—that same primal, instinctual frenzy—had seized him and remained unyielding throughout. He had to acknowledge now that this phenomenon was real. But this was something he had never imagined himself capable of—and for it to have suddenly manifested—at his age—seemed more mysterious than he could grasp.

Craig closed his eyes and steered his mind back to his yoga session. As he proceeded methodically through Shatkarma (cleansing), Asana (postures), and Pranayama (breathing), his immersion into peace and stillness grew all-encompassing. As it did, a simultaneous and unexpected sensibility merged with his accustomed tranquil mind state—a jolting surge of strength and renewal.

He had sensed Golda pressing lightly against the top of his head in the third movement of Plough, and now he felt her again in the crook of his knee as he sat in full lotus, and commenced meditation. It took only seconds for his ego to surrender—his state now transcended into something entirely noncorporeal. The stillness felt infinite, immutable, ecstatic.

For a long time, as he meditated, his mind remained emptied of conscious thought—blissful and undisturbed. But near the end of his meditation session, something completely unanticipated occurred.

Golda suddenly entered his being.

But it was not as if he had become distracted—not as if he had conjured her up—not as if he simply had imagined she was there. This was starkly different. Her very essence had joined him—melded with him. She was present. And her spirit carried with it a depth of urgency and consequence that he had never sensed from her in person.

Golda and Craig finished the meditation session together, their souls in an ardent and intractable embrace. At the end there was a profound sense of completion—of their having shared something unspeakably beautiful.

Then she was gone, and he opened his eyes.

• • •

Craig showered, shaved, and dressed. When he strolled into the kitchen, he found Carolyn brewing coffee and scrambling an egg.

"Ah!" she said, her British accent especially sharp and assured. "Back to a dapper suit and tie. Now I actually recognize you. You look very nice, love."

"You look nice too, Carolyn." She had on a white blouse and a long black skirt that reached down to her ankles.

"I know you don't eat breakfast after yoga. Can I offer you anything at all? A bit of fruit? Some tea?"

"I'll have a small cup of tea with you, while you eat."

"Earl Grey?"

He reflexively reached toward his suit coat pocket to retrieve a packet of green chai tea to hand to her, but stopped himself. "Earl Grey is fine," he said, "with a bit of honey if you have it."

"I'll get that going for you. Was your yoga session a good one?"

"Very good. Your living room rug makes a nice yoga mat." He gazed upward and to the left, then closed his eyes for a moment. "The strangest thing happened while I was meditating. My rabbit—Golda. She joined me."

"Joined you?"

"Not as if I was imagining it. As if she was actually here. Inside me. It was the strangest thing—it felt so real. It was extraordinary—very powerful." He paused. "I wonder what it meant? Do you think she's thinking of me—missing me—wondering when I'll be back for morning yoga?"

"Who can say, love."

"When she was with me—just now—it's hard to know—but she seemed in some way needy. Distressed. Yes! Very distressed. But her being with me—it seemed to soothe her."

"I suppose if you're worried you could call Shoshana. Ask her if there's anything wrong."

"My intuition tells me not to."

"Really? Why?"

"I'm not sure." He looked away.

Carolyn set out her egg and coffee and a cup of tea for Craig. She sat down across from him.

The brief pause enabled him to reset. "Thank you for the tea," he said. He glanced at her dish. "That's not a big plate of eggs at all."

Carolyn chuckled. "Just the one. Got to save room for my habitual scone and tea at ten."

"Right. I remember."

She gazed at him as she chewed. She put down her fork, cocked her head, and affected a flirtatious pout. "It was so lovely, Craig. Last night and this morning. Why haven't we done this before?"

"I don't know. Maybe I'm more comfortable away from home? Away from my marriage?"

"We've traveled together to various regions before."

"But you live out here now. It seems different."

"Well, for what it's worth, I would have been up for it—I mean, before. I was always up for it with you. But you never seemed to be. Regardless of time or place. I'm glad we did it now, though. It was wonderful, no?"

"Yes. Wonderful. Absolutely amazing."

She blushed slightly and sipped on her coffee. "So, you have meetings today and tomorrow? Then fly home Thursday morning?"

"Right."

Carolyn grinned sweetly. "More time for us."

"Yes. That'll be nice."

"I was thinking of cooking something for you tonight, love." A derisive laugh spewed from her lips. "And if it will provide you some comfort, I don't stock bloody fish sauce."

He chuckled. "I'm looking forward to sampling your cuisine, Carolyn. I very much appreciate that you don't stock fish sauce. Just as a precaution, though—lard—chicken or beef stock—gelatin—anchovies—Worcestershire sauce—they're all hidden landmines for vegetarians."

"Good god, you *are* a royal pain. And you don't eat eggs either, do you?"

Before he responded, he took just an instant to applaud his earlier decision not to ask her for green chai tea.

"It's interesting about eggs," he said, "I've actually gone back and forth on eggs for many years. Yoga says no eggs. But I'm pro-choice politically—and not eating eggs could be seen as hypocritical—I mean—if I consider a chicken egg a potential life—then what's an embryo?"

"For Christ's sake, love, do you actually agonize over such bloody philosophical and moral conundrums endlessly like this? You really must stop. It will tear you apart. And it's not good conversation."

He laughed. "I think I'd be lost without moral conundrums. My mind needs things to toss about."

"So I've noted. Anyway, if I use an egg or two tonight, will you run off screaming?"

He chuckled. "No. It's fine. Every once in a while—it's okay. What are you planning to make?"

"It's a surprise, love. I hope anticipating a surprise all day won't topple your finely honed mystical sense of being."

"Ouch! You're in rare form this morning, Carolyn."

"Hardly rare form, love. But you need to see me for who I am. Especially if you plan to keep shagging me like a wild animal. Which, by the way, I hope you do."

"Yes, continuing to do so is in my immediate plans." He smiled. "But what do you mean—when you say that I need to see you for who you are?"

"I'm not easy to be with. Why do you think I was always open to extracurriculars with you, all these years? It's because I've never been with anyone. Never been in any sort of stable relationship."

Craig took a long sip of tea. "That's hard to understand, Carolyn. I mean—you're intelligent, charming, good-looking, outgoing—it's just hard to fathom why you've been single for so long."

"That's sweet of you to say, dear. But it's not hard to fathom at all. I'm a bloody bitch. Men can't put up with me."

He thought a moment. "Geoff did. He put up with you."

Carolyn laughed so hard she shook—she had to put her coffee cup down to prevent it spilling. "Oh my god! *Geoff*? He *worked* for me! He couldn't hold a job without me. That wasn't a relationship. He was a boy toy. Totally dependent upon me. He had to put up with any crap I laid on him. Do you honestly think I'd be with a prat like Geoff?"

"No, actually."

"But, you see, love—it's only the bloody vassals like Geoff who ever put up with my bossiness. I'm a bitchy prima donna." Carolyn finished the last bit of egg on her plate and took a sip of coffee. "Truth be told, dear—I'm dreadfully afraid that you'll come to see it too—and soon enough."

"I see it. I think it may be why I find you so hot."

Carolyn put her coffee cup down. She gazed at him with wide eyes and a surprised, impish grin. "Well, keep that thought, love. It's quite original. And I suppose it provides us some hope."

19

CHOCOLATE

CRAIG SCHUMACHER WAS NOT BOTHERED BY THE heavy traffic as he made his way home from the airport.

It was early evening on Thursday. The flight from DC to San Francisco had been uneventful. Now, as he drove along familiar freeways, the residual elation from his connection with Carolyn was still with him—it felt as though a mangled part of him had been somehow regenerated and made whole.

He had on the same hoodie and jeans he'd worn flying out and was comfortable in them. He opened his home's front door and made his way slowly through the foyer. His right hand pulled his stacked suitcase, garment bag, and satchel, while his left hand held his briefcase. He had barely reached the end of the foyer when he saw Shoshana sitting in the living room, wearing a black caftan. He stopped abruptly and stared at her, his body stiff, his mouth slightly agape. His eyelids scrunched warily.

"Hi honey," Shoshana said.

Her tone was ostensibly soft and gentle. But to Craig it reeked of something ominous—something auguring anguish and upheaval. And though it seemed counterintuitive, that sense of impending unrest felt somehow expected—and even deserved.

"What are you doing here?" Craig asked haltingly. "You're always in your studio on Thursday evenings—doing sessions. Is something wrong?"

"I wanted to be here in person, honey. To explain what happened." Her expression was contrite, her voice hesitant.

Craig stepped to the end of the foyer and into the living room. From there, he could see through the archways into the rear of the house.

It hit him immediately.

"Where's Golda's hutch?" he cried. "It's gone!"

"This is what I need to talk to you about, honey."

"Where is she?"

"Please, sweetie, sit down."

He let go of his luggage hastily—it teetered back and forth on its wheels, endeavoring to steady itself behind him. His briefcase fell to the hardwood floor with a dull thud. He took a step toward Shoshana. His tone grew blunt and urgent. "Where the fuck is she? Where's Golda?"

"Honey—please sit."

"No!" He spoke louder now. "Just tell me. Where is she?"

"I'm so sorry, my love. Golda's dead."

"Dead? How the fuck is she dead?" His intonation turned harsher—his face contorted menacingly. "What happened? For god's sake, tell me what the fuck happened!"

"Okay, honey. Here it is. And I'm so—so—sorry. Really, honey. So sorry. I was here—at home—Tuesday night . . ."

He interrupted. "Tuesday night? You're always at your studio Tuesday night."

"I took the night off. I invited Joe over here."

"The Hauler Guy?"

"Yes. I invited him to spend the night."

"Here? In *our* bed?"

"Oh, honey, what difference does that make? You sleep down in my studio on Friday and Saturday nights. He sleeps in that bed too."

"That's *your* bed—in the studio. This is *our* bed. In *our* home."

"Well . . . I invited him. I mean—you were gone almost the whole week—I had to come home every day to take care of Golda anyway. So, we partied here. And—well—we were playing. He—you know—he has a fetish about brown showers—and having his mistress—you know—force him to eat her shit. I mean he doesn't really want to eat shit—just pretend to. So—anyway—we'd gone to the fetish store—the one in the Haight—and bought a bunch of that dark chocolate—you know, the kind that they make to look like human turds. And we dumped it all out here—on the living room floor—and some out in the foyer. And—well—I made him crawl around and eat it off the floor."

"Don't tell me Golda got into the chocolate . . ."

"I'm so sorry, honey. We must have left some out in the foyer. I just forgot about it. And then things got hot and heavy—with me and Joe, I mean—and I—I guess I never put Golda back in her hutch for the night. And—so then—she got into the chocolate. That's on me, baby. Totally on me. And I feel terrible. Really terrible. And I'm so sorry."

For a moment, he could not speak. He closed his eyes and began to hyperventilate. His tone was shifting now—from rage to pitiable desperation. "You *knew* that chocolate is poisonous for rabbits. You knew that! And you just left it out? And left *her* out—to eat it? You knew she'd eat it!" His eyes began to tear and his lips tremble. "You were so damn anxious to jump into *our* bed with that semi-literate junk-hauling neanderthal that you let Golda kill herself with chocolate? Is that what you're saying? Is that really what you're saying?"

He staggered into the back room and stood where the hutch had been.

"Where is it?" He turned back to face her. "What the hell happened to it? Where's the goddamn hutch?"

"When we found her—the next morning—I'm sure she was already dead—but we raced her over to the emergency animal hospital—just to see if there was anything—you know, any possible thing they could do. But she was gone. I know how much you loved her, honey. If I could bring her back, I would. You know that."

"What happened to the hutch?" He began to sob heavily.

"We thought it would make it easier on you if you didn't have to look at it. I asked Joe to haul it away."

"I want it! I want it here. I want to be able to look at it. And remember her. Tell him to bring it back."

"Oh, honey—I'm so sorry. He told me he was making a run to the dump—that same morning—when he took it. That was days ago, babe. There's no way to get it now. I really thought it would make it easier for you."

Craig said nothing. His sobs became crazed gasps. He fell onto his hands and knees and began crawling about. With frantic lunges, his fingers clawed through the carpet fibers around where the hutch had stood.

"What are you doing?" she asked, her voice now a desolate whisper.

"I'm trying to find something," he blurted between heaving tears. "I don't know—maybe a tiny rabbit turd—a piece of her fur—something—something I can touch and hold onto—something that was a part of her."

He found a tiny wooden shard—it had been a piece of a toy she'd chewed—one he bought for her recently. He clutched it tightly, and then put it in the pocket of his hoodie.

Suddenly, he jumped to his feet and ran to the bookshelf on the opposite wall. He scanned the titles and yanked out a thick text on the care of rabbits. He said nothing but spent a few minutes thumbing madly through its pages, crying as he did. He stopped on a page about two thirds through the book and read carefully, barely moving.

Finally, he lifted his head and glared at Shoshana. "My god," he gasped. "She suffered. The chocolate took hours to kill her. Seizures. Heart failure. She couldn't breathe—she was struggling for breath. Convulsing. Dying here. Right here in our house. Alone. My god! Alone." He wheezed and trembled as he cried.

"The doctor said she probably died in the middle of the night on . . ."

He held a hand up to stop her. His tears slowed. His eyes widened. His frenzied breathing steadied just a bit. "I know exactly when she died," he said, his tone softening. "She came to me. I was meditating. Now I understand. She was suffering—and she found me. Somehow, she found me. Being with me calmed her. We meditated together until she died. At the end, she was at peace. She was released from the pain. She was joyful when we finished—when she said goodbye."

• • •

When Craig poked his head in Bruce's office, he saw that his senior VP was inside, seated in his plush upholstered chair.

"Do you have a minute, Bruce?"

Bruce looked up and responded in his cheerful resplendent baritone. "Sure, Craig. Come on in." He lowered his voice as Craig approached. "I always have time for my favorite VP."

"Do you mind if I close the door?"

Bruce chuckled. "I'm your boss, buddy—I'm supposed to

ask *you* that question! But, sure, close the door if you need to."

Craig shut the door and sat down in one of the guest chairs facing the wide desk. "I've been thinking about that meeting last week," Craig said. "About the layoffs coming up next year."

"Nasty business, eh? I don't enjoy having to conduct meetings like that. I'm sure you didn't like hearing the news."

"You know, actually, it wasn't a surprise. I mean, you and I have worked on so many big projects. They always wind down."

"Absolutely."

"It's the *process* I want to talk to you about. I've given it a lot of thought. We all hate mass layoffs. They hurt people. And they're terrible for morale. I mean, even the survivors wind up traumatized—everybody's unhappy and insecure for a long time. It's just bad all around. I'd like to avoid it—in my shop, anyway."

"We'd all like to avoid it, my friend. But we can't change the headcount numbers—that's a financial reality."

"No. I realize that. I just want to go about it a different way. Everyone is going to just wait, and then do massive layoffs next year—but I'd rather do it gradually—over the course of the next nine months."

"Tell me your plan."

"Well, about a third of my staff is contractors—I won't renew those contracts as the due dates come up—and that'll seem totally expected, given that the project's ending. And then, there's normal attrition—you know, people leave, retire, get pregnant—we won't replace any of them. I'm confident I can reach my numbers—or at least get very close—if I do it that way."

"Can you keep the implementation going successfully if you do that?"

"I'm sure I can. Really, no problem."

"Well, if you say you can—you can. I trust your judgment."

"Thank you, Bruce."

"But how are you going to explain it? You realize—we have to keep the edict hush-hush."

"I'll just say that every big project always has staff reductions when it's done—and I want to get ahead of the inevitable curve—because layoffs are so painful and hurt so many people. So, we'll all sacrifice a little for the rest of the rollout—with slight attrition—but avoid the big pain later on. We owe it to our teammates to do it. You know, Bruce—my teams are accustomed to thinking this way. I won't say that anything definite has been announced to anyone."

"I wouldn't trust most people to pull this off—and they wouldn't want to—I mean they wouldn't want to deal with being short-staffed over nine months and all. But I know you, Craig—you can make it work—so go ahead. We'll have to just keep it between ourselves. Nothing in writing. And I'm not going to inform the higher-ups."

"No problem, Bruce. I'll make sure it goes smoothly."

"I know you will, my friend. Thanks for dropping by."

Craig walked back to his office. His administrative assistant, Basha, an older full-figured woman, was at her desk outside his door.

"Hey, Basha," he said, "I have something I'd like you to get right on. Just one second. It's in my office."

A moment later he was back at her desk, holding a printout.

"There's a conference coming up in Washington, DC, in a couple of weeks. About the expected impact of Y2K. All the details are on this printout. I'd like to attend. I think it will be interesting."

"*Interesting*?" She gazed at him with a quizzical grin. "You hate these things! Whenever the company makes you go to one, you say it'll be a waste of time."

"Well, yeah—I know. But this one might be useful. Oh, and I won't need a hotel room—please just book me into the conference—I'll be staying with a friend."

"Carolyn Winthrop?" she asked with a coy smirk.

Craig laughed loudly, placed his palms on her desk, and leaned forward. He whispered: "Okay. You got me. Hell—*that* didn't take long to get out, did it? It's so bizarre, Basha. You know—if you try to get some information disseminated in a corporation, and you do it through the official channels—half the time it fails. People don't trust it. They're suspicious. But start a rumor in a hallway—whisper it to a few select people—tell them to keep it to themselves—well, then it's almost instantaneous that everyone knows—and everyone believes what they heard."

Basha chucked. "I've known you a few years now, Craig. And I've seen you do it—that exact thing—at least three or four times—you know—intentionally start a rumor to get something out that you really want people to know."

"It never seems to fail." He smiled. "But, Basha, this one wasn't intentional. Still, though, I had a pretty good idea it would get out. I just didn't think quite so soon. Anyway, please just keep it to yourself if you can."

"Of course, boss . . . for all the good it'll do now." She cocked her head and flashed her most ironic smile.

Craig blinked and offered her a sheepish nod before skulking back into his office.

• • •

Craig arose at 4:00 a.m., alone in the large house.

Shoshana was in her studio in Los Altos.

Golda, of course, was gone.

It had been nearly two weeks now that he'd been doing his morning yoga without her. The sessions still seemed somehow misconfigured—eerily hollow and denuded—but he felt that slowly, he was adjusting.

This morning, though, maintaining focus again became difficult. It surprised him, because the past few days had been better. Nonetheless, he pressed through the exercises, and when they were done, he sat erect in full lotus and readied himself for meditation.

But the missing pressure on the crook of his knee, where Golda used to sit, grew palpable—his entire being felt lost without that barely perceptible bit of weight on his knee joint.

Also missing was the pure, tranquil energy that had always emanated from her—had always infused and engulfed him.

He paused and allowed himself to cry.

After a couple of minutes, he felt a bit stronger—ready to try again. He lowered his eyelids and began watching his breath. With each exhalation, he endeavored to relax more deeply, allowing stray thoughts to float away.

He persisted for several minutes, but the accustomed shift in consciousness did not occur. He tried harder to relax his mind and body, but he could not usher in the mind-state he sought.

Then suddenly, without warning, she manifested inside him. It was Golda—but it was not at all like the morning in Carolyn's living room. That visit had been fueled by her emancipation from corporeal pain—her release from the slow inevitable churning of impending death. That visit had climaxed with the bewildering joy and liberation of her soul ejecting itself from her withering body.

No. This time it felt as if she were here to help—that she somehow understood how lost he had become.

Her mystical essence was utterly different now—stronger—

fully adjusted to its disembodied state—ascended and ubiquitous.

He realized that she was now so much more advanced than he—her essence was boundless—massive—as if the sliver of it that was inside him was just a tiny facet of something that could be everywhere and everything at this very instant.

He was honored and humbled to be in her presence. He surrendered to her, and followed her as she guided him. She escorted him, instantaneously, into the meditative state.

Now he was motionless—blissful. At peace.

Golda stayed with him until his meditation session concluded. Then she departed—but somehow a trace of her still seemed to be within him, even when he arose and left the room to shower and shave.

It was as if a bare glimmer of her mystical essence—infinitesimal to her—yet infinite to him—would be part of him always.

He hoped that was the case.

20

FENNEL SAUSAGE AND BLACK FOREST HAM

IT WAS STILL LIGHT OUT ON TUESDAY EVENING, when Shoshana Schumacher greeted Justine Silver at the door of the Los Altos townhouse. As always, the collar of Justine's long black coat was buttoned high, obscuring her chin and mouth, while the huge brim of her wool fedora hung down and shrouded the rest of her face.

"Hi sweetie!" Shoshana said. "It's so nice to see you."

"Oh my god, I'm so late," Justine said as she scampered in, removed her hat and coat, and hung them on the hook in the living room. "It's after seven. I'm so sorry, honey. I really wanted to get here earlier. But I got caught up with a really—like—horrific facial restoration at that funeral home in Daly City."

"Well, I'm sure you did a great job."

"Actually," Justine said with a sly chuckle, "I think the woman looks better now than she did in the picture they showed me—from when she was alive."

The two women sat down across from each other at the small Formica table in the curtained area off the foyer.

Shoshana smiled. "I picked up a couple of containers of that chicken chow mein you like so much. And I got some spring rolls too. We can have some now, if you're hungry, or wait till later, after our sessions."

"We can wait, if that's okay. I'm not hungry yet."

"That's fine. You have a late session at ten, right? Do you have to go home after that, or can you sleep over tonight?"

"I can stay. My friend Claire is so sweet. She's gonna walk 'Chester again tonight and in the morning—you know, she has that big dog that 'Chester likes—so they all go together. And like I told you last time, she's sworn to secrecy about it, if Nigel's ever around."

"Nigel's been traveling a lot, hasn't he? It feels like you've been down here with me—like at least a day or two—pretty much every week for the past month or so. And I really like that you're here, sweetie. But it does seem like a lot of travel for Nigel."

"Yeah, I think most of the time when he's out on the road, he's with that whacko Byron Dorn." Justine giggled. "And who knows what kind of trouble *those* two get into?""Do you ever ask?"

"Oh my god! I'd rather not know."

"Remind me who you have tonight," Shoshana inquired. "I have a session with Phil Math Professor at nine."

"He seems like a nice guy."

"Yeah, nice—but always uptight and kinda nervous. He's sweet, though. And *very* obedient." She chucked. "And who's the session you have at ten?"

"Oh, it's Bill Chest Hole. And thank you again, honey, for letting me see him alone. I mean, he's *your* client."

"No problem, sweetie. With Bill, though, you gotta remember—first thing always—you put your hand all the way inside the cavity in his chest—feel it—rub it—that assures him you accept it. He's really sensitive about it. Like he's ashamed that he has it."

"Got it, honey. I thought it was kind of grody at first—but you know, I watched you do it when we did the sessions together with him—so, I'm fine with it now."

"I guess so, because now he asked for *you*! Alone! You're already stealing my clients!"

They both laughed, as Shoshana leaned across the small table and grasped Justine's hand warmly.

"Well," Justine said, "he really wants to get into this fantasy where his mistress kills him—or maybe doesn't. You know—so, we're gonna do the session in the big bathroom. I'll make him strip naked and tie him up really tight at the bottom of the bathtub. Flat on his back. Then I'll start filling up the tub—like I'm gonna drown him. Then stop. Let a little water out. Then more water so it comes up right over his face. Then let some out. You know, over and over."

"And remember to keep talking to him. Taunt him. Tell him he's been very bad—disrespectful—lax in his duties—and you haven't decided yet whether you want to kill him and get a new slave in his place, or give him another chance. He'll beg for mercy. But if he begs too much, strap a ball gag in his mouth."

Justine laughed. "Oh my god, he might come right then and there, if I do that!"

"You've gotten very good at this, honey," Shoshana said.

"Oh my god, there are so many different men—so many different fantasies. It's kinda like being a shrink, you know."

"Yes. It kind of is."

"So . . ." Justine hesitated a moment, then leaned in a bit closer. "Craig was a client—to start. Right?"

"He was. That was such a long time ago, now. But he *was* a client. He said I was the only Domme he ever went to—you know, it took him a long time to work up the courage to see one. And then, when he decided—he researched every Domme in the Bay Area—anyone who advertised anywhere. And he said he felt a connection to me, just from the ad."

"Knowing Craig—and how thorough he is about thinking through everything—he probably did spend months researching."

"Oh, I'm sure. But the thing is—how exactly did he feel a connection to me, just through the ad? I mean, there's a photo of me in the ad, but my hair covers my face."

"Yeah. That is kinda amazing. He has a sixth sense—like intuition to the max."

"He sort of does."

"So, then—with all the men you see as clients—what made you choose *him*—I mean to be with?"

Shoshana flashed a wistful smile. "He was sweet. So smart. Funny. Accomplished. He made a really good living. And he's gentle—you know—but strong when he needs to be—like when he's at work. And he's the most self-disciplined man I've ever met—the yoga, the meditation, and his vegetarian diet—he's really in wonderful shape. And so healthy." She paused a moment. "You know—at parties sometimes—I make fun of him because he's not big and muscular like some of the men I'm attracted to. It's for fun, but I know he hates it—and I really shouldn't do it—but I do—I just keep doing it for some reason."

"Why do you think?"

"I really don't know. Anyway—I'm not sure it matters much now. This is sad, honey—but we—Craig and I—I think we're drifting apart."

"What? Really? Why do you say that?"

"It's pretty obvious—I mean—if you're around us, it is. I blame myself. I take him for granted. I shouldn't—he's such a great guy—but I do. He doesn't ask for much—just to play once in a while—you know—one-on-one—but I just never feel up for doing it." She wiped away a stray tear with her fingertip. "I guess I always figured—that, you know—from his point of view—that he had to feel like he was lucky to be with me—because I kept him in the BDSM community. But that's not enough, I guess. I really haven't been as good to him as I should have."

"Well—it's good that you realize it—that you thought it through. So—do you think you can fix it?"

Shoshana's lips eased into a sad, fragile curl. "You know how I said he was strong? He is—and I think he's made his mind up—I don't think I can change it. I'm pretty sure he's going to leave me. He hasn't told me, but he's said things that make me feel like—you know—things he might have been afraid to say before—but now—he can just say them—because he doesn't care if we stay together anymore or not. He's cautious—you know—calculated. But I think he'll lay it out for me soon."

"And you think it's too late for you to change anything?"

Shoshana shook her head. Her lips parted slightly to reveal the hint of a crestfallen smile. "I think, in a way, honey, it's *always* been too late—you know—to change anything—at least anything significant. It's like—*he* knows who I am—and *I* sure as hell know who I am. Even if I say I'm going to change—even if I really *want* to change—I'm not really going to, and we both know that."

"I get that it's hard, honey. Are you sure it's really done, though?"

"The thing with Golda—and Joe Hauler Guy—you know, a couple of months ago—that really did it. Maybe he was willing to keep trying before that—but—I think—that *had* to push him over the edge. And—damnit—I can't bring Golda back. Believe me, I wish I could."

"It's such a shame—he seems to really love you."

"He does. He still does. I can see that. He just doesn't *like* me very much anymore—you know—and I really can't blame him. He deserves better. And I don't seem willing to give that to him." Shoshana began to cry. "Why the hell am I such a bitch?"

Her sobs grew heavier. She closed her eyes and laid her head upon her forearms, folded now upon the table in front of her.

Justine rose and walked around to stand closer to her. She lowered her head, pressed her cheek against Shoshana's, and held her tight.

• • •

Having promised their respective wives that they'd both be back home by five to spend the evening, Nigel Silver and Byron Dorn wangled permission to tool around the wineries of Carmel Valley together, for the greater part of Saturday.

Nigel arose early, and after taking 'Chester for an abbreviated walk, lowered the convertible top on his banana-yellow Lotus, climbed in, and—with a palpable sense of having temporarily shed every discernible encumbrance that had been adhering to him of late—darted gleefully across the Golden Gate Bridge and then down the peninsula to pick up Byron in Cupertino.

The two then headed to Carmel Valley, about an hour and a half south.

The wineries they visited specialized in Bordeaux varietals and blends, mostly Cabernet Sauvignons and Merlots. They had tasted the full slate at three different wineries and purchased a few bottles at each.

Now, as they concluded another full set at their fourth tasting, Nigel whispered to Byron, "I'm feeling a bit tipsy, mate. And we still have a lot of driving to do."

"Let's go have a big lunch," Byron said. "That'll sober you up. I know a great place down here."

Paying careful heed to Byron's directions, Nigel navigated the Lotus to a cozy, rustic café a few miles west. Inside, he immediately noticed the open kitchen and the prominent stone pizza oven.

They were seated and handed menus, but as soon as the greeter walked away, Byron said, "Forget the menu, bro. I know the pizza we're gonna share. I have it every time I come. You'll love it."

"Which one is it?" Nigel asked, perusing his menu.

Byron reached over and pointed to an entry near the bottom of the page. It was a thin crust pie, topped with mozzarella cheese, Italian fennel sausage, Black Forest ham, and pepperoni.

When the waiter came back, Byron ordered the pizza and specified extra-large. He was about to request something more, when Nigel interrupted.

"No wine for me, mate," he said. "I'm done."

Byron looked at him with a quizzical gaze. "Well, of course we won't have wine, bro. This is pizza. Only wimps have wine with pizza." He turned to the waiter. "Two mugs of hefeweizen on tap," he said.

As the waiter departed, Nigel asked, "What exactly is

hefeweizen, mate?"

"German wheat beer. Goes great with this pizza. You'll love it."

And Nigel did.

• • •

By the time they started the trip home, they were sated and happy. Other than the whoosh of the whipping wind, the car was quiet—they had seemingly run out of much to talk about.

Nigel was cognizant of the five o'clock curfew they'd set with their wives, and knew that even after dropping Byron off in the South Bay, he'd still have a drive of over an hour remaining to reach San Rafael in Marin County. So, as soon as he accessed the freeway, he bolted into the left lane and, with a constant eye out for predatory highway patrol vehicles, sped north at an electrifying velocity, periodically weaving around any stragglers he encountered. He glanced over to make sure that Byron was still comfortable with the car's top down—and was relieved to see that Byron's face, beneath his shock of wildly flapping brown hair, was scrunched into a subtle but irrefutable grin.

The yellow Lotus pulled up in front of Byron's home just after three-thirty.

"Well, mate," Nigel said, "I've had a cracking time. We'll do it again, soon."

He was somewhat taken aback when Byron replied, "Hey, bro, I want you to come inside. I have something to show you."

Nigel raised his palms apologetically. "Normally—you know, mate—I'd love to. But we have the five o'clock thing. So, I think I'd better take off."

"Don't sweat it, bro—you got time. This'll only take a few minutes. You don't even have to come into the house. I got everything set up in the garage. You really need to see this, man."

Nigel now had the sense that no matter how long the two bickered, he'd wind up being coaxed into the garage anyway, to see whatever it was that Byron had concocted. So, it made more sense to abandon the preliminaries and just head in and get it done.

"Sure, mate, let's check it out."

They hopped out of the car. Nigel left the top down—he felt it was safe on this quiet suburban street. He offered to carry in the box with the bottles Byron had purchased, and when there was no objection, he grabbed it from the trunk. They walked together into Byron's garage.

Once inside, Nigel set down the wine and the two men huddled together over what appeared to be a configuration of video equipment with a small viewing monitor.

"So, what exactly have we got here, mate?" Nigel asked.

"You remember how we've talked a few times—you know, when I said I got some shit on Craig that would bring him down—bring him down hard?"

"I remember."

"Well, let me tell you something you're not gonna fucking believe. His wife—you know—Shoshana. Brace yourself, bro. She's a fucking prostitute."

Nigel's eyebrows screwed into a quizzical stare. Then he spoke softly. "You've got to be wrong about that, mate. It's just not possible."

"I'm not talking about some junkie whore on the street, man. I'm talking high-end. She has her own little brothel—a townhouse in Los Altos. She employs other women—like a fucking madam."

"And how, exactly, do you know all this?"

"I first came across it by chance. But I've staked her place out. Lots of nights. It's undeniable, man. Tricks come by—like every hour. And listen—now I got footage. Almost all of it happens at night, after it's dark—I mean that's when the shit really gets goin'—so, I rigged up an infrared video camera—motion-activated."

"Jesus! This is bloody hard to believe, mate."

"You gotta see some of this footage I put together, bro. It's wild."

Byron started finagling with some of the switches and knobs. Soon, snippets of disjointed action were fluttering across the small monitor.

"I have hours of recordings," Byron said, "but the most recent are the best. It took me a while to figure out the right settings—I mean it's infrared—taken in the dark from a ways away—so it's never gonna be totally like crisp and clear. But you can damn well figure out what's happening."

Byron narrated as the brief clips were displayed.

"So, this is one of the Johns. Look at how this poor fucker is looking all around—scared as shit. He's making sure no one sees him ring the bell . . . And here's another John, this guy's so fat it's hard to figure out how he shoves it in . . ."

Nigel watched as the video stream, along with Byron's narration, proceeded for several more minutes. It was becoming a bit redundant now, and Nigel's focus began to waver. But then a clip appeared which startled him, immediately reigniting his attention. Nigel leaned forward, his gaze, once again, fixed intently upon the small screen.

"This is one of the bimbos she's got working for her," Byron said. "Look at this hag! The long coat. The collar covering her mouth. And the big hat over her face. Jesus, like she's spying for the fucking KGB!"

Nigel's features were dead-still. His focus was steely and unrelenting. He couldn't be certain. The infrared images were a bit hazy. Even *without* a veil or disguise, it would be impossible to discern facial features with any degree of certainty. But the outfit looked too familiar for comfort.

"Oh, bro!" Byron continued. "You're going to love these next few. I got a spot on the street where the angle was perfect. You know, they only open the door just wide enough to let the men in and out—but it's enough to get a quick peek inside—if you got just the right angle. And you can see the getups the girls are in."

They viewed several iterations of women in costumes greeting the Johns at the door.

"Bro—look at this clip—this has to be Shoshana—see, she's really tall—taller than the guy comin' in—and look at what she has on—it's metallic, so it shows up better than a lot of the other clothes—it's like a corset—see—with a pair of handcuffs hangin' off the belt—and look in her hand—that's a whip, bro! Holy shit! What kind of fucking insanity goes on in this place?"

Nigel gazed at the woman's body. Even with the image as hazy as it was, he recognized the shape and contours immediately. He knew Byron couldn't see it, but she was too thin to be Shoshana. Nigel knew exactly who it was.

"I got more, bro. A lot more. You want to see?"

"Hey, mate," Nigel said, in a cadence so stoic and emotionless that it surprised even himself, "this is amazing shit. I'd love to see it all. Every minute of it. But I gotta get home now. You know, the five o'clock thing. But, mate—you've convinced me. What you got going on here is unbelievable. You proved it—I mean, this is dynamite. But man—I really have to think about it—I mean—like what the fuck do you *do* with shit like this?"

"Okay," Byron said, turning off the machine. "Give it some thought. We have a lot to talk about, man. Right?"

"Right, mate! Absolutely. Till then, take care." Nigel grabbed

Byron's shoulder with an affectionate clasp and was off.

• • •

Justine had on a diaphanous, low-cut top and very snug jeans. She'd even applied the barest touch of makeup.

It was just after five when she heard Nigel's car pull into the garage. She smiled broadly as the sound of his footsteps came closer to the living room, where she sat. "Hi, babe," she called in a voice calibrated to reach well into the hallway. "I have a great dinner cooking."

When his footfalls appeared to be just at the room's entrance, she added, with a giggle, "You're two minutes late, babe, but I forgive you."

But when he entered the room, his appearance caused her to flinch and suppress a gasp. Nigel's face was burning red. His eyes glared, his lower teeth jutted prominently, and his jaw was set. His entire body hunched forward, suggestive of a primate readying for battle. His eyelids now began to quiver in rage.

"You forgive *me*?" he screamed, his head leaning menacingly toward her. "You forgive *me*? That's rich. Don't expect *me* to ever fucking forgive *you*!"

On the large couch where she sat, she instinctively pulled back, curled her knees to her breasts, and hugged her legs tightly. "What's the matter?" she pleaded, softening her voice—hoping to de-escalate the situation. "What is it, babe?"

"How the hell can you do this to me? You're a pross! A bloody whore!"

"What are you talking about?"

"Don't play bloody dumb with me—you're a lying bitch! Byron's on to you. The house in Los Altos that Shoshana runs? You heard of it? A nice little place where men drop by every hour. How the fuck could you do this to me? He has video. He has fucking video!"

"Okay, babe. Just calm down. Please . . . I admit it. I won't lie to you about it."

"Oh! So now you won't lie about it anymore? Jesus, that's a bloody relief! Is that supposed to make me feel better?"

"Please—listen. There's no sex, babe. It's more like therapy."

"No sex? Therapy? You think I'm a fucking twat? I know what goes on in these places. What the hell were you thinking? What in bloody hell got you into this?"

"Well, babe—like—you know—you've been away—on business trips—working with the other regions. My funeral director gigs slowed down a little—and then—Shoshana—you know—like started telling me about what she does."

"Jesus Christ, just because she's a bloody brass—that doesn't mean you have to be one! How the hell can you let these fucking whoremongers shove their filthy cocks inside you? I just can't fucking believe it."

With that remark, Justine's demeanor suddenly shifted. Her frightened features now screwed into an indignant scowl. She inhaled deeply, leaped up, and stood a few feet from him. Her eyes confronted his—steady and unblinking.

"Goddamnit, Nigel, stop! Just fucking stop. I told you—there's no sex. I'm not lying to you. Read the fucking ads! They all say it. In capital letters. NO SEX."

Nigel seemed startled. His expression appeared to soften a bit—it was more suggestive now, not quite of contrition, but rather of confusion. He gazed at her for a moment. His voice was a tad softer as he replied, his tone more modulated. "All right. Say—just for the sake of argument—say I believe you—for now. So, what the bloody hell do you do with these guys if there's no sex?"

"Well, Shoshana—er—actually she goes by Delilah—she mostly strings guys up and whips them. Or cross-dresses them and pretends to be their mother and spanks them—you know—like with a hair brush. Tells them they've been naughty."

Nigel's mouth hung open and his eyebrows creased. "Jesus. And what the bloody hell do *you* do?"

"I specialize in people with death fantasies. Embalming. Cannibalism. Preparing bodies for viewing. Mummification. Fantasies about being murdered—you know—punishment—like for being a bad slave."

For a moment, Nigel appeared unable to process what he'd heard. His face contorted into a mystified stare. He spoke to her now in a hoarse, perplexed whisper. "Jesus Christ, babe! You're getting paid to service perverts? How on Earth? Good god!"

Nigel began pacing about the living room. "All right," he muttered as he strode back and forth. "All right—I have to think—have to make sense of this." He stopped and faced her. "Listen. All this. This can't get out. No one can find out that you've been doing this. It'll ruin me. Byron has video." He paused a moment. "Granted, it's all shot from the street. And hazy. But it'll ruin me if it gets out!"

"But you said Byron's aiming all this at Craig. Not you."

Now he raised his voice again. "Don't be a doylem! If he figures out you're in on it too—he'll turn on me in an instant. It's becoming more obvious to people that maybe *I* should be next in line—instead of him. So, now, *I'm* a threat too. I have to stop him before he does something with the footage."

"How exactly are you going to do that?"

Nigel began pacing again, shaking his head and mumbling incoherently. He paused for a moment, turned to her, and started to say something—but he caught himself and resumed pacing—faster now—his muttering even more frantic and desperate.

Finally he stopped and stepped closer to her. His tone now grew cold—analytic—devoid of emotion. "All right. Listen. This may sound farfetched. But think about it. And you know I can pull it off."

"Pull off what?"

"I have to bloody kill him."

"Oh my god! What? What did you just say?"

"I have to kill him—Byron. There are ways to do it."

Now Justine's features tightened and she raised her voice to nearly a shriek. "Are you crazy?"

"No. He's a fucking overweight sick alcoholic. Nobody will question for a moment if he drops dead. I know a guy. You met him. Warren Jaggers. I grew up with him in Leeds. You know—I have dinner with him every now and then—when he's in town for a convention or something. He broke free from the Leeds gang just before the cops caught onto him—and he made it across the pond, just like me. He's a bloody doctor now, if you can believe it. He can get me some kind of injection. Or powder. Simulate a heart attack. We can get away with it."

"Nigel," she screamed, "you're fucking insane. You're not killing *anybody*! Think about it. Please—think about what you're saying. If you actually believe that people finding out that I did a few sessions as a dominatrix will ruin you—think about what a fucking murder charge will do to you."

"We can get away with it! He's told me about it. Several times. When we had dinner. I suspect he's actually helped someone do it over the years—but he won't say. Anyway, look at it, babe—with Byron they'll never suspect. Never try to look for anything—poison or whatever. Because he's a fucking overweight sick alcoholic—so you expect him to drop dead. Almost like, well—he deserved it—for how he treated himself all those years. But even if they looked, they'd have to know what to look for. The stuff Jaggers uses isn't detectable by the usual tests—which they won't run anyway. And Jaggers says that if you pay off a funeral director you can trust, they can embalm the body in a certain way so there's no trace at all! So, don't you see? When he dies, Adelle will want *you* to do the preparation of the body. We'll volunteer to do it free—cover all the costs—because you're in the business. She'll jump on it. You can cover up any possible evidence. You know, needle marks, residue in the organs. Brilliant! It's brilliant!"

"You're fucking insane," she roared.

They stared at each other silently for a moment.

Now Justine's face relaxed. Her voice modulated into a timbre that was more forbearing, yet still steadfast and direct. "I'm not doing any such thing, Nigel," she said. "And neither are you. You're upset. You're not thinking straight. Listen to me, babe. This whole thing about killing somebody—oh my god—it's not even worth talking about. This is San Francisco for god's sake. Nobody here gives a shit about this kind of stuff. They have fucking leather festivals south of Market Street every summer. The fucking mayor drops by. Why are you even worrying about this?"

Nigel remained silent and motionless for what seemed a long time.

When he finally replied, his tone had grown calm, measured. "All right—maybe you have a point. I agree—a murder rap is bad. And Byron isn't exactly on to you—not yet, anyway. He knows it's Shoshana—and he knows there are other women—but he hasn't pegged *you*—not right now, at least. So, I need to work through it—before he figures it out. I need a strategy—need to gain the advantage. You made good points. babe. But I still need to think about it. We got to do bloody *something*, babe. We can't just do nothing. There has to be something we can do."

21

AUBERGINES

EARLIER THAT MORNING, BYRON DORN AND NIGEL Silver, along with Craig Schumacher's other direct reports, had attended a special meeting Craig had called.

Now, for lunch, Byron and Nigel headed to a small restaurant not far from the office. Nigel was unfamiliar with it, but Byron had assured him they'd have a fine lunch.

The eatery was located south of Market Street. The further the two walked from downtown, the more rough-hewn the tenor of the streets became. The narrow, dead-end alley they finally turned into had only a few decrepit storefronts along one of its sides. Bits of garbage were strewn against the edge of the cracking sidewalk. Nigel noticed a dead pigeon decaying on the asphalt abutting the alley's opposite wall. He raised his head and glanced about warily as they proceeded.

The inside of the café was dark, but not quite as uninviting as Nigel had feared. Its walls and floor were raw wood, and a high raftered ceiling mitigated its claustrophobic proportions. The two men showed themselves to one of the small, uncovered butcher block tables and sat down.

The menu was hand-lettered on a large black chalkboard

hanging on the far wall, illuminated by a lone light bulb above it. It boasted a dozen self-proclaimed "hulking submarine sandwiches" and nine beers on tap. Nothing more.

A young waitress in a snug tee shirt and jeans approached and asked if they'd like a couple of beers while they decided on sandwiches. Byron glanced at Nigel, gesturing that he'd handle the beer order. "Two large mugs of the Belgian wheat," Byron said to the waitress, then turned back to Nigel as she walked away. "It's great beer, bro."

"Looking forward to it, mate," Nigel said as he studied the board. "Which sandwich do you fancy?"

"My regular—the mortadella, capicola, salami, and provolone. Good shit, man. But you really can't go wrong—they're all good."

"Hmmm. There certainly are some intriguing choices."

The waitress set two huge mugs of beer with foamy heads on the table. "What'll you guys have?" she asked.

Byron placed his order. The waitress turned to Nigel.

"The eggplant parmesan sub," Nigel said, gazing at the board, "that looks interesting. I think I'll give that a try."

"Good choice—thanks, guys," she said, and scooted off.

Byron Dorn took a long swig, draining nearly half his mug. "You know," he said, "that meeting we all sat through today—the whole big-shit deal that Craig made out of it—you know, having it here on a Monday morning—had to attend in person—tellin' everyone to postpone their travel plans till Tuesday—what a fuckin' crock o' crap. Me and you could have been up in the Northwest region, like we planned, and just phoned in. Now, we'll miss a day up there. And for what? A bunch of bullshit."

"We'll just stay a day longer, mate. No need to get mardy about it."

"It's just the whole damn snobbery," Byron said. He paused a few moments as he quaffed down the rest of his beer, and held up the empty mug to signal the waitress to bring him another.

Nigel took a sip of his brew and awaited the rest of Byron's tirade.

"Yeah—the fuckin' snobbery," Byron went on. "It leaks off Schumacher like he's drippin' with it—his team always has to be the clean white knights. When the fuck did layoffs become some kind of evil demonic thing? We've all been laid off in our lives. We lived. So now, we have to hassle and squirm for the next nine months—movin' people around like a goddamn jigsaw puzzle—so he can strut around and say he didn't lay anybody off?"

"So, you're pissed at Craig because he's trying to avoid layoffs?"

"Damn right. Jesus! Fuckin' layoffs—they're just a fact of life, man. They happen. Everybody gets laid off sometime or other. Big shit. Bite the bullet and deal with it. Schumacher's plan is a bunch o' crap." Byron scowled and shook his head. "So, bro—are you *with* me on this?"

The waitress came by and delivered Byron's fresh mug. She took the empty one away.

Nigel took another small sip of beer and raised his mug in Byron's direction. "Cheers, mate—nice brew," he said. "Thanks for turning me on to it."

They clinked glasses. "So . . . " Byron pressed. "You *with* me on this?"

Nigel pondered for a moment before replying. "Well—about the layoffs—I can see both sides, mate. Really. I mean, you're right—sometimes layoffs are inevitable. But you can't argue with what Craig said about them being bad for morale. I mean—they just are. So, if you can avoid them, then why not? And no matter what you think of the guy—you'd have to admit that the loyalty—the rank-and-file motivation—on all of Craig's teams—is really champion."

Byron was in the middle of another huge gulp, but he stopped abruptly and slammed his mug down on the table. "Jesus Christ, bro! You sidin' with *him* on this? You turnin' wimp on me?"

"No, no, mate. I'm with you. A hundred percent. What I'm saying is—it's smart to pick your battles is all. Look, juggling people about for nine months—is it a bother? Sure. But for guys like you and me with big teams—it's a piece of cake. Not to worry, mate. Let's just focus on what's important."

"Well—I suppose."

The sandwiches arrived and were placed on the table. Each enormous sub had been sliced in half and set atop a brown paper napkin inside a flimsy perforated plastic basket. Byron dug into his with a gusto that seemed to Nigel an amalgam of impatience and rage.

Nigel lifted one-half of his eggplant parmesan sub up to eye level and examined it closely, turning it this way and that. He took a cautious bite and focused closely upon its taste and texture as he chewed. Finally, he swallowed, and almost immediately an enthusiastic smile unfurled across his face. "Brilliant!" he exclaimed. "Who knew? A sandwich of breaded, fried aubergines and cheese. With tomato sauce—instead of mayonnaise. Terrific concept, mate. I'd have this again."

Byron finished his second mug of beer and signaled the waitress for a third. She pointed at him from across the room and nodded.

"You're really chugging the beer, mate," Nigel observed. "Didn't you tell me you never drink till five? Only coffee during the day?"

Byron's features screwed into a dejected grimace, and he shook his head in disgust. "Yeah—usually only coffee—but this goddamn meeting Craig called—it got me all worked up. Shit!"

He took two huge bites of his sandwich—filling his mouth to the point where he needed some awkward preliminary contortions before he could close his lips and gnaw upon it in a reasonably presentable fashion. He grew quiet.

The waitress delivered another beer, and Byron took a short swig. He lowered his head a moment, then looked up. "Listen, bro . . . sorry for yellin' at you just now. It's just this fuckin' meeting this morning—and the whole goddamn layoff thing—it's got me on edge. I mean, I shoulda seen it comin'. It always comes eventually on big projects—but, you know, now it's real. I gotta tell you though—this meeting today—it did make me realize one thing. That now's not the right time to make my move with the Shoshana deal. Not till the department settles out—and the Y2K thing is finished. That's at least nine months away. And who the fuck knows—by then Craig's old-hat—and over-paid—so they may not even keep him around at all. And if they do keep him, he'll be on thin ice—and he'll be more likely to cooperate when I spring it."

"That's good thinking, mate. I agree completely. We should wait."

The two men finished their lunch and took a leisurely walk back to work. As soon as Nigel reached his office, he closed the door and called Justine. She wasn't home, but he left a message on the answering machine: "Good news, babe. We've got time. The big project's winding down—so Byron's gonna wait. No rush to do anything now. Huge relief."

• • •

Craig Schumacher flew into Washington, DC the evening before the conference started.

His intent was to avoid as much of it as practicable.

The conference, dealing with ramifications from Y2K-related technology upgrades, was a three-day affair, beginning on a Tuesday morning and concluding Thursday afternoon. Each day featured several large presentations in auditorium settings and various smaller breakout groups for interactive discussions.

As Craig fully expected, the few sessions he did attend were tedious affairs that went on far longer than they needed to. And worse, many were nothing more than thinly veiled sales and marketing efforts by consulting firms.

But he had noted, with annoyance, that there were a few people in attendance who knew him, and who might be happy to create trouble for him should the opportunity present itself. So, Craig was scrupulous to be seen about the venue, and even to join the potential scandalmongers for a lunch or two, to safeguard against anyone becoming suspicious of his absences.

Despite the burdensome nature of this meticulously orchestrated subterfuge, Craig still managed to spend bits of each morning, and almost all of every afternoon, away from the conference, wandering about the nation's capital, taking in the local attractions. He even managed to fulfill a lifelong dream and spend some time in the dinosaur halls of the Smithsonian Institution—exhibits he'd always wanted to compare with the fossils on display in New York's Museum of Natural History, which he'd loved visiting as a boy.

After lingering in the Smithsonian's dinosaur halls till almost five-thirty on Wednesday evening, he finally tore himself away and caught a cab to Carolyn's house.

When she greeted him at the door, they briefly embraced and kissed. He then followed her into the kitchen, where she had a couple of pots cooking on the stove. She stirred one a bit, checked the other, then turned back toward Craig. "Let me fetch you a soda water, love," she said. "And I'll pour myself a bit more chardonnay."

She replenished her wine and presented his club soda over ice in a tall glass, garnished with a lime wedge. They toasted.

"So, love," she said with a sly grin, "were you successful in evading every dreadful session of the conference today?"

He chuckled. "Well, not *every* session. As I told you last night, I'm trying to appear to be attending in good stead—in the eyes of the people there who know me, anyway."

"And I'm certain you're doing a smashing ninja job of it."

"Well, let's hope. There are some old adversaries there who'd love to make my life miserable if they had half a chance."

Carolyn set down her wine glass and walked closer to him. She stroked the lapels of his suit coat and arched her back just slightly to gaze upward into his eyes. The very tops of her breasts, fringed by the filigreed lacework of her red bra, became evident as her blouse collar spread.

"The last two nights were wonderful," she said. "Looking forward to more. I'm so glad you found an excuse to visit. It's astounding how well this is working—no?"

"Yes, it's been fantastic."

"Our lovemaking. It's the best I've had."

"For me too," he said.

Carolyn cupped his cheeks gently in her palms and drew him down. She rose onto her toes and kissed him passionately. She lowered herself and began to pull away, but before she did, she snatched at his fly and delivered an unnerving squeeze to the erection straining against the cloth of his suit-pants. She snickered as she backed off and retrieved her wine glass. "Got to check on the food, love," she purred as she returned to the stove.

He took a few steps toward the small kitchen table, turned one of the chairs so it faced her, and sat down. "Our lovemaking," he said, "when we're in the throes of it—it's all-consuming. I forget about pretty much everything else. I'm just in the moment."

"That's sweet, dear. I feel the same. I forget about absolutely everything." She turned her head to look at him—her voice grew soft and solemn. "And speaking of 'forgetting,' love—I've been meaning to ask—are you quite over the death of your rabbit? I know how awful that was for you." She glimpsed the stove for a moment and stirred the contents of one of the pots.

He spoke softly. "Not really. Not entirely." He paused. "I'm not sure I ever will be—not completely. I have a theory about this sort of thing. I liken it to Swiss cheese."

She spun around and gazed at him with a quizzical smile. "Swiss cheese, eh? I really must hear this."

"Through life—especially as we get older—we suffer losses. Sad, sad losses—of people—and—of beings we loved very much. Each loss leaves a hole in our hearts. Those holes never go away. So—as we get older—our hearts become like Swiss cheese. Full of holes—but now—so finely aged. The holes enable that. It's like the pain inherent in them imparts wisdom—and acceptance—as we go through the years."

"You're a dear, lovely man. Patient to a fault—but bloody sweet." She smiled warmly and returned part of her focus to the stove, while continuing to glance intermittently at him. "I wanted to say again, love, how truly sorry I am about your rabbit. I know she meant so much to you." She thought for a moment. "I *am* curious though—if you don't mind talking about it. How did she get the name Golda? It seems like an odd name for a rabbit."

"Actually, Shoshana named her that. 'Golda' was just the first part of it. Her full name was Golda My Hare. You know, a play on the name of the Israeli prime minister."

"Oh. How droll." She paused. "But, you know, love—hares and rabbits—they're different animals. So, the name really doesn't make sense."

"Shoshana was never big on such distinctions."

Carolyn put the spoon down and turned toward him fully. "Speaking of Shoshana—have you talked to her about us yet?"

"A little. I mentioned that I'm having sex with someone out here. You know—she thinks that's great. We're supposed to be in an open marriage—but mostly it's just open on *her* end—so she's always encouraging me to have other partners—sort of frees her up to do more of it herself without quite so much guilt, I suppose."

"So—do you *have* any other partners?"

"Hardly. Lately, none at all. It's not really what I'm into. I mean—I'm more comfortable being with *one* person—being completely fulfilled by that person. I think Shoshana realizes that you and I are getting more serious—but I didn't get into it explicitly."

"Why not?"

He flicked his tongue at his upper lip as he gazed at her. "Because I'm a bloody patient—bloody slow—bloody cautious, bloke." His laugh that ensued began as a muted chuckle but quickly grew loud and buoyant.

She chortled along with him, then spoke softly. "I can be patient for a while too, love. I know this is a big change for you—if you decide to do it."

"Carolyn—everything with us just gets better and better as we go. It's amazing for me. And the truth is—Shoshana and I haven't been sexually active together—not for a while anyway."

A soft smile curled her lips and crinkled her eyelids. "For us, it's the total package—isn't it, dear? I mean—we can talk—we can laugh—we can make wonderful love. It all seems so effortless—so natural."

"Yes. That's exactly it, Carolyn. The totality of the package.

That's what I've never had." He took a long swig of his club soda, then thought for a moment. "Look," he said, "I need to come clean with you. Like I told you—this is the best sex I've ever had—and I really *am* falling in love with you. But for me—it's different. I mean—well—it's a long and convoluted story. But I think you need to know."

"Know what exactly, love?"

"Okay, then . . . I'll lay it out, and hope we can make sense of it." He took a deep breath and exhaled slowly. He continued, hesitating between words as he spoke. "So, the thing is . . . I've always been into . . . well . . . BDSM. You know, bondage, pain—sadomasochism. Submission. I'm a submissive—or a bottom. Sexually, I mean. I assume you've at least heard a little about this sort of thing." He assessed her features—she appeared to him more intrigued than upset. That was a great relief. He was about to go on, but she started to speak.

"You know, love," she said, "I must confess—I suspected some sort of strangeness or deviance on your part—I don't know quite why—and I wasn't at all certain how it might manifest. So—here it is—now I know." She grinned broadly. "Do you realize, love, that British school teachers in prim and pretty dresses have been paddling young ill-mannered boys for ages—never realizing that the boys were turned on by it. Or at least that's what some maladjusted British lovers of mine have admitted to me. But I don't know much more about S-and-M than that. It seems to me a harmless bit of business though—I mean—if it provides some fun in the bedroom on occasion—and everyone's on board."

"For me, it's been more than that. It's been intrinsic to who I am. Shoshana's a professional dominatrix—that's how I met her."

"Really? You were a client?"

"She was the only pro I ever tried. It took me a long time to work up the gumption to do it. Before that, I just fantasized—tied myself up—imagined—daydreamed." He chuckled. "I have a pretty vivid imagination."

"So . . . do you miss it? With me, I mean? You don't seem to."

"That's the crazy thing about all this, Carolyn. I don't miss it at all. I wouldn't even *want* to do it with you. What we have is so real. It's so much a part of who we actually are. We don't need roleplaying or psychodrama."

"No, we certainly don't appear to. And it does seem like a bit of a bother—I mean—to fuss with ropes and such—when we can just jump each other's bones and be ecstatic—no?"

"I agree."

She cocked her head and retrieved a memory, her eyes peering momentarily upward and to the left. Then she looked back at him and spoke softly. "So—I think I see now what you were getting at, love—it was a while back—do you remember? I made some comment about men finding me too controlling—a bit of a bitch—and you said something about maybe it was why you were so turned on by me?"

"I remember."

"So—when you jump my bones—it's like the dominatrix is kind of built into the substrate?"

"Very well put. That's exactly it. But it's *real*. It's not play—not something that I have to separate from reality—not something that winds up splitting my life into arbitrary—you know—isolated—compartments."

She smiled and whispered, "I love you," then turned back to tend to the pots.

He got up from his chair and nuzzled behind her, caressing her gently and kissing her softly on the side of the neck.

"I'm cooking, love," she said with a snigger—the ring of her

London accent especially haughty. "You'll have to wait till later to jump my bones. You *can* control yourself till then, I trust."

He backed away a couple of steps and laughed. "Speaking of bones, I saw the dinosaurs at the Smithsonian today. Magnificent. You know, as a kid, I'd spend hours in Manhattan, at the Museum of Natural History. They had dinosaur skeletons there too. Not nearly as many. But still—a whole giant room full. God, it's been so many years. But today, at the Smithsonian, I got that same chill that I used to feel. You know, you're looking at bones that are sixty-five million years old—they even have some you can touch—and they're from these massive, incredible creatures that dominated the Earth. Now, though, when I look at them, there's another component—something nobody understood when I was a kid. They're not actually extinct—dinosaurs, I mean. They've evolved into birds. In a way, it's even more amazing. And stirring. It's like—in order to survive—they had to learn to fly. An absolutely impossible feat. Yet somehow, they accomplished it. I mean, it's true. But it's unbelievable. Just miraculous."

She turned and gazed at him. "I think we—all of us, love—are capable of incredible change—when it's what we really need."

• • •

The conference held its concluding session on Thursday, disbanding somewhat earlier in the afternoon to afford attendees ample time to catch their flights home.

Craig had arranged to defer returning to California till Friday and spent the latter part of Thursday afternoon conferring with key leaders in the company's regional office—culminating conveniently in an extended meeting with Carolyn and her boss Rick—which dragged on until Rick begged off, fearing his wife's wrath for being late for dinner. The result was the precise outcome Craig and Carolyn had schemed—an empty office from which the two could depart together without engendering sordid speculation.

Carolyn cooked dinner while Craig made some calls back to team members in the San Francisco office—the time-zone differential enabled him to snag his targets before their workday ended.

The two shared a lovely dinner, sitting side by side on the living room couch, plates laid out on the coffee table in front of them. The meal was interspersed with impromptu breaks for caressing, kissing, and fervent pawing—each hiatus initiated by Carolyn slamming her fork down on her plate and shouting, "Snogging time!" Her British intonation seemed to Craig especially pronounced during these vocal ejaculations—he found the imperious resonance to be viscerally arousing.

When they were done eating, she edged over so that their bodies touched. She laid her head on his shoulder and rested her hand on his thigh.

"So, love, I've cooked you three meals since you've been here. Have you enjoyed them?"

"Oh yes. And I believe I've told you—every night, in fact—just how wonderful they were."

"Tell me again."

He chuckled. "They've all been absolutely delicious. You're an extraordinarily gifted chef. Every bite was scrumptious."

"I was very careful to avoid all those nasty buggers you mentioned—you know, chicken stock, Worcestershire, anchovies, and such—so you can rest assured that despite how bloody annoying you are—with your seemingly endless stack of self-imposed restrictions—I made certain that your carefully guarded inner temple is still pristine."

He laughed. "Ooh! That hurts—but the result is very much appreciated. When I trust the cook, I can just relax and eat—and not worry about anything. It's so nice."

"Did you notice how I took English specialties and substituted for the meat—you know, with mushrooms, and aubergines, and such—and then additional cheese and eggs—so I gave you all the yumminess of traditional British fare—without disrupting your so-carefully-guarded spiritual purity?"

He laughed again. "Despite your relentless sarcasm, you're taking superb care of my mystical inner sanctum. And I thank you."

"I'm especially proud of what I did with the shepherd's pie—and also the Cornish pasty. Those two are always made with meat—back in the UK, I mean. And they came out delish. Now, the dairy tart I made *last* night—that's pretty traditionally just goat cheese, eggs, and cream—and perhaps some olives and figs—so I didn't need to massage that one much."

"You know, Carolyn . . . " he spoke slowly, measuring his words. "We've talked about the possibility of my moving in here with you . . . at some point . . . and if I were to do that . . . well . . . I think you'd need to make some small adjustments to what you're cooking."

She lifted her head and looked at him. "Adjustments?"

"I mean—I realize that this was a *visit*. And by definition, a sort of special occasion. So, the very rich kinds of food you prepared were apropos. And very, very delectable. You're a great cook. But, you know—on a regular basis—I can't eat such rich food. I mean—the amounts of cream, and butter, and cheese, and eggs—they're astronomical. That wouldn't be sustainable for me—you know—every night. Left to my own devices, I focus mostly on vegetables, whole grains, legumes, nuts—some fruit—very small amounts of dairy. And very occasionally an egg. On a daily basis, I mean."

She emitted a ferocious snort and violently jerked away from him on the couch. Her eyebrows shot downward atop angry eyes, and her jaw jutted forward. She stared at him a moment and took a frantic inhalation, before raising her voice.

"What in bloody hell? You're suddenly complaining about my cooking? What a goddamn shithead you are! First you go on and on about how delicious it is, just to tell me you don't want to eat it anymore? You're a rude fucking ingrate! I worked my bloody ass off on those dishes—I did it for *you*—to show you I love you—and now you throw *this* at me? I really can't believe you're saying all this."

"No, no. You're misinterpreting. These dishes are wonderful—for special occasions—and I look forward to wallowing in them—again. It's just—they're not sustainable for healthy, daily, consumption. For you *or* for me! I *know* you can cook lighter vegetarian food. You're absolutely capable of it. You're a *fantastic* cook. You have incredible skills. You'll be a master at it. You just don't have the confidence because you haven't done it."

"Oh, cut the crap with all the damn flattery. You're trying to bloody manipulate me. Maybe you can play the people on your teams at work—but you can't play *me*—not about *this*—not here in *my* bloody kitchen. This is how *I* cook! I've gone out of my way trying to convert dishes to vegetarian—because I'm trying to please you—and now I get this?"

She shoved him away from her as she rose from the couch.

"Jesus!" she cried. "You're a rude fucking ass. You can sleep in the guest room tonight. I'm bloody-well done with you!"

With that, she stormed into the main bedroom, slamming the door behind her.

Craig sat motionless on the couch for a few moments, staring at the spot in the hallway where she'd disappeared from view. His lips parted and spread into an awkward, confused grimace—his teeth clenched hard. *Well*, he thought, *that didn't go exactly as planned.*

He considered knocking on the bedroom door and trying to talk it out, but it seemed to him that doing so had a far greater likelihood of inflaming the situation, as opposed to calming it. Instead, he cleared the coffee table and carried the plates and glasses to the kitchen sink, where he methodically washed and then loaded each one gently into the dish rack—endeavoring to clear his thoughts—hoping that a serene mindset might coax his intuition to emerge and guide him as to what action he should take.But even after finishing the dishes and standing motionless for an extended time at the sink, it still seemed to him that patience and inaction were the only viable alternatives. He wanted desperately to go to her, to seek some sort of reconciliation—but that urge was emotionally charged. He knew that approaching her prematurely could make matters worse—and he knew instinctively it was not yet time. So, he dejectedly made his way into the guest room, rummaged through his carry-on bag until he found the book he'd brought with him on the plane, and sat down on the edge of the bed to read.

He had inattentively scanned only a couple of pages when Carolyn walked through the open door. She stopped a few feet from where he sat.

"So sorry, love," she said haltingly, her eyes and mouth seeming to stretch toward him in supplication. She took a step nearer. "Please forgive me. I should never have jumped on you like that. And I said really nasty things that I didn't mean. Can you ever forgive me?"

He put the book down. "Of course I forgive you."

She sat down beside him on the bed, and leaned gently against his side. "Thank god you're such a bloody patient—and truly kind—soul. Not many men would put up with a shirty tirade like that. I suppose it comes along with being a bitch—which you say turns you on—but probably not so much after a disgraceful display like that." She wiped away a tear with her finger. "The thing is, love, you caught me off guard. But now—I guess I've had some time to think about what you said—you know—get some distance from it—and from all that anger. But you know—when you said it—it seemed to me like—well—like you were challenging something that's such an important part of my identity. Everyone I know tells me I'm a great cook. But I'm a great cook because everything is full of meat, and cream, and cheese, and eggs, and salt. Because they're bloody delicious ingredients. I depend on them. I always have. I have to tell you, love—I honestly don't know if I can cook the way you ask and make it any good. And then you're taking away from me one of the few things that I'm really exceptional at."

He put his hand on her shoulder and pulled her tighter against him. She leaned her head upon his shoulder.

"Carolyn—I think you're exceptional at a *lot* of things. That's the truth. Believe me, I'm not trying to manipulate you with praise. Everything I've said—it's just the way it is. And among the things you're exceptional at—you're a great chef. That's irrefutable. *You* know it, and *I* know it. And, something else I know is that people cook fantastic, healthy, vegetarian food. I've tasted it in restaurants. I've seen people cook it on television. Read about it in lots of vegetarian cookbooks. You are such a gifted chef. Just as gifted—probably far *more* gifted—than lots of these people I've seen and read about. So, I *know* you can do it. Will there be a learning curve? Sure. But I have absolutely no doubt you can become one of the best healthy-vegetarian chefs around—if you really want to do it. The only thing holding you back is fear."

"All right. If you believe in me, I'll try it. This is your last night here for a while, so I'll have lots of time to practice. Send me recipes if you have them. I'll buy some cookbooks and try to find some of those cooking shows on the telly that you talked about. Why do I have no bloody doubt they're on the public network?"

He smiled. "Thank you, Carolyn. I really appreciate it. And, if you hit a snag—try to think about it the way the Italians look at cooking. If you get really good ingredients, you know, fresh vegetables, things in season, and you let them shine—kind of treat them minimally and with respect—it's pretty difficult to really fuck it up."

"Oh, I'm sure people find ways . . ."

He chuckled. "Not you. And listen—if you like, when I come out the next time—we can cook *together* too. I'll be your obedient and infatuated sous chef."

She laughed softly. "You've been so sweet. Thank you." She kissed him on the cheek and sat up straight. Turning to him with a smirk, her voice resumed its more confident, smug demeanor. "Enough chitchat, love. Get your hot ass back into my bedroom. You need to fuck the living daylights out of me—and more than once. For god's sake, it's our last bloody night together for a while!"

22

SARNIES

JUSTINE SILVER CONSIDERED THE SMALL GOURMET market in downtown San Rafael absurdly overpriced. It was just a five-minute drive from her home, but she rarely visited. Every now and then, however, if the occasion seemed to call for it, she'd make a quick stop. Whenever she did, she'd find herself hopelessly immersed in its sumptuous ambiance—everything impeccably displayed—the aromas of the obscure fruits and vegetables, and the finely aged cheeses, irresistibly enticing.

The fact that she had driven over there this Saturday afternoon, however, was prompted far more by spite than by any purely epicurean pursuit.

Now that the big Y2K project was winding down, Nigel's work-related travel had dwindled to nearly nothing. Justine was relieved to be spending evenings at home with her husband—and even more relieved that he was fraternizing far less, in distant cities, with that creepy wretch Byron Dorn.

But she hadn't yet been able to wean him away from his weekend winery sojourns with Byron, which she felt stripped huge chunks out of almost every one of their Saturdays or Sundays. Nigel insisted it afforded him a way to monitor Byron and protect them against any negative repercussions from the secret surveillance. But increasingly, Justine was dubious. She was convinced that more and more, it was just a convenient excuse for early day-drinking and for decadent "bro-time."

And she felt neglected.

So, while stewing in the house over Nigel's being gone yet again—this time tooling around Sonoma wineries with Byron since mid-morning—she'd hatched a delectable plan for sandwich-based revenge. Her plot had at its heart what she'd always known as British tea sandwiches—though Nigel insisted that no one in Great Britain ever called them that. He referred to them as cucumber sarnies. He'd explained that they were too posh for tea where he'd grown up in Leeds—but he'd become addicted to them when he'd spent time in London.

What Justine was sure of, though, was that whenever she put out a platter of cucumber sarnies, Nigel devoured them ravenously.

She arrived at the gourmet market in the early afternoon. She stayed only long enough to purchase a loaf of incredibly fresh white sandwich bread, two crisp organic English cucumbers, a perfectly ripe lemon, a small block of locally sourced cream cheese, and a diminutive crock of the shop's homemade mayonnaise.

Back at home, she made a quick stop in her backyard herb garden to snip sprigs of dill and chives. In the kitchen she washed and dried the herbs and chopped them finely. Into a stainless-steel bowl, she then added the cream cheese, mayonnaise, dill, chives, and a squeeze of lemon juice. She sprinkled just a touch of garlic powder, kosher salt, and freshly cracked black pepper over top, before whisking it all into a succulent spread. She sliced the bread and the organic English cucumbers, and apportioned out exactly enough for an overindulgent lunch—for one. Satisfied now, she hacked off the crusts and sliced the sandwiches into small dainty squares.

Then, she retrieved from the refrigerator the bottle of fine champagne she'd put in to chill just prior to visiting the shop. Her features crinkled into a contented smirk as she extracted the cork and poured. She watched with a grin as the bubbles erupted to nearly the top of the delicate crystal flute, then quieted and settled back down. With serene focus, she patiently splashed a few more iterations into the glass, to raise the level nearly to the top.

It was three in the afternoon when she sat down to eat.

Nigel had promised to be home from Sonoma at four.

She hoped to time it such that when Nigel arrived, he'd find her sipping on the last drops of champagne. There would be an empty platter on the table, and directly in front of her a plate containing the barest remnants of his beloved cucumber sarnies—dregs just sufficient to be recognizable as to what they once had been—but with nothing substantial enough left for him to enjoy even a morsel.

And she planned a long, enthusiastic dissertation regarding the awesome quality and freshness of the ingredients, all procured from the San Rafael gourmet market.

• • •

The unassuming winery sat just off a narrow road traversing two tranquil grape-growing regions in upper Sonoma County—Russian River Valley to the south and Dry Creek Valley to the north.

The banana-yellow Lotus pulled into the small gravel lot alongside the tasting room, and squeezed in among the three cars already parked there.

Nigel Silver and Byron Dorn had just exited the Lotus when the huge, slow-moving dog that patrolled the winery's grounds nuzzled up to greet them. This initiated a familiar litany of obliging rituals prior to their stepping into the tasting room. First, they lavished rubs and scratches on the slothful, long-haired dog. Then they made a quick stop in the lavatory. Finally, they spent a few minutes gazing through the wire fencing that enclosed the enormous chicken coop, replete with its array of multi-hued hens and their rows of white, brown, and speckled eggs.

Once inside the nicely appointed tasting hut, they sampled the array of whites and reds being offered, and shared brief updates with the likable fellow who always manned the pouring station on Saturdays. They purchased a few wines to take home and also selected a bottle of Petite Sirah, redolent with hints of black pepper and chocolate, to enjoy with their picnic lunch.

After settling the bill and packing the wines for home in the trunk of the Lotus, they walked up to one of the remote picnic tables nestled among the tall trees on the top of the hill above the tasting room. They carried with them the opened bottle of Petite Sirah, two clean glasses, and the bag of sandwiches and chips they'd purchased at the small grocery just down the road.

They sat down beside each other on the wooden bench. When they peered out over the picnic table, the expanse of neatly tended vineyards appeared to stretch for miles, with endless bunches of grapes sparkling in the late morning sun.

"Lovely view," Nigel said.

"Yeah, it is."

"I promised Justine I'd be home by four," Nigel said as he rolled open the top of the large paper bag, pulled out the two wrapped sandwiches and the bags of chips, and set them onto the wooden table.

Byron stood for a moment, to more carefully wield the full bottle of Petite Sirah, as he began to fill the two glasses. "Yeah, I told Adelle I'd be home by five," he said, "and I'm an hour south of you—so—same thing. No sweat, bro. We can hit two or three more wineries after lunch—easy—and be home before the wives get apoplectic."

Nigel chuckled. "You know, mate, Justine and Adelle are rather different, when it comes to most things. But their internal clocks—you know, for getting their knickers in a twist when their husbands are out—are synchronized quite precisely."

Byron laughed loudly and his shoulders heaved, causing the bottle to jiggle as he poured. A few drops of the dark wine dribbled down the outside of one of the glasses. "Shit!" he muttered with a sardonic grin. "Don't want to waste any of the good stuff."

"I think we're fine, mate."

"So—I hit my number to avoid any layoffs," Byron said as he sat down. "And there's still two months to go. I guess you were right. It wasn't really that big a deal. Did ya hit your number yet?"

"Just yesterday, in fact."

Byron raised his glass, and the men toasted and sipped. "Good wine," Byron said as he began to unwrap his sandwich. "Well, I guess even though Schumacher's still an asshole about all kinds of other things, he was probably right about this. When layoffs get announced and our team doesn't have any—the staff will feel good about it."

"I reckon so. Like you said, that's two months away. Are you still planning on waiting—I mean, to act on the Shoshana video stuff—you know, till everything settles out?"

"Yeah. I suppose that's the smart thing to do. Who the hell knows what's gonna happen then? Better to wait and test out the waters."

"Good thinking, mate. By the way, have you been able to

garner any more information from the video footage? You know, figure out how many women work with Shoshana? Maybe identify any of them?"

"Nah. I really haven't watched it that much. And frankly, I don't give a shit about the other girls. They may be a bunch of pervert whores, but I'm just doin' this to have somethin' to hold over Schumacher. The other girls don't matter to me."

Nigel smiled. "Makes perfect sense, mate. I couldn't agree more."

"Sandwiches look good, bro. I'm starved."

The two men tore into their food, washing down hastily chewed mouthfuls with enthusiastic gulps of wine.

But, as he chewed a particularly large chunk of sandwich, Byron's body suddenly seized. He expectorated bits of food and wine onto the table in front of him, and began hyperventilating.

Nigel slapped Byron between the shoulder blades a couple of times to help clear his airway. "What's wrong, mate? Are you all right?"

"Jesus!" Byron wheezed, still breathing hard. He forced his words out, interrupted by frequent, aborted rasps. "I'm having—one of my—bad memories. They come—sometimes—like an attack. But always—when I'm alone. I can't believe it's—happening—when I'm here with you."

"Well, just calm down. Relax. Tell me about it. It'll help if you talk about it."

"Jesus! I—can't."

"Sure you can, mate. Just tell me."

Byron's breathing slowed slightly. His facial muscles and upper body appeared to unclench just a bit. "Okay. For this one—I was—maybe twelve—thirteen. I got sent away to summer camp—for five weeks. There was this girl there—Wendy Klassen—I kinda liked her, you know. But she was totally into theater shit. She was part of this group—they were putting on a musical—you know—rehearsing all the fuckin' time—gonna perform it the last night we were there. I could barely find a chance to see her—with all the rehearsals. But finally, there was a little time. I made my move—we got kinda tight—you know, makin' out—the way kids do—standin' up—clothes on—leanin' against a wall or somethin'. I kinda don't know how I managed it—I was really shy—but somehow, I worked up the courage, and did it."

Byron smiled for a moment, but then his face abruptly tensed up again. He grimaced and gritted his teeth.

"Calm down, mate. Just tell me the story."

"Yeah. Thanks." He took a deep breath. "Okay—I'm all right now. Anyway—I'm walkin' with her one night—from the mess hall where we had dinner—I'm walkin' her back to the girls' bunks. I wanna stop and sneak behind some tree and make out—but she's goin' on and on about this midget kid . . ."

"Midget kid? I think you're supposed to call them little people, mate."

"Whatever. Back then we called 'em midgets. And this story happened back then." Bryon relaxed a bit and took a long breath. "Anyway, the camp was doin' this musical—I'll never forget—*Finian's Rainbow*—because it has a big part for a leprechaun, and this midget kid was playin' the fuckin' leprechaun. So, Wendy's goin' on and on about how talented this midget kid is—singin', dancin', actin'—won't shut the fuck up about how talented he is."

Byron was calmer now. He reached for his wine glass and took a large gulp.

"You think it's wise to drink that now, mate?"

"I'm good. You were right. Talkin' about it is good. I've never come down from it this fast." He chugged his glass and poured himself another.

"So, mate, finish the story."

"Oh. Yeah. So—I was gettin' sick and tired of just hearing about this midget kid and how talented he was. So, I start tellin' Wendy that I write songs—set poems to music—you know—tellin' her that *I'm* talented too. Maybe, even more talented than him."

Nigel chuckled. "You wanted her to stop yakking about the *little* person, and make out with *you*."

Byron laughed. "Kinda. Yeah. I just wanted her to see that I had talent too. You know what I'm sayin'. But it all went bad. She got totally pissed. Started screamin' that the midget kid had more talent in his little finger than I'll ever have in my whole life. I remember—she said those exact words—*more talent in his little finger than I'll ever have in my whole life.* That really hurt, bro. Then she pulled herself away from me—you know, we'd been walkin' together back to the bunks—and I had my arm around her—and she just rips it away and storms off—screamin' that I should never talk to her again—never even look at her again. Jesus—I was just tryin' to tell her I wrote songs."

"Well, that was a long time ago. You seem better now, mate. Good to talk these things out."

"Yeah. Thanks, bro. I appreciate it."

Byron downed what was left in his glass and took a huge bite of his sandwich. As he chewed it, he reached for the bottle and began to pour himself another round.

Nigel watched for a moment as the wine swirled from the bottle into Byron's glass. Then his gaze wandered out to the noiseless acres of vineyards with their sparkling grapes.

But an instant later Nigel's reverie was shattered by a loud crash. He looked back to the table. The wine bottle had fallen from Byron's hand and smashed both glasses. Wine coursed upon the table's surface. Shards of broken glass were everywhere.

Nigel's first impulse was to thrust his hands out to try to corral the mess, but just as he did, he heard an eerie squeal beside him. When he spun his head, he saw Byron seizing violently.

Nigel's jaw slackened. He watched as Byron lurched upright, his body quivering, his face burning red. Frantic croaks eked from Byron's throat. Now, Byron stiffened, his face contorted in agony, and he slapped both his hands over his chest.

"Oh fuck!" Byron gasped in a barely discernible whisper. "I think it's my heart!"

Byron's rigid frame suddenly crumpled. His eyelids lowered, and his head and upper body slumped forward until they rested motionless upon the wooden table.

Nigel leaped up. He jerked Byron around and laid him down on the hard wooden bench. As Byron lay immobile on his back, Nigel felt his friend's neck for a pulse and pressed his ear against Byron's chest to check for a heartbeat.

Without hesitation, Nigel straddled Byron where he lay, centered his hands on Byron's chest, positioned his shoulders so they were directly over his hands, locked his elbows, and began chest compressions, counting aloud for each one, until he reached thirty.

"Two breaths now," Nigel whispered to himself.

He tilted Byron's head back, pinched his nose shut, and then took a breath. He immediately lowered his head, sealed his lips over Byron's, and exhaled. He glanced over to make certain Byron's chest rose.

It did.

He repeated with another breath.

Without pause, Nigel rose and initiated another set of chest compressions. But this time, as he administered them, instead of counting, he screamed as loud as he could. "Help! Help!

Goddamnit, I need help! Help me!"

But even as he yelled, he wondered who could possibly hear him from where they were, isolated, on top of the hill.

When it seemed to him that he had administered about thirty chest compressions, he dipped down and dispensed two more breaths.

As he pulled himself up for another set of chest compressions, he was astounded to see the enormous, long-haired dog who'd greeted them running up the hill. The dog stopped a few feet from where Nigel stood.

"Good boy! Good boy. Get help! Go get help!"

The dog raced off. "Jesus," Nigel whispered. "I didn't think that dog could run."

He started chest compressions, again, counting with each one.

Just as he finished the set of compressions, the friendly fellow who poured wine there every Saturday appeared, the dog at his side. The man seemed out of breath, but as soon as he saw what was happening, he said, "Oh god! I'll call the paramedics. The fire station is just down the road. They should be here fast. Hang in!"

Nigel dispensed two more breaths as the man and dog dashed back down the hill.

The man was true to his word. Just a few minutes later, Nigel heard the ambulance's siren growing louder as it approached.

• • •

Much to Justine's surprise, Nigel stormed through their front door at five minutes after three, nearly an hour earlier than she expected him. She had taken just a few sips of champagne, and only the very first nibbles of her perfectly composed cucumber sarnies.

She sighed in frustration upon seeing him. Nigel was *never* early coming home from these winery romps with Byron. Of course he'd choose today to do it—just to thwart her exquisitely imagined scheme of culinary vengeance.

But then she noticed how agitated he was. His clothes were disheveled, and he was breathing heavily.

"Oh my god, what's the matter?" She leapt up and moved toward him. "I expected you to be late—and you're early. You're—like—*never* early. Are you okay?"

Nigel gazed at her for a moment before he spoke. His eyes were stretched open wider than she'd ever seen them, and his mouth formed a crazed, paralytic chasm.

"Holy fuck!" he finally screamed. "Byron had a heart attack!"

"What? What did you just say?"

"Byron fucking Dorn. He had a goddamn heart attack."

"Oh my god!" she howled. "You killed him?"

"What?"

"Goddamn you!" Her voice was frantic now. "You said you wouldn't do it. You swore to me. And now you went ahead and did it. What the fuck is the matter with you? You killed a man! Now what the hell are we going to do?"

"He's not dead," Nigel said, in a confused, hoarse screech. "He's alive."

"He's alive? That's even worse! Now they'll figure out for sure that you tried to kill him. You fucking bastard!" She stepped closer and slapped him viciously on his chest, just below his neck.

"I didn't kill him. I didn't even *try* to kill him. I saved him."

"What do you mean you didn't try to kill him? You mean he just suddenly had a heart attack—like on his own—after you talked about giving him some secret poison to bring one on? You expect me to believe that?"

"Babe, he's a fucking overweight alcoholic who hasn't

exercised since Neville Chamberlain was prime minister. And he eats more meat in a day than you eat in six months. Damn right he had a heart attack. And I saved his bloody life. He's in the fucking emergency room. Right now. Up in Sonoma. Adelle rushed up there to be with him."

"And *you* saved his life?"

"I bloody did."

"How?"

"With CPR."

"You know CPR?"

"Oh yeah, babe. You should have seen me. I was like bloody Superman. I saved the bloke's fucking life!"

"Since when do *you* know CPR?"

"I took a class—years ago, when I first got to the States—things were kind of slow—I thought it might be an interesting way to meet women."

Justine just stared at him. Her mouth was agape—her lower jaw dangled loosely—and her head tilted to an angle suggesting a mind-state wedged between bewilderment and incredulity.

"You can call the hospital," Nigel said, "and confirm what I'm saying to you. They'll tell you that I saved Byron's life. The doctors and nurses said I was a bloody hero."

Justine swallowed hard and thought a moment. "All right," she said hesitantly. "I guess I'm convinced." She paused and then smirked. "Only *you* would fess up to having such a moronic reason for learning CPR."

He chuckled. "It actually worked. A tad, anyway. I met a couple of very pretty lasses. Didn't go anywhere—but we had a hell of a crack practicing breathing into each other's mouths."

Justine sighed. "Oh my god—you're grody to the max."

"I knew you saw *something* in me—way back when."

She realized that he was eyeing the sandwiches and the

champagne. "Well," she said, her voice displaying just the slightest hint of reluctance, "I guess if you're a bona fide hero, I should let you share these sarnies with me."

"I thought you'd never ask." He laughed and sat down.

"I'll get you a plate. Oh, and here . . ." she slid her champagne flute over to him. "You can start on that. I'll pour myself another glass."

Soon they were seated across from each other, munching on sandwiches and sipping champagne.

"These sarnies are choice!" he said, voraciously popping the delicate squares into his mouth.Justine grabbed a few more sandwich pieces and put them on her plate to protect them from his frenetic onslaught. She had no doubt he'd gobble up the rest before long.

He talked while he stuffed more squares into his mouth. "It was a right kerfuffle, babe. First, up at the winery when the paramedics finally got there. Then they put him in an ambulance. I told them I'd follow in my Lotus. Then—inside the hospital—the nurses and doctors—all telling me I saved my friend's life. I called Adelle, and she got up there pretty fast. Thanked me—she was bloody hysterical—but *very* grateful. And then she went in to be with him. And I came back home."

"Oh my god, isn't it weird? It wasn't that long ago—you said you wanted to kill him."

He chuckled. "Well, you talked me out of *that* pretty quick. But, you know—before all the drama happened—I probed. Without him realizing, of course. About the videotape—and Craig—and all that. It's interesting. Byron said he didn't care about the other women. He said it, flat out. He wasn't even looking at them. So, we were home free anyway."

She took a long swallow of champagne, then put down her glass. "And if he'd said that he recognized me? Would you still have saved his life?"

Nigel pondered a moment. "Good question, babe. I hadn't thought about that."

"Well, would you?

A sly grin slowly materialized on Nigel's face. "Does anybody really know what they'd do if something totally unexpected happened? You know, reacting in the spur of the moment? All that adrenaline flowing through your blood—who actually knows what they'd do?"

"Oh my god, you really won't say, will you?"

"Well, I'd like to think I'd do the right thing."

"So—then—you'd save him?"

Nigel chuckled. "If that was the right thing."

"Jesus, Nigel!"

"How about some more fizz?" he asked with a broad smile.

She reached for the champagne. "I'll pour us *both* some more. After this conversation I'm sure as hell going to need it."

23

EGGPLANT CAPONATA

IN THE BAR AREA OF A WELL-APPOINTED RESTAURANT in the Logan Square neighborhood of Chicago, Craig Schumacher and Carolyn Winthrop shared a small, cushioned booth. Carolyn sipped on a cosmopolitan, while Craig nursed a club soda, garnished with a lime wedge.

They were chuckling.

"Bloody clever of you, love," Carolyn said, "conjuring up the need for both of us to attend this useless seminar in Chicago. Jesus! What's the precise name of it? 'How to wind down a large Y2K project' or some such nonsense? Shutting down is the easy part. And it's pretty bloody obvious how to go about it."

"Senior management was happy that I'd decided to attend—without being forced or coerced." Craig laughed. "Anyway, it really can't do any harm. Everything's winding down now. Nobody will miss us if we're away for a few days."

"And how goes your ninja plan to avoid layoffs?"

"We're done!" he said with a broad smile. "Every one of my

teams hit their number. We won't have to lay off a soul."

Carolyn took a small swallow of her cosmopolitan. "Bravo. Did it go smoothly, love?"

"Pretty much went perfectly." He pondered for a moment—and after a hesitant gulp of club soda, he reassessed. "Well, except for this one incident. I'm still bothered by it. Do you remember Hashim Hayat?"

"Oh, yes! Nice fellow—quite brilliant—Pakistani, as I recall, no?"

"Right. When you were in San Francisco, I'm sure you remember old Cliff Stanley—heavy-set fellow—he still manages my utilities team—you know—the guys who write all the little peripheral programs that kind of hold everything together? Well, Cliff is a very skilled and experienced manager—but that team has to write code in every conceivable language—and Cliff's not technically up to supervising that. So, Hashim Hayat's been basically running the technical side of that team since day one."

"And Hashim's a contractor, no?"

"Exactly. And a really good man. I didn't want to lose him. So, before anything was announced about hiring freezes, I called Hashim into my office. I told him that I can't say anything official, but at some point as the Y2K project winds down, there's sure to be a hiring freeze and termination of contractor positions. So, I offered him a full-time position—as an employee—to protect him."

"And he said no?"

"He said no. I told him that he's higher-level than any of the other contractors—you know, essentially a manager—that it might be hard for him to find a new gig at that level. And I said that he fit in so well here—did great work—was very well-liked by everyone."

"I'm sure he didn't want to take the pay cut," she said. "Independent contractors at that level earn a very high hourly wage. And they keep it all—they don't share it with an agency or a firm."

"Yes, but with no benefits. No health insurance. No safety net. I don't know. Maybe he just didn't believe me. Thought I was trying to snow him into making less money."

"Do you think there was a personal trust issue, love? You know, him being a Muslim—and you a Jew?"

"No. I'm sure it wasn't that. Hashim and I have talked like friends many times. He must have just thought it was a corporate ploy. I practically begged him. I told him once the freeze is announced I wouldn't be able to help him. But he wouldn't budge."

"So, I guess when the freeze was announced, his contract ended, and he was gone?"

"Yes. But that's not what haunts me." Craig took a long breath and shook his head sadly. "Hashim came back to visit me in my office—oh, about a month and a half later. He said he couldn't find anything—pleaded with me to hire him. And I couldn't. You know—the freeze was in place—no exceptions. And you know—Hashim's a middle-aged guy—he has a wife and kids. So, not finding work was really hard on his family. He said, 'Can't you sneak me in somehow? As a personal favor?' I said I wish I could but I can't. I said I'd help him with references—to find a job somewhere else—but that was all I could do. And then . . ." Craig paused and took another long swallow of club soda. "I said—you know—I told you this was coming. I offered you a position when it was possible."

"And what did he say?"

"He just bowed his head—sad—mortified, actually—and he said, 'I know—I know.' And I asked him—why didn't you believe me? And he just bowed his head even lower, and said it again, 'I know—I know.' You got to picture this, Carolyn. Hashim's a big, imposing man. Maybe, six-one—surely over two hundred pounds. Receding hairline. Going gray a little. Just standing there—almost crying. 'I know—I know.' It was heart-wrenching."

Carolyn took a slow, pensive swig of her cosmopolitan. She put her glass down and gazed at Craig with an adoring smile. "You're such a sweet man. So compassionate. I don't think there's another vice president on the planet who'd choose that as the one story he'd tell—when asked about downsizing a large department. Or even care about someone like Hashim."

"Thank you," Craig said softly.

She reached across the small table and put her hand on top of his. "Enough about work, love. So, tell me. Have you talked to Shoshana? About us—about your moving out here?"

"I've been doing it in dribs and drabs."

"Dribs and drabs? Why is that?"

"She pretty much had it figured out—and early on. She knows exactly what's happening."

"Oh? And, how is she handling it?"

"It's interesting. On one hand she seems sort of reconciled to the separation. But I think there's a part of her—it's somehow—I don't know—maybe as if she's still trying to hold on to a piece of me. She keeps hitting me with this argument—you know—ostensibly looking out for *my* welfare. That you and I are unsustainable—because I'm wired for BDSM—and it's impossible to change that—any more than someone can change being gay or trans. And—how I'm eventually going to miss it—and I'll resent *you* for my not having it."

"And do you believe that?"

"No."

"No? Not at all?"

"Look, I'm always going to have fantasies. I know that. But what does that really mean? I've had fantasies my entire life. And what I've found is—they're actually more than sufficient."

"More than sufficient?"

"It's funny, Carolyn. I used to think they were like a poor-man's substitute for the real thing." He chuckled. "But it turns out, the 'real thing' is just a fantasy too. Only it's played out with other people. And when you play it out with other people—well, then two things always happen. First, because you're really doing it—the things you're doing—by necessity—they become less intense. I mean in terms of pain and subjugation, you know, because the fantasies can be extreme. But if you really played them out, they'd be unbearable—untenable. And then, there's also all the time and energy you put into it—with the costumes, and toys, and arranging the logistics. It's a lot. And, when it's all done, you actually don't have anything lasting to show for it. Really. Nothing." He gazed into her eyes and smiled. "The way you put it once—months ago when we were talking. For me that's what's key here—that the dominatrix is in *your* substrate. And it is. And it's all I need. Because it's real."

She flashed a wicked grin and her face suffused with a fierce reddish sheen. She downed what was left in her glass and leaned toward him. "You know, love," she whispered, "it's far too early to eat. Let's have a late dinner tonight. Because—right now—you're going to take me back to my room—where you'll jolly well jump my bones."

• • •

Adelle Dorn answered the door and greeted Nigel with a cursory hug. She led him into the living room, where Byron was reclining on a leather chair, with a plaid woolen blanket covering his legs and lower body.

"How are you doing, mate?" Nigel asked.

Byron lifted his head a bit. His words seeped out in a strained murmur. "Hey bro. Nice to see you. I'm gettin' by—you know—a little better every day." He shifted slightly in the chair, to address Nigel more directly. "But hey, bro—I gotta thank you again—you saved my fuckin' life, man. I owe ya, big."

"It was nowt, mate. Any friend would have done the same."

"Not many people know CPR," Adelle said, with her customarily shrill inflection. "You're special that way, and we'll always love you for what you did."

Nigel glanced at Adelle. "Thank you," he said with a warm smile, "that's very kind." He turned back to Byron. "So, mate, will you be coming back to work?"

"Hell, no!" Byron said, with the slightest hint of a croaking chuckle.

"We're moving back to Tampa," Adelle said. "The truth is—we never belonged out here in Northern California—all these uppity left-wing crazies—we've had enough."

"That's right," Byron said. "And I'm goin' on disability. Probably stay on it till I qualify for Social Security."

"Sound!" Nigel said.

"You know," Byron added, "Adelle has a cousin back in Tampa. Me and him, for years now, we talked about buyin' into some little Italian place. You know—pizza, pasta, salads—some wine. He'll do the heavy lifting. But I'll hang around. Supervise the cooks. Take a cut—in cash—you know—to hide it from the IRS." He smirked. "Gotta keep my disability."

"What are the doctors telling you?"

"Oh, that I should be okay if I take it easy. They got me on meds."

Adelle's tone grew more pressing. "They told him he needs to change his eating and drinking habits. And walk every day."

"Are you going to do that, mate?"

"Well—I suppose I ought to eat a little less. Maybe, when we get to Tampa, we can get ourselves a dog—you know—a small one. I'll take her for a walk now and then."

"You going to cut down on the drinking?"

Byron laughed. "Nah!"

Adelle scowled. "We'll see about that," she whispered.

"Well, I wish you all the best, mate," Nigel said. "We'll keep in touch."

"Yeah, sounds good." He paused a moment. "Hey, bro—you want the recorder and the videotape—you know—the Shoshana brothel stuff? I sure as hell don't need it now. But who knows? Maybe you could pull off somethin' with it."

Nigel consciously tightened his features to keep from signaling the relief he felt. "Sure, mate. I'll take them. I'll probably never use them—but who knows." He laughed. "You know, someday, maybe twenty years from now, Justine will force me to clean out the garage—and I'll probably find them on some shelf—covered in dust—eroded past any deciphering. And I'll toss them out with all the other junk I find. But they'll conjure up some fond memories." He flashed a sly grin. "Anyway, as you said, mate, you'll certainly have no use for them in Tampa—puttering about in your Italian café."

Byron looked down. His hoarse whisper grew uncharacteristically reflective. "Actually, bro, all this got me thinkin'. If I really did the kinda thing I was plannin'—you know, tryin' to take Craig down with the tapes—if I really went through with it—then one of these days, the thing I did would just be another one of those scary memories that jumps up and haunts me. You know, attacks me. And this one would be the worst—because I really shoulda known better by now."

Nigel walked over to Bryon, leaned down, and gave him a hug. He shared a brief hug with Adelle.

Byron pointed to the dining room. "The recorder and the tape are right on the table there, bro. Grab 'em on your way out."

Nigel was careful to shield his complacent grin as he secured the fruits of Byron's clandestine surveillance. Barely turning his head, he offered a melodious "Cheerio," and departed.

As soon as he got home, Nigel poked about the garage and found a heavy steel pipe. He smashed the tape cassette to pieces. Then he tossed the recorder and the shattered shreds into the trash can and went inside the house to see Justine.

• • •

When the meeting concluded, Craig Schumacher rose from his seat at the large circular table in the corner of his office and walked to his desk. He set down the pile of diagrams and documents upon which he and Nigel had been working.

Nigel Silver also had a large heap of papers. He was still sorting them and stuffing batches into his briefcase, when Craig returned and stood beside him.

"I have every confidence that you'll do great with this," Craig said as he raised his hand and rested it affably on Nigel's shoulder. "Your leadership skills are exceptional—and people enjoy working for you."

"I appreciate your confidence, boss," Nigel said. "I feel good about it. I'll keep you in the loop."

The men shook hands, and Nigel left the office.

They'd spent the past two-and-a-half hours working out the details of rolling Nigel's and Byron's departments into one unit, to be headed by Nigel. With the staff reductions, both entities were now significantly smaller—and would need to coordinate closely in keeping all the new systems running smoothly.

Craig took a breath and slowed his thoughts. He ambled over to the guest chair adjacent to his desk and sat down. He swiveled in his seat so that he could gaze out the large corner windows, and took a few minutes to review how the meeting with Nigel had gone—most specifically, the things he'd chosen to emphasize to help Nigel grow as a manager.

In the course of their discussions, what Craig had stressed most passionately was delegation. He and Nigel had breezed through the more perfunctory tasks of developing new organizational charts and mapping out revised responsibilities for each individual team. But what Craig wanted Nigel to internalize viscerally was that managing a more diversified department entailed distancing himself further from the details—which in turn entailed letting go—and putting much greater trust in his direct reports.

And as Craig thought back upon it now, he was pleased—it seemed to him that he'd delivered an appropriately balanced message—and that Nigel had responded positively to it. Craig was especially glad that as they spoke, he sensed in Nigel a genuine willingness to accept that things would be done differently by his direct reports than he himself would have done them. And Nigel seemed to be able to properly juxtapose the importance of assuring quality, setting direction, and facilitating collaboration with the seemingly contradictory needs of deferring to the expertise of the people closest to the work, and allowing his people to operate in the manner that best suited them.

Craig stood up, nodded, and flashed a contented smile.

It occurred to him that although he had cleared this reorganization with his senior vice president, Bruce, a few days prior, it would be appropriate now to stroll over to Bruce's office, and if he found him in, to let him know how well it was proceeding.

Craig closed his door behind him and began walking down the hallway. But as he approached Bruce's office, something felt amiss. When he got close enough to see clearly through the large glass window, he realized the room was completely empty—shelves bare—surfaces clean—wall hangings stripped.

Traces of any former inhabitant had been obliterated.

Craig stood motionless, surveying the barren space. An eerie sense of foreboding now engulfed him. *How could this have happened so quickly? Without me knowing? He wasn't even given the opportunity to say goodbye.*

Craig pondered a moment. He was certain that this was just an initial salvo. Surely, more was to follow.

He heard footsteps behind him. He turned and saw his admin Basha hurrying toward him. "Thank goodness I found you, Craig," she said. "They just called an emergency mandatory meeting—for you and the other VPs. It's at eight tomorrow morning. It'll be in that executive meeting room on the top floor—the one a few doors down from the boardroom. The president will be leading it. The message said that you need to bring your numbers—whatever that means."

Craig nodded and spoke softly. "Thanks, Basha." He glanced for a moment back into Bruce's barren office. Then his eyes met Basha's again. "This isn't good."

"No," she said, "I'm sure it's not." She touched his arm gently. "I'll clear your calendar for the entire morning, Craig. It sounds like this meeting might go on for a while."

• • •

A few minutes before eight in the morning, Craig Schumacher was the first VP to enter the meeting room. He exchanged nods with the company president, who was already seated at the head of the table. Craig politely took a place down at the other end. Although he'd never had an extended one-on-one conversation with the president, Craig had shared brief exchanges with him in the course of larger meetings, and was at ease in his presence.

The president was not, however, alone at the head of the table.

Immediately to the president's left, along the table's curve, was a stocky, bull-necked man, whom Craig recognized immediately. The man's appearance had always struck Craig as a contradiction—a purposeful and duplicitous one. His fine silk ties sported flawlessly configured Windsor knots, always thrust conspicuously upward by ornate gold collar pins—his suits were peerless and impeccably tailored—and his hair was perfectly coiffed. Yet, Craig imagined that the fellow would have been far more in his element in a hooded sweatshirt, wielding a crow bar or a baseball bat.

The man's name was Hunter Brosnan. He was a senior partner in the prestigious consulting firm with whom the company president had been doing business of late.

They had never conversed directly, but just from the way that Hunter Brosnan carried himself—and from snippets of overheard hallway conversations as well as from bits of gossip seeping through the ranks—Craig had formed a strong intuitive sense of who the man was. Politely termed a "change agent," Brosnan was, in fact, the type of consultant who specialized in the dirty work of tearing down and ripping apart. When senior executives had led their enterprise into a quagmire, the escapades of people like Brosnan enabled those executives to broadcast the impression that strong, revitalizing change was now at hand. It had always seemed to Craig that rerouting existing resources in the right direction would have been a much more humane, pragmatic, and efficacious course of action. But mass purges were viscerally compelling—and far more likely to ensure that senior executives retained their positions.

What often went overlooked was the sort of moneymaker that partners like Hunter Brosnan were for their consulting companies. Inevitably, for some extended period of time, the shattered void left by Brosnan's destruction would need to be filled by armies of young, eager, and obedient recruits from Brosnan's own firm, generating prodigious income.

As Craig had been mulling all this over, the other vice presidents had filtered into the meeting room, and had now taken their seats.

The president opened the meeting without niceties or salutations—just a single blunt announcement:

"I fired Bruce yesterday afternoon."

Craig was shocked.

He had fully expected the president to warble on, employ polite corporate-speak, and say something akin to, "With the big Y2K project winding down, and responsibilities changing, Bruce got another offer, and we agreed by mutual consent that he should leave. I thank Bruce for his fine service, and wish him the best."

Instead, the president had chosen to declare, flat out, that he'd fired him.

And it was not just the words the president had used. The tone of his voice, his facial expression, and the thuggish body language of both the president and his associate Hunter Brosnan, conjured in Craig's mind the precise image of godfather and consiglieri in an organized crime film.

The president went on to say that the company had reached an inflection point—that the need for radical change was urgent. He did give brief lip service to the fine work completed on the Y2K project, but only to point out that its conclusion signaled that a completely different corporate reality was now present.

By now, though, Craig was only half-listening. The president's words blurred together as filler in Craig's mind. He knew what was afoot. A strange but not unfamiliar physical sensation soon manifested in the back of his throat—as if the flesh there had been scraped and set aflame. Craig knew what it meant—it was his intuition warning him to be hypervigilant. But Craig required no such exhortation here. It was clear to him what was happening.

The president concluded his statement about the need for impending change. Then he got up. "I'm going to leave now," he said, "and I'm turning the meeting over to the gentleman on my left." He gestured in that direction and said, "This is Hunter Brosnan. Some of you have already met with him. He's a senior partner with the consulting firm we're working with. For now, all of you will report to him. I want you to know that Hunter and I have set the date for the mass layoffs we've been planning—they'll take place a week from Monday. Hunter's going to run that—he'll discuss with you exactly how we're going to pull it off—and I want it done exactly how he says."

As the president walked toward the door of the meeting room, Hunter Brosnan slid into the seat at the head of the table. He waited until the president had shut the door behind him before he began:

"For months now, all of you have had your target numbers—the headcount your team needs to get to by a week from Monday. I have the numbers here. I'm going to go around to each of you and make sure that the numbers I have jibe with yours. We'll look at the total number you need to hit and then—based on your current headcount—how many people you'll need to identify to be laid off a week from Monday to reach that."

Brosnan skipped about the table to verify each VP's

numbers—ostensibly to match the order on the list he had in front of him—but perhaps, Craig thought, for another reason.

As Craig suspected, Brosnan saved him for last.

The two agreed immediately on the total headcount Craig's team needed to reach. Then Brosnan said, "All right, Schumacher—so—based on that number—how many people do you need to lay off a week from Monday?"

"None," Craig said.

There were audible gasps in the room, followed by ghostly silence.

Brosnan waited a moment to respond. "None?" he asked.

It was clear to Craig that Brosnan knew, coming in, that his team had already reached its number. But he thought it best to feign naïveté—and to use to his advantage the fact that he had anticipated, and had thoroughly rehearsed, the salient points he now needed to present on the matter.

"I've worked on this for the past nine months, sir," Craig said. "I've always kept a fairly high percentage of contractors on my team—around a third all told—anticipating that a reduction would eventually come. The rest of the cuts, we got to by normal attrition—we haven't replaced anyone who left during the past nine months. I wanted to reach my number without the traumatic effect that layoffs tend to have on morale. I cleared it with Bruce, back when all this started."

"*I* didn't know about it," Brosnan said. "The *president* didn't know about it either."

"It's possible that Bruce didn't mention it."

Brosnan leaned forward. "Bruce is gone, Schumacher. I assume you've noticed that. And even if Bruce had mentioned something about it—even if you two had a written agreement—you know what that would be worth now?" Brosnan reached down into his briefcase and pulled out a single blank sheet of white paper. "This is what it'd be worth, Schumacher." With a condescending scowl, he tore the paper into four pieces and smashed them onto the table.

Tension in the room grew palpable.

"Now, I'm going to ask you again, Schumacher, how many people are you going to lay off a week from Monday?"

"None, sir," Craig said. "There's no need. I've reached my number."

"Wrong answer," Brosnan said. "You're going to identify five more people, and lay them off a week from Monday."

"And why would I do that?" asked Craig, remaining calm. "If I've met my number already, why would I need to lay off more in addition?"

Brosnan's complexion reddened as he glared at Craig. His voice took on a gruff, threatening tone. "Because every other department will be laying off people on that day—hundreds of people altogether. And if your team doesn't lay off anybody, it will look like you're getting a pass—special treatment—and I won't have that."

"So," Craig said, speaking slowly and deliberately, "you want me to lay off five people—five innocent people—layoffs that will be devastating to them as human beings—as well as being hurtful to the morale of the rest of the team—just for appearances? That's absurd. We could just explain how I went about it differently—met my number in a different manner. It's not difficult to understand."

"Schumacher, I'm not discussing this any further. Identify five people by the end of the week. And if you don't—I'll fire *you*—and I'll put someone from *my* firm in your place, and *he'll* lay off five people. Got it?"

Craig said nothing.

Brosnan leaned back in his seat. His voice resumed its prior, more relaxed tone. "That'll do it for this meeting. But I want you all to know that you'll be receiving performance evaluations over the next couple of weeks. I'll be doing those and meeting with you one-on-one to discuss them. I'll let your assistants know when they're scheduled for. Oh, and I want you all to submit the names of the people you'll be laying off—to me, with a copy to HR—by Friday."

Brosnan rose from his seat and headed toward the door. Everyone else in the room dutifully followed suit.

• • •

Early the following week, Craig Schumacher was summoned for his performance evaluation.

A large meeting room on the building's top floor had been converted into an office for Hunter Brosnan. Craig entered the room and was immediately struck by the extravagant, yet meretricious nature of the furnishings. Brosnan gestured to Craig that he take a seat at the table in the far corner. Brosnan left him sitting there, alone and in silence, for two or three minutes, while he ostensibly completed some paperwork. Finally, he walked over and sat across from Craig, placing a small pile of documents onto the table.

"I see you found five more people," Brosnan said.

"I did."

Brosnan glanced at his sheet of notes and smirked. "You found pregnant women who wanted time off, and people who were looking to leave anyway, and told them about the nice severance package they'd get if they opted into the layoff."

"Yes, that's how I went about it," Craig said, fully appreciating the level of invasive scrutiny, as well as the time and effort, that Brosnan had put into uncovering that information.

"And that gets right to the heart of the matter, Schumacher—the thing I want this performance evaluation to really be about."

Craig said nothing. He scrutinized Brosnan, who had paused and appeared to be thinking. Craig suspected that Brosnan knew exactly what he was about to say and how he planned to phrase it. The brief silence was purely for effect—intended to be disquieting—intimidating.

Craig suppressed a grin.

"You don't behave like an executive," Brosnan finally said. He looked at Craig and awaited a response.

"I don't behave like an executive?"

"That's right. That's it exactly. You don't behave at all like an executive."

"What about my team's results?"

"I can't argue with your team's results, Schumacher. They're the best in the enterprise. You know that—you've seen the metrics. But I don't like the way you go about it—or the perspective you take. It's not appropriate for an executive. The president agrees with me on that—and by the way, so do your peers."

Craig took a few seconds to cement the wording of his response—given the combative nature of the discussion, he opted for phrasing that was succinct and direct: "Don't you think that my team's results are directly related to the way I behave?"

"I just told you, Schumacher, nobody likes the way you behave."

"Well, the people on my *team* like it. And if my team's results are so good, maybe other executives should follow *my* example. Behave the way I do."

"There you go again. This is exactly what I mean. Your peers—the other VPs who report to *me* now—*we're* the group you should have allegiance to. Not the people who report to you. Those people are expendable. You don't seem to get that."

"I feel a sense of responsibility for the people who report to me. They spend a significant percentage of their lives here. If they feel good about that, if they feel trusted and supported—then they're not just happier—they work harder—they care more—they're more loyal. It's a win-win."

"That's not an appropriate approach for an executive to take. Your priority needs to be the company—the bottom line. This is business, Schumacher. Not some hippy commune."

Craig took a calm, deep breath. "But you do acknowledge that my team's results are extraordinary."

Brosnan closed his eyes and shook his head in frustration. He grimaced and sighed.

Craig experienced some pleasure in annoying him this way but kept his features unemotive.

Brosnan now tried a different tack. "It's entirely possible," he said, "to like the results of something, but disagree with the process of how you got there. You have to acknowledge *that*, Schumacher."

The fact that Brosnan felt the need to retreat for a moment from his brute force approach and try instead to outreason Craig, felt like a small victory. Craig was quite certain that Brosnan couldn't compete with him in dialectical discourse. And Craig had given this topic a great deal of thought.

"Yes," Craig said, "it's certainly possible to like the results of something, but disagree with the process of how you got there. But that argument is only applicable when the approach is Machiavellian—you know, hurtful, cruel—insensitive. In my case, you disagree with the process because it's honest, collaborative, and compassionate. And you do so even though it leads to superior results. To be *kind* and effective is clearly preferable to being *cruel* and effective—unless you're some sort of sadistic maniac. So, sir, unless you truly *are* a sadistic maniac, your argument makes no sense."

Brosnan's tone grew sharper. "It makes perfect sense to *me*, Schumacher. And in our current situation, that's really all that matters."

"It may be all that matters—and your assertion of power may be incontestable—but it doesn't make your logic sound. Your argument is still specious."

"Schumacher, this is exactly why so many of your peers and superiors find you exasperating—and despise working with you. You're smug and condescending. As if *you* know what's right, and everyone else is a bunch of idiots."

Craig blinked slowly and looked away.

Brosnan flashed a self-satisfied grin. "Anyway, Schumacher, there's no point talking about this anymore. None of it matters now. I'm here to execute the roadmap that the president and I came up with. And it has your IT department going into a minimalist maintenance mode. The official announcement will come out later today. We're going to outsource everything we can outsource—that means anything generic—the network, operations, backups, devices, email—we'll just have a small in-house maintenance shop for the customized applications. So, there'll be a lot more downsizing over the next six to twelve months. A *hell* of a lot more. There won't be much left, Schumacher." Brosnan paused, and leaned back in his seat. He struck a leisurely pose—his elbows rose to rest on the plush, upholstered arms of his chair—his fingers intertwined a few inches from his chin. His lips curled into a patronizing smirk. "I don't think any of this is a good fit for you anymore, Schumacher. Don't you agree?"

Craig looked at him, but did not answer.

Brosnan's tone grew even more barbed. "My advice, Schumacher, would be for you to start examining other employment options. If you get going now—and do it willingly—then you can accomplish it on your own terms. It looks much better on a resume that way."

"I'll consider it," Craig said. "I assume we're done?"

"Yes, we're done. Oh, I do have written copies of your performance evaluation. You're free to sign one and take one with you—or not. Your choice."

"I don't think I'll need it," Craig said. He rose from his seat and left the office.

• • •

Carolyn Winthrop was in her kitchen, stirring the contents of a hot skillet. A dish towel was slung over her shoulder, and the slightest sheen of perspiration covered her face.

She snuck a quick taste and smiled broadly.

On the counter, next to the stove, an illustrated hardcover cookbook was open to a page featuring eggplant caponata. Though the book was brand new, the open pages were already splashed copiously with olive oil and tomato sauce.

A piercing ring snapped her out of her cooking reverie. Her head twisted and she scowled at the phone across the room. She decided not to answer it—let her machine take a message. If it was a junk call, perhaps they'd just hang up and not leave a message at all.

"Hi Carolyn," the voice on the recording began, "it's Craig. I hope you're doing well. I wanted to call and . . ."

Carolyn's eyes spread wide and her lips rounded into a tiny circle. She hurriedly turned the burner down and tried to toss the large cooking-spoon onto the counter as she pivoted—but she stumbled, causing the spoon to clatter about and fall to the floor. She left it lying there and dashed to the phone, hastily drying her hands before lurching for the receiver.

"It's you, love!" she cried. "What a nice surprise."

"What are you up to? Do you have a few minutes to talk?"

"Actually, love, you've caught me working on my vegetarian cooking repertoire. Just as I promised."

"Oh, that's wonderful. How's it going?"

"Remarkably well. I continue to astonish myself with my innate bloody talent for this sort of thing. This is my third go-round with this wonderful recipe—eggplant caponata. Are you familiar with the dish, love? It's an Italian appetizer."

"Yes, it's one of my favorite things."

"Quite remarkable, isn't it? Not even a shred of dairy, and it's so delicious. The first time I made it, I followed the recipe exactly, and it was fine—but now I've amped up the garlic and capers—and added green olives to the eggplant, along with the black ones. It's a damn masterpiece. It's supposed to be just an appetizer, but with some crusty whole grain bread, and a bit of green salad, we could make a nice meal of it—cuddling on the couch while we eat."

"That sounds divine."

"I didn't expect a call from you at this hour, love. Aren't you still at work?"

Craig chuckled. "Yes, but just barely. I tendered my resignation today."

"Oh my god!" she screamed. "Congratulations!" She paused a moment, self-conscious about her level of exhilaration. She attempted to check it, at least a tad, but soon realized the change was indiscernible. "I'm sorry, love—I realize that quitting a job is not usually cause for such celebration. But in this case—I'm just so happy. You know, I really did figure this was coming—as soon as I heard the announcement about downsizing the IT department."

"Yes, that was pretty much the final straw."

"I knew you were dead-set on waiting until the project wound down completely—you know, to make a clean break of it—but this downsizing announcement—it seemed to absolutely be cause for a change of plans."

"It was, indeed."

She laughed, and allowed her exhilaration to modulate to what she deemed a more appropriate level. "I had assumed you'd take a few days to mull it over, love—but apparently it only took you one. I'm quite surprised."

"I pretty much decided as soon as I heard about it. But even so—you know me—I always run my internal checks, just to be sure."

"Oh, yes. I bloody know."

"But I'll certainly have some amusing stories to tell you about the new regime—and how they viewed me."

She chortled. "Oh dear. I can only imagine."

"And you know, when I resigned, I suggested they offer Nigel the position of running what's left of things. I didn't know if they'd pay any attention to how I felt about it. But I was surprised—they said they already planned to do that. Anyway, Nigel just called me and told me he accepted."

"Well, good for him."

"It is. I think he'll do well. He's a fine young man."

She paused a moment. "Nigel doesn't like me one bit, does he?"

Craig laughed hard. "No. Not one bit, I'm afraid."

She sniggered. "Well, to each his own, I suppose." Carolyn took a few seconds to phrase her next question. "So, love, what do you plan on doing when you move out here?"

Craig grinned. He hadn't actually committed to moving in with her. But he supposed that it had become obvious from their discussions that he eventually would. So, rather than continue to chide him for his overly cautious decision making, Caroline had asserted the Dominatrix in her substrate and declared it a done deal. That realization provoked a brief but agreeable tingling in his groin.

"When I come out—well, look for a job, I guess. My resume is rock-solid. By now, I'm a legitimate expert in implementing large projects. And, my resigning here just when the implementation ended looks totally organic. I assume I'll find something fairly quickly—you never know, of course—but I'm optimistic."

"Did you ever consider consulting, love? I know you hate those buggers—but you'd be terrific—and not like them at all. You could move from one big project to the next. Even oversee teams doing several simultaneously. And you'd be able to bring your rare fount of ethics and honesty to a field quite deeply devoid of it."

Craig chuckled. "Well, that all sounds lovely, Carolyn—but I think I'd need my own firm to do it the way I'd really want—and I'm not at all up for opening a business. You know how it is—that sort of thing takes lots of selling and marketing. I hate all that. And I'm dreadful at it."

"But I'm not, love. And neither is this other fellow I know. Actually, you know him too. Do you remember Elias? A bit younger than us—I think he had a gig briefly with your team in San Francisco some years back. He's out here now, looking to start a boutique firm. Specializing in managing big projects. We've talked. You'll remember him. He was very impressed with you."

"Oh yes, Elias. I remember him well. A good guy—honest and straightforward—highly ethical—compassionate. Actually, *I* was impressed with *him*."

"Elias and I could handle the sales and marketing end of it, and support you in every way you need. And as for the sales—he's a dear, and people trust him. And me—well, love—you know how irresistibly ingratiating and charming I am. So—you can hire good staff—and supply your personal ninja magic for managing all the big projects we find for you. And Elias and I will certainly help you out—we can even manage teams under you. And think about this, love—between you and Elias, there'll surely be enough bloody honesty, integrity, and compassion in the company to suck in even a haughty bitch like me."

Craig laughed, then took a few moments to consider what she'd proposed. "You know, Carolyn, I never thought I'd say this about being a consultant—but the way you laid it all out, it actually sounds pretty damn good. I think there's even a decent chance we could make it work. It's sure as hell worth giving it a try. Don't you think?"

"Oh, I do."

24
WHOLE DUNGENESS CRAB

DUNGENESS CRAB SEASON HAD JUST COMMENCED IN the Bay Area.

Justine and Shoshana were in Tiburon on a clear Monday afternoon, seated across from each other in one of their favorite seafood restaurants. The wall beside their table was clear glass from floor to ceiling, affording them a magnificent view of the Golden Gate Bridge in the distance—and the Bay's gurgling white foam, assaulting the rim of land, just feet from the eatery.

The two shared a bottle of champagne while savoring the restaurant's featured special: whole Dungeness crab, steamed and served with vegetables and roasted fingerling potatoes.

"I have to tell you, sweetie," Shoshana said, "I've been kind of sad since you stopped doing sessions with me down in Los Altos. I really miss our time together there."

Justine took a sip of champagne. "I'm so sorry, honey. I miss our time together too. But—you know—I really just decided that it wasn't right for me anymore. Oh my god, I enjoyed it for a while—and I loved just being with you—but things are kind of different now. Nigel's home every night—and like, all of a sudden, there's all this restoration work coming my way."

Shoshana put down her glass and smiled. "I'm so glad you're finding more restoration work. I know that's what you really love doing."

"It really is. And, I have to tell you—when we were doing sessions—you know, working with clients who were, like, *pretending* to be dead—it wasn't the same at all. You know, the dead *feel* different—they *smell* different. There's something so quiet and peaceful about them. I mean, for me—when the clients were pretending to be dead—it was almost like—I don't know—maybe almost *disrespectful* to the people I work with who really *are* deceased. Does that make any sense, honey?"

"It does. And I totally understand."

"And, you know, with the Y2K project ending—it's not just that Nigel's not traveling anymore—it's that he's not spending time with that creep Byron Dorn anymore either. Thank god for that."

"Right. Did Byron and Adelle move back to Tampa yet? I knew they were planning to."

"They left a couple of weeks ago. So, Nigel and me—we have a lot more time together—it's nice—it kind of feels like we're rebuilding something."

"That really *is* nice, honey. I'm so happy for you. You and Nigel are good together."

The two fell silent for a time. Around them, the restaurant was quiet. The only sounds they heard were the crackle of their pincers shattering the animals' exoskeletons—the nearly inaudible squishes and taps of their tiny forks piercing meager mounds of flesh—and the occasional sip and swallow of champagne, followed by the muted ping of the glasses' bottoms returning to the table.

After a couple of minutes, fueled by the champagne, Justine finally raised the subject she'd been, until then, too uncomfortable to broach. "I'm really sorry, honey—you know—about what you and Craig are going through."

"Yes, it's hard," Shoshana said softly. "I appreciate your being here for me."

"Did you ever find out exactly who Craig's seeing out in DC?"

"Yes—a woman he worked with—she'd been out here for a few years—but recently, she moved back east. Carolyn Winthrop."

"Oh my god!" Justine cried. "Nigel used to work for that woman. He hates her—says she's a raging, controlling bitch."

"Well, that's who it is."

"Jesus!"

"And get this. They're not just going to be living together. They're also going to be business partners. They're starting some little consulting firm—the two of them and another guy."

"Oh my god! People say it's like totally a mistake to work with the person you live with. It gets claustrophobic—and like, conflicting—you know?"

"I agree completely. And I have to be honest. I truly think—between this consulting firm idea—and the vanilla sex that the two of them have—there's a whole lot wrong with what Craig's trying to bite off. I just don't think it's sustainable for him."

Justine took a long, slow swallow of champagne and thought about how to word her response. "I agree with you totally, honey," she said, "and I know how sad and frustrated you are about all this. I need to say though—well, Nigel says it—and you know, he's worked really closely with Craig for a while now—he says Craig's the kind of guy who can make pretty much anything work when he puts his mind to it."

Shoshana's eyes welled with tears. She took a couple of deep breaths and spoke in a hesitant murmur. "He *is* amazing that way. He really can—pretty much—make anything work." She paused for a moment. "I guess, though—somewhere along the way—he just decided that making it work with *me* wasn't worth it anymore." Shoshana's soft tears gave way to heavy sobs. She lifted the cloth napkin from her lap and used it to dry her face.

Justine reached across the table and held Shoshana's hand. "I'm sorry, honey," she whispered.

Shoshana raised her head and flashed the hint of a faint, ironic smile. "You know," she said, "it's really sad—for both of us. But honestly—I hate to say it—but he's right. We're done. We've probably been done for a while, but it was just so convenient for us not to acknowledge it."

"You two were always very different from each other."

"Tell me about it," Shoshana said with a forlorn snigger. She glanced down at her dish. "For god's sake—just look at what I'm eating! A Dungeness crab—a whole freaking animal—lying dead, right here on my plate—staring up at me—and I'm cracking its bones and tearing it apart. It would gross Craig out totally." She looked up, gazed into Justine's eyes, and sighed. "But dear, sweet Craig—he'd never say a word—just look away—and wish I wasn't doing it." Shoshana offered a dejected shake of her head. "Really. We're so totally done."

"Yes, honey. I agree. You two are done. But *you're* gonna do great."

"I guess so. But it'll take a while."

"Oh my god, it always does."

• • •

For his long road trip, Craig Schumacher took only the barest essentials.

The rest, he'd packed in boxes for cross-country shipment. He was surprised how much of what was in those shipping cartons turned out to be books.

There really wasn't all that much else.

There were, of course, some clothing and shoes—his work wardrobe and his more casual attire. But clothes had never been very important to Craig, so he hadn't amassed a huge collection—only what Shoshana had purchased for him over the years.

And he'd identified a few of his favorite pots, pans, and kitchen utensils—he'd packed those for shipping as well. He knew that Carolyn was well-stocked with those sorts of things, but these were items he'd owned for a very long time—their value was more sentimental than utilitarian. He felt Carolyn would understand, and not resent his desire to add them to her kitchen stockpile.

He had a small cache of personal BDSM toys. He'd taken quite a while with them—touching and caressing them—savoring their textures and heft—striking himself briskly on the arm with some—and binding or gagging himself momentarily with others. It felt like a farewell to something that he believed he'd outgrown. He decided to leave them for Shoshana—he assumed she'd find them and realize that his abandoning them was part of his new direction—and that she'd incorporate them into her professional collection—accepting them, perhaps, as a farewell gift.

He had opted to make the road trip to Maryland a leisurely one. He'd reserved rooms in small hotels along the way such that he'd never drive more than four to six hours a day. He planned long yoga and meditation sessions each morning before he set out, alone and at peace, onto the highway. And he charted a northern detour that would allow him to meander through Yellowstone National Park for a day and stop to see Old Faithful and a few other sites, as he headed east.

He understood that in many of the small towns, the kind of food he wanted would not be available. But on trips like this in the past, he had lived for days at a time solely on provisions from two chains present in almost every freeway rest stop. Subway made a sandwich of nothing but vegetables and avocado slices piled into a twelve-inch whole-wheat roll—and Starbucks concocted a latte made of chai tea and soy milk. He found it funny that while he never partook of either of these offerings when home in the Bay Area, he found them comforting and flavorful when he consumed them in his car or hotel room, alone, in quiet rural parts of the country.

There was one more item he took with him.

At first, he was embarrassed about it, and wondered where in the car he could hide it. But, in the end, he propped Zippy up in the front passenger seat and buckled him in with a seat belt.

Zippy was a very old toy—a stuffed cloth chimpanzee—so worn now that his clothes were torn in many places—one round ear was only half-attached—and one foot had been lost forever, the bottom of the leg tied with an old shoelace to keep the stuffing from falling out.

As Craig pulled away from the house, the chimp's presence in the seat next to him prompted a long and poignant recollection:

His parents had bought Zippy for him when Craig was very young—probably three or four. Craig had chosen the name Zippy because there was a real chimpanzee by that name on a popular children's television program.

But when Craig turned twelve, his parents told him he'd outgrown the toy and threw it in the garbage—a paper sack from the grocery store that sat on the floor in the corner of their small kitchen and was carried down to the big bin in the apartment house cellar when full.

That night, young Craig could not sleep. He lay in bed, picturing Zippy alone in the bag—soon headed to the dump where he'd be crushed and mutilated. Mangled pieces of him would be enveloped forever by greasy food scraps and other disgusting waste. Craig cried for a long time, then snuck out silently into the kitchen, retrieved Zippy from the bag, and took the chimp into bed with him.

He never again allowed Zippy to be taken from him.

It wasn't long after rescuing Zippy that something began happening to Craig. Every time he ate, he'd picture the live animals that had been slaughtered to provide him with the meat, poultry, and fish on his plate. Soon, he found it repulsive to eat these things—but his parents insisted that without them in his diet, he would not survive.

About four years later, when Craig was sixteen, he took the subway into Manhattan on a Saturday afternoon and found himself wandering around the aisles of a secondhand bookstore in Greenwich Village. It was there that he came across the first book he'd ever found on yoga. It had an extensive chapter on the physiological and spiritual benefits of a vegetarian diet. After a good deal more reading from various sources, he became certain that his parents were wrong. Despite their furious protests, Craig stopped eating animals.

Craig glanced again at Zippy in the seat beside him. "It's just you and me for the next two weeks, pal," he said.

But he knew Golda's spirit would be with them as well.

• • •

Shoshana had made Craig promise that before he headed east to catch the interstate for his long journey, he'd stop at her studio in Los Altos, for one last goodbye. It was out of his way, but he never considered saying no.

She was alone in the studio when he arrived. It was late morning—too early for sessions. She invited him in. They stood facing each other just inside the front door.

"Would you like to sit down for a few minutes?" Shoshana asked.

"I won't be long," he said. "It's probably better if I stand. I really need to get on the road."

"Okay, sweetie."

After a brief awkward silence, Shoshana's lips rounded into a melancholy halo, and her eyelids slid to half-mast. She spoke softly. "Well, I guess this is it, huh?"

"I guess so."

"Oh," she said, "I heard from the realtor today—some details on the house—you know, putting it on the market—and the estate sale. We'll be able to divvy it all up after that."

"Yes. Hiring the mediator was really a great idea you had. She's so helpful—just facilitating everything."

"I'm so glad we're not making it adversarial," she said. "And isn't it funny—that whole giant beautiful house—and all the gorgeous furniture inside it—and really, in the end—neither of us has any use for it."

In Craig's mind flashed the vivid image of a rabbit's hutch—he'd have use for that, he thought. But he kept it to himself. Instead, he said, "I know you'll have no problem finding a new live-in submissive."

"I don't know that I'll necessarily be looking for one right now." She took a small step toward him. "I had a great one in you, sweetie." She paused and dipped her head. "And I squandered it. I know that. And I'm sorry. But I really don't think I could have done better and still have been me." She pondered a moment. "Maybe I'm better off just keeping a harem of playthings. For a while at least. I think I need to reassess the whole thing."

"This has been such an important relationship for me, Empress," he said softly. "I'll never forget it. And I'll always love you."

"I'll always love you too, sweetie. And I hope that what you're trying works out for you. I know how you're wired, babe. And it's a big leap you're trying to make. But I do hope for the best."

"Thank you. I'm convinced it's exactly what I need."

She fixed her gaze upon him. Her features softened into a mournful smile. "Let's just remember the good times," she said.

"We sure had some of *those*."

Their embrace was that of old and dear friends. Within its tight grasp was not even a nominal suggestion of anything more.

END

AUTHOR BIO

Robert Steven Goldstein is the author of five novels. His first, The Swami Deheftner, about problems that ensue when ancient magic and mysticism manifest in the twenty-first century, developed a small cult following in India. His second novel, Enemy Queen, a sexual comedy of manners set in a North Carolina college town, was a finalist in the category of cross genre fiction for the International Book Awards. Robert's third novel, Cat's Whisker, probes the perceived rift between science and spirituality; it was longlisted for the prestigious Chanticleer International 2021 SOMERSET Book Award for Literary and Contemporary Fiction. His fourth novel, Will's Surreal Period, about the peripatetic machinations of a dysfunctional family, was longlisted for the Chanticleer International 2022 SOMERSET Book Award for Literary and Contemporary Fiction. Golda's Hutch is Robert's fifth novel. He and his wife Sandy live in San Francisco; over their thirty-six years together, they've shared their home with an array of dogs, cats, rabbits, turtles, and parrots, each of whom has displayed a unique personality, startling intelligence, and a profound capacity for love. Robert has practiced yoga, meditation, and vegetarianism for over fifty years. Learn more at www.robertstevengoldstein.com.

Printed in the USA
CPSIA information can be obtained
at www.ICGtesting.com
LVHW091107211024
794382LV00002B/50

2 370001 948181